T0129735

PICARD ROSE FROM HIS CHAIR . . .

. . . stepping forward until he stood directly behind the conn and ops consoles, as though the movement might bring him closer to the person pleading for aid.

"Our reactor coolant tank has ruptured, and our environmental system has failed. Send any available transports for evacuation!"

Picard's eyes locked on the viewscreen and the uncounted asteroids drifting all around the ship, as if he might locate the caller by sight alone. Somewhere out there, among all the tumbling and drifting rock, someone needed their help.

STAR TREK®
A Time to Sow

DAYTON WARD
&
KEVIN DILMORE

Based on
STAR TREK: THE NEXT GENERATION®
created by Gene Roddenberry
and based on STAR TREK: ENTERPRISE™
created by Rick Berman & Brannon Braga

POCKET BOOKS
New York   London   Toronto   Sydney

The sale of this book without its cover is unauthorized. If you purchased this book without a cover, you should be aware that it was reported to the publisher as "unsold and destroyed." Neither the author nor the publisher has received payment for the sale of this "stripped book."

This book is a work of fiction. Names, characters, places and incidents are products of the authors' imaginations or are used fictitiously. Any resemblance to actual events or locales or persons, living or dead, is entirely coincidental.

An *Original* Publication of POCKET BOOKS

POCKET BOOKS, a division of Simon & Schuster, Inc.
1230 Avenue of the Americas, New York, NY 10020

Copyright © 2004 by Paramount Pictures. All Rights Reserved.

A VIACOM COMPANY

STAR TREK is a Registered Trademark of Paramount Pictures.

This book is published by Pocket Books, a division of Simon & Schuster, Inc., under exclusive license from Paramount Pictures.

All rights reserved, including the right to reproduce this book or portions thereof in any form whatsoever. For information address Pocket Books, 1230 Avenue of the Americas, New York, NY 10020

ISBN 978-1-9821-3497-6

First Pocket Books printing April 2004

10 9 8 7 6 5 4 3 2 1

POCKET and colophon are registered trademarks of Simon & Schuster, Inc.

Manufactured in the United States of America

For information regarding special discounts for bulk purchases, please contact Simon & Schuster Special Sales at 1-800-456-6798 or business@simonandschuster.com

ACKNOWLEDGMENTS

We'd like to thank John Ordover, editor of the *A Time To . . .* series, for the opportunity to participate in one of these high-profile projects featuring the work of several authors. As readers and fans of *Star Trek* books long before either of us got the harebrained idea that we could write, we became accustomed to names like David, Friedman, Reeves-Stevens, and Carey as staples for efforts on this scale. That anyone might consider us capable of holding our own at the level established long ago by these fine writers is a reward unto itself.

Thanks also to the other writers involved in this effort: John Vornholt, Robert Greenberger, David Mack, and Keith R.A. DeCandido. Everyone pitched in well beyond the efforts of simply writing their own story, offering insights and advice on one another's manuscripts to make this entire affair a truly collaborative effort.

Last but certainly not least, thanks very much to the many readers who've expressed their enjoyment and appreciation for the stories Kevin and I write. One of the most common questions we ask whenever working on a project is "What would a fan want to see?" That question and the mind-set it evokes influences everything we do, and we hope it shows in the stories that end up in your hands.

Prologue

Translated from the personal journal of Hjatyn:

WRITING IS NOT SOMETHING I have practiced much of in the past, at least in any capacity that did not involve my work, but the crisis that is befalling us compels me to record my feelings and thoughts. I am sure that others, possessing superior education and clarity of thought, are at this very moment recording these events so that future generations might read and reflect on this time in our history. Still, I feel an obligation, almost a compulsion, to do the same.

I know I should report to the school to conduct my scheduled classes, but I am finding it increasingly difficult to remain focused on my responsibilities. With each passing day, those things I once considered important and even enjoyable in life seem to be losing their significance. More than once, I have fought back the growing sensation that I myself am becoming progressively inconsequential.

I am afraid.

My wife, Beeliq, keeps telling me there is nothing to fear, yet with each new day she spends more and more time at the office of the colony administrator. She acts as one of his assistants, which puts her in a position to know if anything was wrong.

What I am no longer sure of is whether she would tell me. Since our earliest days of courtship, she has never kept secrets from me, at least to the best of my knowledge. That she seems to be holding back now only deepens my anxiety. Is it possible she has been ordered to keep information even from her husband?

Still, despite her best efforts, the worry in her eyes is unmistakable.

It is a look that becomes more obvious on those rare occasions that we can share a meal together. Neither of us seems to have an appetite, however, and more often than not the food goes uneaten as we watch the latest news feeds from Dokaal. They seem to be on all the time now, even in our classrooms at the school. With the communications channels overloaded by everyone trying to reach family and friends, the feeds are our only other contact with our homeworld.

At first, the images of destruction were rare, only one or two a season. Certain parts of the world had always suffered from quakes, after all. Such disturbances were given their just due by the media, appearing as part of the daily news broadcasts transmitted to the mining colonies from Dokaal. People worried about loved ones who might be living in affected areas, and memorial services were held on the rare occasions it was learned that relatives had fallen victim to tragedy. There might also be discussion regarding the type and amount of aid the various regional governments might provide, but ultimately, such news was usually forgotten quickly.

Things are different now.

Quakes seem to be erupting every few days at different locations around the world, and the effects seem to be getting worse each time. Barely a week ago, we received the news that the capital city of Wyjaed suffered widespread damage when a quake struck there in the middle of the night. Rescue efforts continue with unrelenting intensity just as they have since the beginning, but hundreds of thousands are feared dead.

Last night's broadcast brought news of the most recent incident. We sat aghast and watched journalists fight back tears as they reported the loss of the entire island nation of Saorquiln, destroyed by tidal forces generated as the result of a massive undersea quake. My friend Rueq and a few others living in our colony had relatives there, and we sat up through the night waiting for any word of survivors. According to the accounts we have seen, it appears that all of the island's inhabitants were lost.

The reports and images, coming from nearly every city now, are perhaps more disturbing because we are helpless to do anything. Out here, among the asteroids, we are days away even with our fastest ships. Besides, what would we do once we got there? Even those with the proper skills and knowledge do not yet seem to know what is happening.

On another of the colonies, the wife of my friend Caesi has been in constant contact with the ministry on Dokaal, but even her position as colony administrator has gained her nothing. No one seems able to explain what the scientists are calling "recurring irregular seismic disruptions beneath the planet's surface." They do not yet know what caused the quakes to begin, why they continue, or whether they will get worse before they finally stop.

One theory that seems to be gaining support in the scientific community is that this is a natural geological phase for the planet. Many scientists are searching for evidence that such an event might have happened long ago, perhaps even before life evolved on our world, but I do not understand how this knowledge will help stop the quakes.

What if they never stop?

More alarming to many is the notion put forth by several prominent spiritual leaders: that this is "the Reckoning." Many religious groups have long felt that our people have been drifting away from the principles Dokaa laid down at the start of our civilization. They believe she is angry at us and that the quakes are a punishment for abandoning our faith in her. Though this specific penalty is not recorded in our people's most sacred texts, the wording is sufficiently cautionary that it is enough to send waves of concern through our more devout people.

As for myself, while I have always attended services with Beeliq, I have never accepted these beliefs with her level of conviction. I know that she is seeking comfort and perhaps forgiveness in Dokaa's embrace, much as she did after her brother died in the mines. Though I did not do so then, part of me wants to join her in prayer now.

The colony administrators are doing their part to keep up a brave front. They repeatedly tell us to go about our lives as best we can, working in the mines or at the various stations supporting the miners and their families. Despite their efforts, the activity is doing little to ease everyone's concerns. My friends and others talk before and after our classes, and I overhear conversations in the Concourse Module when we go to shop or eat. Everyone, everywhere, all across the different colonies, seems to be asking the same question.

What is happening?

2151

Chapter One

THOUGH IT WAS NOT UNUSUAL for him to be called to the bridge at such an irregular hour, Captain Vanik was still surprised at the summons. After all, given their current assignment, what could possibly be so pressing?

Located well within the admittedly small sector of the galaxy that had been mapped and traversed by Vulcan ships, this area of space was one Vanik had traveled numerous times during his fifteen years as commander of the *Ti'Mur*. Other than its status as the location of a single minor conflict during the protracted war with the Andorians, the region offered little of interest. None of the planets in the area's lone star system were habitable, and they contained nothing of scientific or strategic value. The only quality the area possessed, in Vanik's opinion, was that it had few distractions to delay a vessel's journey to some other, more appealing destination.

Has this somehow changed?

He had only just settled into his evening's meditation

when the message came from the officer on duty. Well aware of her captain's routine, Sub-commander T'Lih would not have intruded on his private time unless she believed it was a matter for his attention. Whatever it was that had prompted her call, it must be quite fascinating indeed.

Of course, Vanik reminded himself, *further speculation serves no purpose. My questions will be answered in short order.*

The turbolift slowed to a halt and the doors parted to reveal the *Ti'Mur*'s bridge. Triangular-shaped, the command center was widest at the rear stations, with rows of control consoles to either side and angling inward until they met the immense viewscreen dominating the forward bulkhead. Unlike other areas of the ship, where lighting was adjusted in order to simulate the daily cycle on Vulcan, Vanik preferred the command center's illumination to remain at normal levels regardless of the time of day.

Each of the bridge's key stations was manned despite the lateness of the hour, just as they would be during prime shift, yet the captain also noted a crew member operating the secondary science console. A visual inspection of the weapons station showed that the defensive systems were not active, meaning that no threats to the ship had been detected. Even from across the room, he could hear the two separate conversations taking place between members of the bridge crew and detected nothing untoward being discussed.

Stepping from the turbolift, Vanik nodded in greeting to T'Lih as the subcommander noticed his arrival.

"Good evening, Captain," she offered as she rose from the command chair at the rear of the bridge. Like every other member of the ship's complement, T'Lih wore the standard gray uniform of the Vulcan Space Service. Impeccably tailored to her physique, the uniform possessed no decorative accessories save for the small rank insignia on the left side of her collar. Like Vanik's own, her features were lean and angular, but while his hair was gray and full-bodied, T'Lih wore her black locks cropped close to her skull in a manner that served to highlight the severe upswing of her pointed ears.

"And to you, Sub-commander," Vanik replied. "So, what is it that has attracted your interest?" Rather than take the proffered seat T'Lih had vacated, he chose instead to pace the room's perimeter, walking a slow circuit with hands clasped behind his back as he waited for the subcommander to make her report.

Moving to join her captain, T'Lih replied, "Fifty-two point six minutes ago, our long-range sensors detected an object traveling at warp one point three. A review of our data banks shows that it is of a type and configuration unknown to us."

"Life signs?" Vanik prompted.

"No, Captain. The object appears to be an unmanned drone. It is transmitting a recorded message that repeats at intervals of four point seven minutes. Translation efforts are already under way, and I have also ordered an attempt to determine the drone's origin point based on its current course heading."

Vanik nodded, pleased with the report and the subcommander's initiative, which also logically explained the presence of additional science personnel on the bridge. "Is it close enough for visual inspection?"

By way of reply, T'Lih summoned the attention of the

junior officer working at the main science station. "Lieutenant Serel?"

The object that appeared on the bridge's central viewer in response to the science officer's commands was unlike anything Vanik had seen before. It consisted of a bulky cylindrical module mounted above a trio of squat engine bells. The cylinder's outer shell was composed of metal plating, and Vanik could see the join lines as well as the heads of dozens of fasteners that presumably attached the individual plates to a skeletal frame. Two antenna dishes were affixed to the cylinder's flanks, one of which appeared to have suffered damage. In fact, pockmarks and other blemishes were clearly discernible across the surface of the small craft.

"The damage is consistent with the effects of ion storms we have seen on our vessel's hulls," Serel reported from his station. "According to our scans, exposure to such a storm most likely occurred approximately eleven point six years ago."

"What have you learned about its level of technology?" Vanik asked.

"Though we will have to retrieve the drone in order to complete a thorough investigation," the science officer replied, "its propulsion system looks to be quite rudimentary. I would theorize that the warp drive was of an experimental nature, perhaps the first such test made by whoever constructed the object."

Interesting, Vanik thought. Given that the craft was obviously primitive, in all likelihood a first-generation deep-space vessel, that it had survived such an encounter relatively intact and still able to transmit data was a testament to its designers' craftsmanship.

Could this drone be the initial step toward first contact with a new species? Though he had worn the uniform of the Space Service for seventy-six years, he had participated in only one other introduction to an alien race. Vanik had to confess that the opportunity to do so again presented an intriguing notion.

He heard a telltale tone from Serel's console and turned to see the junior officer rising from his chair. "I have a report on the status of our translation efforts, Captain," Serel said as he crossed the bridge to stand before Vanik and T'Lih. "The object has sustained considerable damage during its journey. Much of the message is garbled beyond our ability to decipher. However, I was able to isolate several passages. The people who constructed the drone call themselves the Dokaalan, and the device itself was not launched from their homeworld as part of an exploration initiative. Rather, it seems that the message is a distress call."

Vanik's right eyebrow rose in response. An entire planet calling for help? What could have prompted such a desperate act? "Did the message include a reason for their plea?"

"Yes, Captain," Serel replied. "Their planet was undergoing global seismic events that threatened to destroy it, and science specialists among their people predicted total obliteration within one of their years. Though they had discovered the ability to travel at light speeds, they possessed no space vessels capable of transporting people to another habitable planet. They therefore sent out a trio of unmanned craft in the hopes of contacting someone who could come to their aid."

Already beginning to surmise the likely outcome of

this scenario, Vanik was nevertheless obligated to consider what course of action, if any, he could undertake in response to the distress call. "Are we able to determine where the object originated?"

Turning to the secondary science station, T'Lih said, "Sub-commander Taren?"

"According to our sensor scans of its onboard systems," Taren replied, "it appears to have traveled on a constant course at a consistent speed for thirty-eight point three years. This places its likely origin point in an area of space that according to our databases is presently unexplored."

It took little effort for Vanik to comprehend the futility of the Dokaalan's actions. Even if the drone had been able to travel at a faster speed, had its creators not understood the improbability of making contact with anyone possessing the resources to render assistance on such a scale? Perhaps they had, and yet the dire situation they faced nevertheless compelled them to make the attempt.

"Given what has already been learned," Vanik said, "and presuming the Dokaalan scientists were correct in their original predictions, it would seem the time to provide assistance has long passed." It was an unfortunate determination to reach, he knew, but the facts currently available to them seemed to support no other conclusion.

"Captain," T'Lih said, "we could deploy a reconnaissance probe back along the drone's original course. It will take several months to reach that area of space at the probe's maximum speed, but it will be able to ascertain what ultimately happened to the Dokaalan homeworld."

It was a logical suggestion, and one Vanik at first supported. However, as this matter involved a species never before encountered, it was an issue that would have to be decided upon by the Vulcan Science Directorate. Only that august body possessed the authority to permit any interaction with a new race, a precaution intended to prevent the accidental introduction of technology, science, or even ideas that might prove too advanced for a culture not yet ready to possess such knowledge.

Besides, the *Ti'Mur* had other priorities. High Command had instructed Vanik to deviate from its current patrol in order to observe the latest activities of *Enterprise,* the deep-space exploration vessel recently launched by the humans from Earth. Though the humans themselves held little interest for him, Vanik nevertheless had kept abreast of their progress, especially regarding their efforts to perfect warp travel and push farther away from the confines of their own star system.

It had long been the opinion of High Command that the humans bore watching. Though they had proven to be somewhat innovative in their own way, they had also demonstrated that their inexperience in dealing with a larger celestial community, to say nothing of their own arrogance and overconfidence, likely would be their undoing.

Since *Enterprise* had left Earth, its crew and particularly its captain had managed to make quite a nuisance of themselves. That much was amply demonstrated when the vessel departed Earth on its inaugural voyage, deep into the heart of the Klingon Empire of all places. Only fortunate happenstance had prevented their initial contact with the Klingons from dissolving into an unmitigated disaster, and Vanik believed that the ultimate ramifications of the haphazard encounter were yet to be realized.

Then there was the recent debacle that had unfolded at the monastery on P'Jem. The *Enterprise* captain, Archer, had revealed the presence of the top-secret observation facility hidden beneath the monastery to Andorian operatives. Now that station and the vital data it provided about ship movements and other activities within Andorian space was gone, and the damage Archer had inflicted on Vulcan's intelligence-gathering operations would take a long time to repair.

Given all of that, Vanik could understand High Command's wishes that the Earth ship be monitored. He simply did not agree with the dispatching of a *Surak*-class vessel to do it. He hoped that *Enterprise* would be able to avoid trouble for the few days until the *Ti'Mur* was relieved by another vessel.

"Sub-commander T'Lih," he said, "prepare all of the information you have for transmission to High Command. In the interim, divert from our present course long enough to retrieve the drone, then adjust our course and speed to make our appointment on schedule."

"Yes, Captain," T'Lih replied, and set about relaying the necessary orders. As Vanik paced back to his command chair, he watched and listened as his bridge crew turned to their various tasks, satisfied that they would carry out their duties with their usual impeccable efficiency.

Settling into his seat, the captain realized he was actually looking forward to what a full examination of the alien object might reveal. If nothing else, the effort would pass the time until the rendezvous with the Earth ship.

It would be up to High Command and the Science Directorate as to whether a vessel was sent to discover the origin of the alien drone and perhaps to learn what had happened to those who had dispatched it, but Vanik for one hoped the attempt was made. Given the calamity they had apparently suffered, it would be unfortunate if the mystery of the Dokaalan were to remain unsolved.

Chapter Two

At ONE TIME, Admiral Forrest could differentiate among the various types of headaches that had always plagued him. There were those caused by stress or muscle tension or too little sleep, for example. Then there was the newer variety of discomfort he experienced on increasingly frequent occasions, invoked whenever he read one of Jonathan Archer's more colorful status reports from the *Enterprise*.

These days, however, Forrest divided his headaches into only two categories: those caused by Ambassador Soval, and the rest of them; and Soval's score was growing at an exponential rate. Though he didn't have a headache at the moment, Forrest nevertheless mentally added another mark to the list as he walked into his office and saw the Vulcan waiting for him.

The beginning of another wonderful day.

"Good morning, Ambassador," Forrest offered in what he knew to be a vain attempt at pleasantries. "How may I help you today?"

Dressed in his normal ensemble of flowing, earth-toned robes, Soval stood before the admiral's desk with his hands clasped in front of him. Forrest could not be sure, but he thought he saw the Vulcan's jaw clench. Something was definitely annoying the ambassador this morning.

"I understand that Captain Archer has managed to get himself into trouble again," Soval said, "and this time he required the assistance of one of our vessels to extricate himself from his predicament."

Movement outside his window caught Forrest's attention, and he looked up to see a Starfleet shuttlepod flying past. It was ascending into the sky, doubtless on its way to one of the space stations or drydock facilities orbiting Earth. The spaceframe of a new long-range space vessel was being assembled up there right now, he knew, and hundreds of engineers and other specialists were currently hard at work constructing the hundreds of components that would combine to create the next NX-class ship. He was looking forward to tomorrow, when his schedule would permit him the opportunity to go up there and see the status of the formidable project for himself. It certainly was a more appealing prospect than anything listed on his agenda for today.

Is it too late for those guys to come back and pick me up?

There was no way he would retreat from his current guest, of course. A man not easily intimidated, Forrest had long ago learned to handle personalities even haughtier than Soval's. "And Starfleet is extremely grateful, Ambassador. Please pass on my thanks to Captain Vanik and his crew. I also intend to submit a letter of commendation to the Vulcan High Command for their actions." Shrugging, he smiled and added, "I guess it was just good luck that the *Ti'Mur* was nearby." It was an effort to keep from smiling as he heard Soval exhale, an action on par with a heavy sigh of frustration from a human.

Of course, Forrest knew it was anything but coincidence that the Vulcan vessel had been in the vicinity when two *Enterprise* officers were trapped on the surface of the comet they had discovered. According to Archer's report, they had been under scrutiny by Vulcan ships for weeks. Though no explanations had been offered, Forrest was certain the directive had come because of Archer's actions on P'Jem.

His exposure of their secret surveillance facility hidden beneath the monastery there had not sat well with the High Command. They had been against the *Enterprise*'s launch and its subsequent long-range exploration mission to begin with, feeling that humanity was not yet ready to venture into the cosmos on its own. That Archer and his crew already had logged a handful of notable mishaps since leaving Earth had only exacerbated the Vulcans' unease. Undoubtedly, they would want to take steps to insure that Archer could not do anything else to interfere in their affairs.

"I have been in the company of humans long enough to recognize sarcasm when I hear it, Admiral," Soval said. "It is one quality of your people I have not yet come to appreciate."

Despite his best effort to remain composed, Forrest could not resist the opening. With a smile he asked, "Ah, so we have other qualities that you *do* admire?"

There was a moment of silence as Soval appeared to consider the words, and Forrest was sure he saw the ambassador's jaw tighten yet again. *I think Archer's right, and Soval* has *been spending too much time among us lowly humans.*

Finally, the Vulcan said, "I do admire your tenacity and desire to expand your horizons, Admiral, as these are commendable goals. My concern, however, and it is one shared by many of my people, is that you refuse to temper such determination with patience. Surely you can admit that your ignorance of the galaxy you inhabit already has been a source of great disruption?"

The compliment, wrapped as it was within the criticism, was still high praise indeed. Forrest knew that the ambassador had spent a great deal of time on Earth in the decades following first contact. He also had been one of the many voices of Vulcan dissent when Zefram Cochrane and Henry Archer had begun work on the Warp 5 project, all while Forrest himself was little more than a wide-eyed teenager contemplating a four-year stint in the navy in order to earn money for college. As Cochrane, along with the elder Archer and hundreds of others, labored to expand the limited warp capabilities of his original *Phoenix* spacecraft and those efforts began to bear fruit, Soval had been there, always warning that the "humans were too brash and were moving too fast for their own good."

And now this, a grudging accolade *for* humans from one of their most vocal detractors?

Could Soval actually be mellowing in his middle age? *Wishful thinking, Admiral.*

Deploying his best diplomatic charm, Forrest said,

Dayton Ward & Kevin Dilmore

"Ambassador, it's true that Jonathan Archer is not the experienced commander one might like to have in charge of the *Enterprise*. No human possesses such experience, and the only way we're ever going to acquire it is by going out there. Will we make mistakes? I don't doubt it, but in the end I trust Archer's judgment."

"I hope your confidence is not misplaced, Admiral," Soval replied, "and that Captain Archer obtains the experience he seeks before he commits a transgression that does real, lasting damage."

That's the Soval I know and love, Forrest mused.

Attempting to change the subject, the admiral held up the padd his aide had given him. "Since you're here, there is another matter I was hoping we could discuss. Starfleet received word yesterday that the Vulcan Science Directorate has updated its databases, and one item in particular caught my interest."

Though tight-lipped when it came to sharing technology, the Vulcans had been very forthcoming with other information, such as interstellar cartography and navigation. Despite their misgivings about *Enterprise*'s mission, that information exchange had become much more frequent and detailed following the ship's launch.

"This probe that the *Ti'Mur* discovered," Forrest continued. "Is there a final decision on what to do about it?"

Soval's eyebrow rose in response. Clearly, he had not anticipated this new question. "The Directorate is still examining data collected from the device. Why do you ask?"

Forrest paused, taking a moment to ponder the Golden Gate Bridge, visible across San Francisco Bay. Fog enshrouded most of it, but the view was still clear enough that he could see a lone sailboat navigating the bay as it headed out to sea. A wistful smile curled the corners of the admiral's mouth, and not for the first time he wished it could be him at the wheel of such a tiny vessel.

"It's a fascinating discovery," he said. "I was thinking of sending *Enterprise* to investigate."

His position at Starfleet naturally precluded Forrest from undertaking any of the long-range missions planned for *Enterprise* and future NX ships, the next of which would be ready for launch nearly two years from now. The delays and setbacks encountered during the development of the advanced warp program had seen to it that he and his contemporaries would live vicariously through the experiences of younger men like Jonathan Archer, A. G. Robinson, and those who followed such promising leaders into that vast, unknown frontier.

With that in mind, the idea of sending Archer and his crew to learn the fate of the Dokaalan appealed to the admiral. It also seemed to present an opportunity to give the *Enterprise* a mission unlikely to further irk the Vulcans.

Judging by Soval's reaction, however, that was not an opinion the ambassador shared.

"According to our calculations," Soval replied, "it would take your vessel months to reach the probe's point of origin, even traveling at its maximum speed. Besides, there would be nothing to investigate when they arrived."

Forrest replied, "I know that whatever happened to the Dokaalan was a long time ago. Still, they had the means to launch that probe. What else might they have left behind? Don't you wonder about that, or what finally became of them?" The Vulcan's position seemed a bit simplistic, the admiral decided. There was no telling what kind of artifacts of their civilization the Dokaalan might have left behind. The possibilities were endless.

"Scientists on Vulcan examined all of the information transported within the craft's limited computer storage facility," Soval said. "Using that information to extrapolate a series of computer models, they determined that seismic forces eventually tore the planet apart. Given that conclusion and the Dokaalan's limited technology, it is logical to assume that their civilization was destroyed by whatever cataclysm befell their planet. There would be little use sending your ship, Admiral. That part of the galaxy is still uncharted, and it will be some time before we ourselves undertake any exploration of the region."

Forrest shrugged. "Seems like the perfect reason to go." Speaking the words, he was unable to ignore the various photographs, paintings, and sculptures adorning his office, each of them representing key vessels and moments in naval and Starfleet history. He almost wanted to append the obvious question to what he had already said: Was "going there" not the reason for constructing ships like *Enterprise* in the first place?

"As we have already discussed," Soval countered, "Captain Archer and his crew seem to have enough difficulty staying out of trouble in this part of the galaxy. There is no point in compounding their work by sending them on a long and arduous mission with nothing to gain."

If he had not known Soval better, Forrest would have sworn he detected the slightest hint of amusement in the ambassador's voice.

Not likely.

Still, the admiral felt compelled to agree with his counterpart. There were countless things for *Enterprise* to discover right here in their own neck of the woods. Perhaps, one day, when Starfleet had many ships at its disposal, some lucky captain and his or her crew would be able to seek out the ultimate fate of the Dokaalan.

One day. . . .

2378

Chapter Three

"I AM ZAHANZEI, first minister to the people of the planet Dokaal. I speak to you as the leader of a people in desperate need of assistance from anyone who might hear this message."

Though he had watched the recording twice already, Jean-Luc Picard once again found himself drawn by Zahanzei's appeal as if seeing it for the first time.

"Catastrophic seismic forces are tearing our world apart, and our most experienced scientists believe that total destruction is inevitable. Our planet is the only one in our solar system capable of sustaining life, and we do not possess the resources to evacuate our people to a suitable world in another system. We have only just recently discovered a means of propulsion that would allow us to complete an interstellar journey, but our level of technology is limited. Our calculations tell us that there is insufficient time to build vessels capable of

carrying a sufficient number of our people to safety in order to insure the preservation of our race."

Standing before a window offering a picturesque view of a thriving city, the Dokaalan leader's visage was noble and thoughtful, as would befit a person in his position. Tall and thin, he was humanoid in appearance. His skin, possessing a light blue tinge, was free of any blemishes that Picard could see. Deep maroon eyes peered out from beneath a prominent brow, while only small holes represented where the ears and nose might be on a human's head. Completely devoid of hair, his skull tapered to an almost arrow-shaped chin. Despite his stately bearing, Zahanzei still seemed to possess a vulnerability held only barely in check by the need to carry out the duties of his office for the benefit of those he governed.

"Therefore, I ordered the creation of these three small probes, one of which has traveled to you and carries with it my plea on behalf of my people and my world: Please help us."

As the recording completed and the *Enterprise*'s senior staff turned back to the conference table and each other, Picard knew that already their minds had set to work. He could almost see them ordering their individual lists of responsibilities to support a rescue operation on the scale they believed was coming.

"How soon do we get under way, sir?" asked Commander William Riker from where he sat to Picard's right, giving voice to the concern and determination that was evident on the faces of the others.

As he regarded those faces, however, he felt a twinge of regret, knowing that it fell to him to dash those plans and remind them of the reality of their current lot in life.

"Three weeks ago," Picard said, "the *U.S.S. Crazy Horse* discovered a small probe of unfamiliar design adrift near the Jeluryn Sector. It had suffered massive damage during its rather lengthy voyage, and engineers aboard the *Crazy Horse* weren't able to retrieve anything of value from its onboard computer system. What they did discover, however, was that this was not the first object encountered from these people. According to Federation data banks, another such device was encountered by a Vulcan ship more than two centuries ago."

"Two centuries?" said Deanna Troi, seated next to Riker and sporting a confused expression. "We're just now learning about it?"

Picard nodded, resisting the urge to smile at the counselor's confusion. "The Vulcan Science Academy spent several months analyzing data retrieved from the first probe. They concluded that the planetary disaster described by First Minister Zahanzei occurred decades before the first probe's discovery, and well before Starfleet possessed any sort of deep-space exploration capability. The Vulcans advised against sending a ship to investigate, and the matter was closed."

"Earth was taking a lot of advice from the Vulcans in those days," said Lieutenant Commander Geordi La Forge, "but it's hard to believe that anyone in Starfleet could resist the urge to find out where that probe had come from. It sounds like just the mission to give to one of those first long-range ships."

Seated next to La Forge, Lieutenant Commander Data replied, "It was a very active, almost chaotic, period in Earth history, Geordi. With only a single vessel of sufficient capability available for such a task, Starfleet's priorities did not allow for a mission of extended duration at that time. By the time such resources were available, Earth found itself embroiled in conflicts with both the Xindi and the Romulans."

In response to the android's words, Picard could not help but glance to the rear wall of the observation lounge and its array of replicas portraying the lineage of starships named *Enterprise* dating back more than two centuries. Grimly, he reminded himself that in addition to the promise of peaceful exploration, the replicas also represented decades of conflict, both victorious and damaging.

Picard almost smiled as he watched the exchange between the two colleagues. Even in the face of what was shaping up to be little more than a milk run, La Forge and Data were trading information both relevant and trivial, just as they would if they were attempting to solve a looming crisis. *Some things will never change.*

"Once the Federation was founded," he said, "and with a whole host of new friends, to say nothing of enemies, Starfleet's charter and mission initiatives took them in other directions. After a time, verifying the fate of a single planet which was already believed destroyed for years was lost in the shuffle of larger concerns."

A student of history, Picard was intimately familiar with that period in Earth's evolution from a single civilization to one of the founding parties of what was now a Federation of more than one hundred fifty worlds. Such a feat, carried out in the space of little more than two centuries and accompanied by all manner of ancillary accomplishments and setbacks along the way, would have been more than enough to obscure any desire to investigate the presumed destruction of one planet.

Leaning forward in his chair until his forearms rested on the conference table, Riker said, "I don't understand. If there's nothing we can do for these people, then why show us the message at all?"

"It seems," Picard replied, "that Starfleet Command wishes us to chart the area of space where the probes are believed to have originated, and see if we can determine what exactly happened to the Dokaalan and their world."

"Sir," said Lieutenant Christine Vale, the *Enterprise*'s security chief, from where she sat at the far end of the table, "wouldn't an actual science ship be better equipped for such an assignment?"

Tugging on the lower edge of his uniform jacket, Picard replied, "Perhaps, Lieutenant, but Admiral Nechayev believes that under the current circumstances, the *Enterprise* is the perfect ship to head up this mission."

A bitter aftertaste remained even as he spoke the words, but Picard vowed he would reveal none of that irritation or disappointment to his subordinates. Vale's point about sending a science vessel in search of the Dokaalan was a valid observation, but there was also the simple matter that no science vessel, or captain of same, was currently believed to be a hindrance to Starfleet.

The recent confrontation with the demon ship at the Rashanar Battle Site, as well as the annihilation of the *U.S.S. Juno* and several Ontailian warships, was still fresh in many people's minds, particularly Picard's. There were those in Starfleet, many of whom he once had called friends, who believed that his best days as a starship captain were behind him. It did not soothe his emotions to know that the perception was one manufactured to preserve the dignity of the Ontailian government in the face of their own missteps during the incident.

A valuable ally to the Federation in the current post–Dominion War reality, the Ontailians could ill afford a political incident within their own society. Such a disruption might cause them to withdraw their Federation membership, an option viewed by many on both sides as highly undesirable. The only way to ensure the stability of the Ontailian government was to make certain that blame for the demon ship incident was directed elsewhere.

In this case, that meant Picard. Though officially cleared of culpability for the loss of the *Juno* and the Ontailian ships, so far as the public and Starfleet were concerned, the captain had nonetheless committed a grave error. Many within Starfleet were asking whether Picard had finally begun to succumb in the face of the numerous traumatic experiences he had suffered over the length of his career. Was he still up to the task of commanding a starship, much less the vessel carrying the most renowned name in Starfleet history?

Despite the confusion, resentment, and even outright anger with which some officers in the highest echelons of Starfleet viewed him, Picard had managed to find an unlikely ally in the persona of Admiral Alynna Nechayev. It was she who ultimately had submitted the recommendation that, given the political and strategic challenges facing the Federation, an officer of Picard's experience and talents could not be dismissed from Starfleet so long as he was willing and able to serve. To Picard, the admiral's support had come as a near total surprise.

Picard and Nechayev had clashed more than once over the years, particularly in his handling of the lone Borg his crew had recovered nearly a decade ago, and with it, the discovery of a possible way to destroy the entire Borg Collective in one fell swoop. He had been unwilling to unleash what he considered a genocidal tactic, even on the Federation's most formidable enemy, and that decision had invoked Nechayev's wrath. The *Enterprise* captain had weathered that storm as well as several others that followed, and a mutual grudging respect had developed along the way, with each officer knowing that Starfleet was better off with the other than without.

Though a Starfleet tribunal already had ruled on Picard's actions with respect to the loss of the *Juno* and the damage done to relations with the Ontailians, temporary though that might have been, Nechayev had taken it upon herself to watch over Picard and the *Enterprise.* First, she had given them the chance to prove the existence of the demon ship and clear their names. With that issue laid to rest, there remained the much larger burden of giving Picard some needed breathing space and keeping him from becoming embroiled in any other potentially volatile political situations for the time being.

Sitting across from Counselor Troi, Dr. Beverly Crusher said, "What you mean is that Starfleet isn't sure what to do with us, so they're shuffling us out of the way to avoid any more embarrassment while they figure out a plan."

There was no mistaking the torque of the doctor's delicate jaw or the disgust clouding her dark blue eyes, and though he was tempted to admonish her for the comment, Picard refrained. Crusher, along with the entire ship's complement, was frustrated at the chain of events to this point. They deserved to blow off a bit of steam now and then. Better to do it here, among the privileged company of trusted friends, than elsewhere on the ship where subordinates already battling damaged morale might hear them.

"Admiral Nechayev believes that by assigning the *Enterprise* to this mission," Picard said, "her crew and most especially her captain will possibly avoid further controversy for at least a while. Therefore, that is exactly what we shall do." Turning to Data, he asked, "Commander, how long to reach Dokaalan space?"

"At warp eight," the android replied, "we will arrive at the Dokaalan system in twenty-six days, eleven hours, and forty-seven minutes. That estimate is based on long-range sensor data obtained from an unmanned exploratory probe sent to chart that region of space sixty-three years ago. Though incomplete, the data suggests . . ."

"Thank you, Commander," Picard said, circumventing an oration that, while no doubt informative, could conceivably take most of the time the *Enterprise* would spend traveling to its intended destination.

"Though this is supposed to be a low-risk assignment," Riker said, "we're still traveling to a sector that's largely unexplored. I don't think we should go in unprepared."

At the far end of the table, Vale said, "I agree, sir. With your permission, I'd like to conduct a series of scheduled and surprise security drills, as well as request a level-one diagnostic of all defensive systems."

"No problem there," La Forge replied. "My people will need something to do, too."

Picard nodded to the security chief. "Make it so. I leave the details to your discretion, Lieutenant." Turning to Riker and Troi, he said, "Given the length of time it will take us to reach the Dokaalan system, I want you to organize a duty roster that allows for reduced shift rotations for the entire crew. Given recent events, I want them to enjoy as much leisure time as possible." Nodding in Vale's direction and with a small smile, he added, "Feel free to factor in any of the lieutenant's surprise security drills you see fit, however. We wouldn't want to lose our edge, after all."

With a mischievous grin of his own, Riker replied, "Aye, sir."

Before saying anything else, Picard took a moment to regard those sitting around the table, each looking expectantly to him for direction.

Riker, his loyal second-in-command, who during his own career had done almost as much in the name of protecting the Federation way of life as had Picard himself.

Troi, reading him in her own unique way, knowing more about him than anyone ever could.

Beverly, her stately countenance softened slightly with age and yet still consumed by the same drive and passion he had always seen in her.

Data, who even after all these years and without the emotion chip he had been forced to surrender to Starfleet, still managed to convey the sense of wonderment of a precocious child.

La Forge, who possessed a clarity of vision that far exceeded even that provided by his artificial eyes.

Though she had not been a member of the crew for as long as the others, Vale had taken little time to demonstrate her talents and potential. In similar fashion, she had proven herself worthy of those who had preceded her as *Enterprise* security chief, carving herself a position of respect among the rest of the senior staff.

Shipmates, trusted advisors, valued friends. Picard knew that these six individuals, and by extension every person on the ship, would follow wherever he might lead them. While he could learn to accept how outsiders viewed him, it angered him that his crew could be treated as the pariahs many now believed them to be. Regardless of all they had accomplished over the years, despite the very real debt Starfleet and the Federation itself owed this ship and her crew, they had been sent away in the name of political expediency, no longer considered worthy of the esteem Picard believed they had rightfully earned long ago.

You will regain the respect taken from you, he vowed silently to his shipmates. *If it takes the rest of my days, I will see to that.*

When no one responded to his query for further questions and Picard dismissed the staff, only Riker remained, much as the captain expected he would. He recognized the way his first officer's shoulders tensed when he had something to say yet was waiting until the appropriate time. Despite the close friendship they had cultivated over the years, ingrained protocol and discipline would always prevent William Riker from speaking freely until any subordinates were out of earshot.

Watching his first officer waiting for the room to clear, Picard noted the touch of gray peppering the man's temples. The badge of maturity seemed at odds with his clean-shaven face, which gave the commander a look of youthful innocence both men knew had been left behind long ago.

"So we're not really out of the doghouse just yet, are we?" Riker finally asked once the doors to the conference lounge had closed. "They're going to just shuffle us from one meaningless assignment to another?" He rose from his seat and began to pace the length of the conference room. Watching him move back and forth, Picard realized that without his beard to hide the lines of his face, it was easy to see how frustrated Riker was by the visible clenching of his jaw.

Settling back in his chair, Picard replied, "I believe the preferred term is 'low-priority mission,' Number One."

His delivery was just deadpan enough to elicit the desired response, that of catching his first officer momentarily off guard before he noticed Picard's teasing smile. Riker laughed in spite of the frustration he was obviously feeling.

"This isn't like when they sent us to the Neutral Zone during the Borg invasion," Riker said. "At least then I could understand their reasons, even if I didn't agree with them."

Picard found himself concurring with that. His previous capture and assimilation by the Borg during their first attack on the Federation twelve years earlier had given the collective all the information needed to cut a destructive swath through Federation space and right to humanity's doorstep. Only Data's skill and Picard's own force of will, battered into near-total submission by the Borg's invasive procedures besieging his mind and body, had prevented Earth from being crushed by perhaps the most formidable oppressor ever known.

Many were certain that Picard had suffered irreparable harm at the hands of his captors. Still others, notably those who had studied every piece of information about the Borg and any scrap of technology salvaged from the wreckage of that first enemy vessel, believed the *Enter-*

prise captain might still retain vestiges of a connection to the collective. The risk of his becoming a liability or, worse yet, a weapon for the Borg in the event of a future invasion attempt was too great to ignore.

Accordingly, when the Borg had sent a second massive cube-shaped vessel on a direct attack course for Earth seven years later, the newly commissioned *Enterprise,* NCC-1701-E, had been sent away from the conflict. As it turned out, Picard had indeed retained a visceral link to the collective, a revelation he had used to his advantage after defying orders and joining the fight, eventually aiding in the destruction of the second Borg ship.

"This is different," Riker continued, stopping his pacing and turning to lock eyes with his captain. "To treat us this way after everything we've done? After everything *you've* done?"

"We're serving a larger purpose, Number One," Picard replied, hoping to convince himself as much as his first officer. "At least until the situation with the Ontailians is stabilized, Admiral Nechayev feels that assigning us to these types of missions will help minimize our impact to an already volatile state of affairs."

After the truth of the captain's actions surrounding the demon ship was revealed, Starfleet Command had no choice. Despite the belief held by many in those corridors of power that Picard himself should relinquish command, his forcible removal was not an option.

However, the unusual request of the Ontailians had put Starfleet in a quandary. In order to preserve their ally's political stability, it would have to appear that Picard was receiving some form of sanction. Though all of the *Enterprise* crew knew the truth, for which Picard was thankful, the majority of those serving in Starfleet did not.

"Well, if they want to give us milk runs," Riker said, "then we'll just have to log the best damn milk runs they've ever seen, won't we?" Smiling, he straightened his posture in the manner that told Picard the first officer would carry out his duties on this assignment as he would on any other mission, not that the captain needed such confirmation, of course.

Riker took his leave and returned to the bridge, leaving Picard alone in the conference lounge. Turning in his chair to face the line of viewports forming the room's rear wall, he allowed himself several minutes of quiet, watching stars streaking past as the *Enterprise* warped toward uncharted space. Ordinarily it was a view that soothed him, but not today. Unlike other occasions, when he might take satisfaction that he and his vessel were heading where none had traveled before, this time was different. Instead, they were running away, retreating as an unruly child might flee the gaze of an admonishing parent.

As he swiveled away from the windows, his eyes once again caught the display of ships on the lounge's rear wall. Studying them, Picard found himself unable to resist dwelling on the history his vessel shared with those depicted on the wall before him. Individually, each ship's captain had enjoyed triumphs and suffered adversities that rivaled and even surpassed his own. Together, they had woven one of Starfleet's most enduring legends.

Had his actions, either those he had actually perpetrated

or others perhaps destined to be recorded for posterity, sul-
lied that history? If so, was such damage beyond repair?

No, he decided. *I refuse to accept that.*

Alone and in the privacy of his own thoughts, however, Picard could not help noting a disturbing lack of
conviction.

Chapter Four

Translated from the personal journal of Hjatyn:

THINGS ARE getting worse.

We see only the news feeds from Dokaal now. They are constant, transmitting on all channels. Many have quit reporting for their assigned shifts, be they miners or workers in any of the support sections, and have instead taken to congregating in the public recreation areas to watch the feeds for hours on end. Still others have simply retreated to their private quarters, as if trying to find a place of safety.

Beeliq is one of the few who are trying to maintain some type of normalcy. She continues to carry out her duties at the colony administrator's office, while I try to persevere with my classes. School has been all but canceled, though, and we sit with our students and watch the reports coming from the homeworld.

The quakes are growing in number and intensity. Sometimes three or four occur at different locations around the world during a single day. On other occasions, a site already tormented by one quake is subjected to another, adding to the toll of death and destruction. Rescue workers are hampered or even thwarted when this happens, helpless to do anything in the face of renewed devastation. Resources for rescue and recovery have long since been pushed beyond their limits, and those citizens who can volunteer to assist are already doing so. Even their efforts are not enough.

Many here are frustrated at their inability to render aid. I have heard some people talking about trying to return to Dokaal at any cost. Fearful that some might attempt to take matters into their own hands, the colony administrators have placed guards on the few shuttle transports available to us. I guess they hope this will deter anyone from trying to commandeer any of the ships.

The administrators also have threatened to enact special protection measures on the colonists as well, warning that they will restrict us all to our homes and duty stations if order is not maintained. That seems to be enough incentive for most people to restrain themselves from doing anything foolish, but it does nothing to relieve anyone's anxiety over the situation.

For a time, Beeliq and I said little or nothing to one another about the escalating crisis. I know she felt the need to protect me from all of this at first, somehow, but I could always see the stress and fear she tried to keep to herself. I also know that her attempts to reach her parents on the homeworld have not been successful. Nearly a week ago, the news feeds reported a massive quake near the city where they live. The number of people believed dead has been growing with each update. Beeliq knew I comprehended what this probably meant, but I could tell she was not comfortable talking about it.

Even the meals we shared at the beginning and end of each day were quiet affairs. I think that neither of us wanted to talk for fear of the conversation turning to the situation on Dokaal, after which we would both return to our respective silences more frightened than before.

At tonight's meal, however, I finally gave voice to the thoughts plaguing every person on each of the colonies.

Our planet is dying.

Perhaps it was the way I said it, not as a question but as a statement of undeniable fact, but Beeliq only nodded when I actually did say it. She seemed almost relieved, as if a mammoth burden had been lifted from her.

Then she cried, for the first time since her brother's death.

I cried with her, for my grandparents lost on Dokaal, for the friends I had left behind when we were transferred to the colonies, for everyone who had suffered during this catastrophe. We even cried for those left to endure whatever was yet to come.

As for what that might be, people are fearing the worst. The news reports are making no attempts to soften the harsh reality of what is happening to our planet. Plans for evacuation are in progress, and all across the colonies preparations are under way to receive those precious few who will be able to escape the global devastation. It will be but a fraction of the population, a fact not lost on people who have come to realize that our planet's days, to say nothing of their very own, are numbered.

And what about those of us who already live here

among the asteroids? We are trapped here, helpless to do anything except wait for our homeworld to die. What will we do in the aftermath of the coming disaster? How will we survive? Out of necessity, the colonies are able to sustain themselves for the long periods of time between supply shipments from Dokaal, but what will happen when the ships stop coming? We will have more people living here than the colony facilities were designed to support, so adjustments will have to be made quickly to accommodate them.

Caesi tells me that his wife and the other administrators have had plans set in motion for some time to deal with this situation. This means that they have known the awful truth for longer than the public has, and have been preparing. Part of me is relieved because I know that those in charge have retained their focus in the midst of this crisis and are working to give us the best chance of survival.

However, I am also concerned that there may be other facts that our leaders have withheld from us. Perhaps things are more serious than is generally believed, and the administrators are trying to prevent panic from escalating. Were I in charge, I think I would want to inform the people as much as possible, no matter how unsettling the facts might be, and trust that their initial fear and uncertainty would be defeated by their desire to survive and protect their families. I think that displaying great faith in those you lead would better allow them to trust in your guidance.

In the days ahead, I think that both the people and our leaders will need such trust if we are to survive.

Chapter Five

SUNRISE on Qo'noS.

Since arriving on the homeworld as the Federation's ambassador to the Klingon Empire, Worf had yet to tire of the magnificent view afforded by the trio of large windows forming his office's back wall. Beyond the transparasteel barriers, the sun was just beginning to highlight the skyline, burning a fiery red and bathing everything in its harsh crimson hue.

Before his current position brought him here as a matter of course, he had visited Qo'noS only sporadically since leaving with his parents for Khitomer at the age of six. Most of those visits had not been under pleasant circumstances, so it was with no small amount of comfort that he was able to sit here, as he did most mornings before beginning his official duties, simply to relax and take in the vast metropolis before him. Worf had decided long ago that the First City was at its most peaceful during this time of day.

It was also one of the few occasions where he felt a

true connection to the capital. Just as the robes he now wore as a symbol of diplomacy shrouded the beating heart of a warrior, a blanket of tranquility covered this, the very cradle of the Klingon Empire and the countless soldiers who had served it over the centuries. How easy would it be to simply sit here, ignoring the numerous appointments and responsibilities conspiring to drown him in a sea of bureaucratic chaos, and just watch the city come alive for the start of a glorious new day?

"They're calling for rain later this morning," a voice said from behind him.

Perhaps I will try again tomorrow, Worf amended silently, sighing in amused resignation as he turned from the windows to see Giancarlo Wu standing in the doorway leading from his office.

As always, his chief aide was impeccably dressed, his black trousers and shoes accentuated by a dark blue shirt and maroon vest. Wu affected an aristocratic air that in Worf's eyes was ideal for the types of diplomatic and social situations the ambassador found himself navigating, which was a good thing.

Having served at the embassy for nearly a decade, Wu's seemingly unmatched familiarity with the political minutiae that consumed so much of Worf's time, to say nothing of his superior patience for it, had proven invaluable time and again. In fact, the ambassador even had sent his aide on various missions of his own, comfortable in the knowledge that Wu's consummate skill and experience were more than enough to handle whatever was required.

"Good morning," Worf said, knowing that Wu already had been in his own office for at least an hour. As was the human's habit, he was here before sunrise each day and did not depart until the evening hours. It was normal for him to leave Worf to work alone upon his own arrival, his entry to the ambassador's office signaling the official start of the day.

"And to you, Ambassador," Wu replied before glancing down at the omnipresent padd in his right hand. Studying the device, he affected an amused expression. "I have good news and bad news. Which would you prefer to hear first?"

They both knew it was a rhetorical question. Within moments of their first meeting two years earlier, Worf had directed Wu never to withhold any information or soften it in any way, no matter how unpleasant it might be to hear. He had expected his aide to resist those instructions at first, as it had probably been Wu's habit to dissemble out of concern for the sensitivities of human diplomats. The man had instead embraced Worf's preference for direct dialogue in true Klingon fashion.

Tapping commands into his padd with such speed that Worf thought the melodic tones generated by the individual keystrokes might actually blur into a single extended whine, Wu said, "The emperor sends his regrets at having to cancel the audience you requested with him next week. He has urgent business offworld and will have your meeting rescheduled upon his return."

Worf nodded. "Notify his office that I will submit a new request through official channels and appreciate any assistance they can offer in selecting an alternative appointment." There were protocols to be observed, after all, and His Excellency was free to honor or dismiss such requests at his discretion. As it was, Worf considered it a personal honor that any sort of explanation for the cancellation of their meeting had been offered.

Of course, he did enjoy a closer relationship with Kahless than most Klingons, including those currently serving on the High Council. After the revelation that clerics at the monastery on Boreth had created a clone of the original emperor in a scheme to provide what they perceived as sorely needed leadership to the troubled Klingon Empire nearly a decade ago, Worf had been the first outsider to meet with him. Later, he had convinced Gowron, chancellor of the High Council at the time, to install the cloned version of the empire's greatest and most storied warrior as ceremonial emperor to the Klingon people. And two years ago, Kahless was instrumental in aiding Gowron's successor, Martok, in surviving a *coup d'état*. With honorable warriors such as Chancellor Martok—Worf's friend and mentor—leading the way, and Kahless's guidance, the Empire would regain its former glory.

Though Kahless had expressed his eternal appreciation to Worf, the ambassador had always been careful not to give the appearance of using his friendship to curry favor, particularly after taking on his diplomatic posting. Worf would not dream of circumventing the normal process for an audience with the emperor.

"On a brighter note," Wu continued, "Chancellor Martok passes on word that he still expects you for dinner this evening, assuming your schedule permits, of course."

Worf smiled at that. Despite his aide's straight delivery, there was no mistaking the humor behind the words. After all, even if one were brave enough to casually dismiss an invitation from a chancellor of the High Council, it was sheer foolhardiness to do so when that same person was also the ruler of the House to which one belonged.

"Assuming there are no interstellar incidents in the offing," he replied, "please advise the chancellor that I will be there."

Nodding, Wu made another entry into his padd. "Here's the best news of the day. Your son sent a communiqué that he has been granted leave from the *Ya'Vang,* and plans to be here in about two weeks. Can I assume your schedule will permit a brief vacation for his benefit?"

Though he knew Wu did not, and could not, mean anything else by asking the question, Worf realized that at another time, he might well have considered not making plans with Alexander. To say that their relationship had been strained from the beginning was an understatement of galactic proportions. After years of struggling to understand one another, father and son had finally reached a point where they enjoyed each other's company. Alexander's duties aboard the *Ya'Vang* coupled with Worf's own diplomatic responsibilities made those occasions rare, and Worf was thrilled when such opportunities presented themselves.

"Absolutely," he said to Wu. "See to it that any routine matters that might take place during his time here are rescheduled accordingly." With luck, Worf's duties would permit him the brief respite.

After a moment, his aide said, "Ambassador, I've also done some checking with a friend of mine at Starfleet Command. Apparently, a decision has been made regarding the *Enterprise.*"

Worf sat quietly as Wu described the political minefield Captain Picard had left for both the Federation and the Ontailians to traverse, as well as the new "mission" Starfleet had given Picard and his crew. The only outward response he allowed was the tightening of his jaw, his frustration with the situation growing with each second he listened to Wu's report.

He was already fully aware of the incident with the *Juno* and the Ontailian vessels that had been destroyed. Colleagues in Starfleet had kept him apprised of the *Enterprise* crew's treatment in the aftermath of that tragedy. At the outset of the incident, Worf could understand the need to investigate the matter with utmost care, including the possibility that Jean-Luc Picard could have become mentally unbalanced to the point of willfully murdering innocent people.

The very idea was laughable, of course, a fact later confirmed by Starfleet specialists. What galled Worf even more than Picard's initial treatment following the incident was how he and the *Enterprise* crew had been "disposed of," at least for the time being.

Exhaling in disgust, Worf let his eyes wander to the wall of his office where he kept the small collection of mementos he allowed himself. Awards bestowed from both Starfleet and the Empire hung alongside photographs of Alexander and his son's mother, K'Ehleyr, as well as a still-humorous image of him and the command staff of Deep Space 9, dressed in the uniforms of the Earth game called "baseball." His eyes lingered for a moment on his wedding photo with Jadzia Dax, and he paused long enough to send a silent message to her in *Sto-Vo-Kor,* where she now hunted with the other warriors who had honorably given their lives in combat.

For the first time, Worf realized that among the keepsakes was no overt reminder of his time on the *Enterprise.* While he would scarcely have given the observation a second thought only a few years ago, he now found the idea troubling for reasons he could not explain, at least not yet.

Was it because of the situation his former shipmates currently faced, and that he was not there to stand with them?

Opportunities to see his friends on the *Enterprise* had been rare, particularly since he took on his role as ambassador. Other than the time the ship had ferried him to the Klingon border for his first diplomatic assignment on taD, the gateways crisis, and the mission involving the mysterious Malkus artifact, the opportunities had been few and far between. While he knew he was carrying out important duties here on behalf of both the Federation and the Empire, there were times he wished he were still serving in Starfleet, doing his part to look after his comrades. He wanted to help them now, but what could he do from here?

As if reading his mind, Wu said, "You know, with your travel schedule being what it is in coming months, it would not be unusual to request a Starfleet vessel be detailed for courier duty. I'm sure that special consideration would be given if you were to ask for a specific vessel for that purpose, assuming that ship's mission priorities permitted it."

It was an interesting notion, Worf decided, and a tempting one. Such an assignment normally was viewed as an honor by Starfleet brass, even if individual ship crews and their captains regarded the duty as only slightly less glamorous than replacing navigational buoys. Being specifically requested for such a mission was further considered to be a singular privilege. Worf also realized that by having the *Enterprise* as his courier vessel, he would be able to call upon Picard's own formidable diplomatic skills. If nothing else, it would surely be a better assignment than being "banished" to some faraway corner of the galaxy.

For that reason alone, Worf discarded the idea.

Shaking his head, he replied, "No. That could be perceived as using my position to come to Captain Picard's aid." While he did not care how such a move might reflect on him personally, Worf did not want to add further unfavorable light to Picard or the *Enterprise*. Besides, he knew his shipmates would find a way to weather this controversy without his help, and they would do so beginning with this odd assignment Starfleet had seen fit to give them.

"Where is this Dokaal system?" he asked.

Checking his padd, Wu replied, "Beyond the limits of explored space, it seems, out past Cardassian and Tholian territory. Ordinarily it would be a plum assignment, especially for such a passionate explorer as Captain Picard. Under the circumstances, however, anyone with even cursory knowledge of the situation will see this tasking for what it truly is."

Worf agreed. Not actually a punishment, so far as the legal or technical definition of the term was concerned, the *Enterprise*'s assignment to investigate the origin of a distress signal sent more than two centuries ago was a slap in the face to a man of Picard's stature and accomplishments, to say nothing of the rest of his crew.

While the complete details of the so-called Ontailian Incident had been classified, Worf knew that there were those in Starfleet who had called for Picard's dismissal from service in the wake of the *Juno*'s loss. Despite his exoneration, political schemers who had lost face during the incident would be looking for restitution. Publicly reprimanding the *Enterprise* crew, particularly Picard, would not sit well with the numerous allies the captain had garnered over the years. Therefore, all they could do was send him on a mundane assignment and get him out of the way. Perhaps they would dispatch him on another such mission once he had completed this one, and another after that, and keep doing so until Picard finally resigned in frustration.

That was unlikely, Worf decided. Admiral Nechayev was far too shrewd an officer to allow the captain to leave under such circumstances. As she had with other officers on different occasions, she would find a way to protect Picard until the current situation subsided.

As for Picard himself, he was as adept at playing the "political game" as anyone he had ever encountered. His brinksmanship skills were on par with his command abilities, rivaling even the very talented individuals Worf had come across since becoming an ambassador. The big difference between Picard and career politicians, of course, was how and why he put those skills into play, and a key advantage he held over those who would see him removed from command of the *Enterprise* was his seemingly limitless reserves of patience.

Worf smiled at that as his gaze moved to the corner of his desk and to the small leather-bound book he had deliberately placed there. A gift from Picard, it was a reproduction of an ancient Earth text, *The Art of War.*

He had read the book while a student at Starfleet Academy, of course. However, it was not until revisiting it, this time benefiting from many more years of experience, that he realized the volume's multilayered message and just how appropriate a gift his former captain had offered. Despite the book's obvious title, the words of wisdom recorded by the human warrior Sun Tzu centuries ago were not only a timeless guide for battle, but were also applicable to a great many other situations, including politics.

There was yet one more message carried within the pages of the book, Worf realized, one even Picard had not anticipated when he had sent it: No matter how long this "game" went on between him and Starfleet, Worf was certain that his former captain would emerge victorious.

While he knew that Picard would appear confident in any public setting, a pillar of strength to those who looked to him for leadership, what toll would this struggle exact on the man himself? How would it affect him during those moments of solitude he cherished? Though Worf was concerned for his former captain's well-being, both physical and mental, he knew that if asked directly, even in a private conversation, Picard would almost certainly conceal his true feelings.

To obtain the information he sought, Worf decided he would have to go about getting it another way.

Chapter Six

DROPPING THE PADD onto his desk, Geordi La Forge closed his eyes and rubbed his temples, groaning in satisfaction at the momentary relief the action brought. Though his eyes might be artificial, the muscles and nerve endings that received the information supplied by his ocular implants were still nothing but good old-fashioned human tissue, and they were tired.

With days of open space ahead of them and hours of idle time likely to result, La Forge had already begun to straddle the fine line between giving his engineering crew purposeful tasks and loading them up with busy-work. His first impulse as chief engineer was to take advantage of the long haul to the Dokaalan system by putting the *Sovereign*-class ship through a stem-to-stern regimen of diagnostics and system tests. It would be a lot of work, but La Forge had good reason for it.

Even now, three years after the end of the Dominion War, Starfleet's ship-maintenance facilities were still laboring to alleviate the backlog of service and repair requests. The fleet was struggling to return as many ships to active duty as they could in the shortest amount of time possible, so routine and noncritical tasks were being deferred. Engineering staffs aboard many ships, particularly those with limited access to such facilities in the first place due to their current assignments, were taking matters into their own hands. Already formidable technical skills were being enhanced through impromptu on-the-job training as they took on some of the more complex tasks usually performed at drydocks and starbases.

Knowing that the *Enterprise* probably would be out of touch with the level of Starfleet support it had enjoyed in recent years, La Forge and the rest of the department heads had taken care to insure that the ship's stores were fully stocked with all manner of spare equipment and replacement parts to maintain the myriad onboard systems. For the engineering section, this included a few bulkier components not usually carried aboard ship, as well as replacements for items normally diagnosed and repaired only at a drydock facility.

He also knew that their lengthy journey would be just the opportunity to experiment with increasing the graviton loads of the deflector shield generators, or perhaps to replace that pair of power couplings in the impulse propulsion system on which he was keeping watch, and those were just off the top of his head. Even with Captain Picard's desire for the senior staff to afford the crew as much recreational time as possible during the voyage, there would be plenty of opportunities for him to see to his project list and still allow his people some time for rest and relaxation. That in itself would be a welcome change for a ship that typically saw little inactivity.

Not for the first time, La Forge observed just how fortunate he was to lead the complement of engineers assigned to the *Enterprise.* One of the many benefits of serving on the Federation flagship was that, sooner or later, the best and brightest of Starfleet's engineering minds ended up here. He thought of Reg Barclay, who served on two incarnations of the starship before becoming a key player on Project Pathfinder and aiding the *U.S.S. Voyager* in its return from the Delta Quadrant. And there was Sonya Gomez, who began her career on the *Enterprise* as an unsure ensign and now served as a highly capable commander aboard one of the ships assigned to the elite Starfleet Corps of Engineers.

His mental list went on until La Forge paused at the realization that, in the eyes of many, the *Enterprise* might no longer be the destination of choice for the most talented personnel in Starfleet. There was also the distinct possibility that some members of his current engineering crew might start to explore better opportunities for themselves elsewhere. After all, there was little to hone one's skill set in missions like this one.

I don't want to lose good people simply because there isn't enough to keep them here anymore.

It would require an extra effort from him to make sure that his engineers' sense of purpose was maintained. Simply keeping them occupied at their duty stations would not be enough. Lieutenant Vale's idea of running security drills, which would include diagnostic tests of the ship's defensive systems, dovetailed nicely with his own agenda.

With a plan for success already in action, La Forge had also reminded himself that part of the equation was to see to it that his people also set aside less pressing matters and spent some time on more frivolous pursuits.

And that includes me, he mused as he left his office and made his way from the engineering levels to the upper decks of the saucer section, heading for officers' quarters. Walking the corridors, he was comforted by the steady rhythm of the *Enterprise*'s warp drive as the vessel powered toward the Dokaalan system. It was the smooth, strong sound of a well-maintained ship, he knew. Most people eventually learned to tune out the omnipresent thrum of the engines, but La Forge always listened for it, knowing that it would often provide the first clue as to a problem in the heart of his beloved ship.

Finally, he came to one particular door, hoping even as he reached for the call button that his leisure plans also included the person he had come to see.

"Come in, please." Data's voice filtered through the panel positioned next to the door. As La Forge stepped into his friend's quarters, he realized that almost all of the lights in the room had been extinguished. The only signs of activity came from the android himself, seated before the extensive computer station that dominated the room's right wall. Looking up at the engineer's approach, Data said, "Hello, Geordi."

La Forge smiled as he moved farther into the room. "What are you working on?"

"I have been studying the information contained on the two Dokaalan probes, as well as the reports compiled by the Vulcan Science Directorate in 2151. While neither the Vulcans nor Starfleet specialists were able to determine their exact point of origin, there are clues within the probes' recorded messages that may help us narrow our search parameters once we arrive in the Dokaalan sector of space."

Taking a seat in the other chair positioned near the workstation, La Forge admitted to himself that his interest was piqued. "Really?"

"I have been analyzing the visual transmission by the Dokaalan leader," the android continued, gesturing to an image from the centuries-old transmission frozen on one display monitor. "Notice the color of the sun and the orange hue of the sky behind First Minister Zahanzei. This suggests that their planet orbited a star of the spectral class K-1. Given that, the size of the star in relation to the planet suggests an orbital path within the ecosphere of a typical K-1 star as I have plotted here." Tapping a command string into his console, Data called up a tactical display that showed a haze around an orange point of light against a grid demarcating dozens of light-years.

La Forge nodded approvingly. "That seems like the place to start looking, then." It would be simple for Data to take the information he had gathered here and correlate it with the star charts and other navigational aids stored in the main computer. He would be able to determine if this star system was the former home of the Dokaalan long before the *Enterprise* arrived there.

Data said, "I have also cross-referenced the visible characteristics of the Dokaalan race with all available information from Starfleet Medical biological files. Based on the first minister's epidermal coloration, facial physiognomy, and overall structure, he physically resembles fourteen distinct races known to the Federation."

Confused at this, La Forge said, "That's interesting, Data, but I'm not sure where you're going with it."

"I accessed all available geophysical information on the planets to which those races are native," the android replied as he keyed the console again, and La Forge watched one monitor begin to scroll columns of data faster than he could read it. For a moment he mused that the effect would be dizzying—if he had real eyes.

"As common environments lead to common species development," Data continued, "I have compiled a list of naturally occurring elements on those known planets as well as their percentages of concentration. Assuming the Vulcans were correct when they reached their original conclusion that Dokaal indeed exploded due to prolonged tectonic stress, programming our sensors to detect such elements should help us locate planetary debris."

"Um, okay," La Forge said, starting to wonder just how much time Data had devoted to this research exercise. "That's not a bad theory, but . . ."

Entering yet another string of commands, Data called up a new image to one of the display monitors. "And here, I have created a mathematical construct of the planet's geothermal explosion, starting with the mass of a typical Class-M planet. Such destruction is likely to have exerted enough force to propel fragments of the planet in this manner."

"Uh, Data?"

Focused on his report, Data continued, "Lack of surveys in this region prevents us from accounting completely for any gravitational effects of surrounding stars or planetary bodies. It does, however, give me reason to believe that fragments of the planet could be encountered as soon as . . ."

"Data!"

The android halted and turned to face him. "Yes, Geordi?"

La Forge took one look at his friend's somewhat quizzical expression and laughed a bit. "Data, this is all very helpful, but did Captain Picard ask you to put it together?"

"The captain tasked me with tightening the focus of our search in an attempt to determine the probe's origin point within the shortest amount of time," Data replied. "He was not specific with the details of his request, so I have exercised my own initiative in order to provide the most comprehensive investigation possible."

Smiling, the chief engineer put a hand on Data's shoulder. "Data, I know you love doing this kind of thing, but when the captain said he wanted the crew to take some time off during the trip, he meant you, too. I think you've accomplished enough for one day, so what do you say about finding something relaxing to do?"

"I do not understand," the android replied. "You said this information would prove useful in our mission. Should I not continue?"

"Oh, I'm sure it will, Data," La Forge said, trying to explain himself without sounding too condescending. "I'm sorry. What you're doing *is* important. I thought that maybe you were just working so hard at it because you were bored."

"While I did experience sensations comparable to boredom on four separate occasions after the installation of my emotion chip," Data replied, "I have found no such variations in my motivational subroutines since the chip's removal. I do not believe I remain capable of boredom."

"I see," La Forge said in a soft voice, finding himself taken aback by his friend's stark admission. In the wake of the incident with the demon ship, Data had been ordered to surrender his treasured emotion chip to Starfleet scientists. The slightest pleasure or the deepest pain were foreign sensations to him once again. Perhaps it was a blessing that he would be incapable of even aching for his own loss, and La Forge now realized that he himself had not taken the time to appreciate the full ramifications of his friend's choice.

With all of the activity surrounding the status of Captain Picard and the *Enterprise* in the wake of the demonship incident, the engineer had not taken the time to seek Data out and discuss his decision and its results in detail. Now he wondered whether he might have been unconsciously dodging the topic.

"Data, I'm sorry," La Forge said. "I just realized that was a pretty thoughtless thing for me to say."

The android nodded, appearing almost to console him rather than the other way around. "It is fine, Geordi. Without emotions to offend, I am the best individual on whom you can demonstrate your thoughtlessness."

Laughing aloud at that, La Forge suddenly felt as though he had been caught in a temporal loop that had tossed him into a conversation with his friend that could have occurred more than a decade ago.

In many ways, that was precisely what had happened. This "version" of Data, without Dr. Noonien Soong's emotion chip, seemed more like the person he had met during the Farpoint mission, his first assignment aboard the *Enterprise,* than the close friend he had accompanied to the Starfleet tribunal.

According to the reports detailing the battery of diagnostic tests Starfleet technicians had performed on Data, the android's memory banks had been unaffected by the emotion chip's removal. His ability to access information regarding their travels and missions together appeared to have remained intact. However, without the chip to enhance his personal recollections of his experiences, his drawing of information from those memory files would carry the emotional warmth and impact of an encyclopedic database.

"It just occurred to me," La Forge said, "that in a lot of ways, you're starting over, aren't you?"

Appearing to mull over the engineer's words, Data paused several beats before responding. "I had not considered that before now. According to my self-diagnostics, my internal calculations are now performing at a rate that is 2.6877 percent more efficient than when the emotion chip was an active part of my systems. My current processing rate is within 0.0023 percent of my efficiency rating on Stardate 48642.8, my last internal diagnostic before the chip was installed." Nodding, he added, "In a manner of speaking, I suppose this does mean that I am starting over, at least in some ways."

La Forge forced a smile, well aware that his friend, in all likelihood, had no clue that he really *had* changed. He wondered if Data had felt compelled to discuss the situation with anyone, or whether it might help him, or perhaps both of them, to better appreciate what this all meant.

Deciding to take advantage of the opening, he asked, "Would you like to talk about it?"

"Would that make you feel better, Geordi?"

I guess it's dumb for me to think it might make you feel better.

"Yes, Data, I think it would." La Forge considered several possible avenues of inquiry before finally deciding it best to start by keeping things simple. "Have you noticed anything different in your ability to operate or perform your duties? Aside from the increased efficiency, I mean."

"I have not."

"Have you sensed any, well, unexplained interruptions in your routines or protocols? Any lapses in function?"

Data shook his head. "I have recorded no such lapses."

"Your positronic brain and its accompanying programming have adapted over the past few years in order to function with your emotion chip," La Forge said. "Its removal is sure to affect, at least in some way, your overall operating systems. Do you sense any . . . loss?"

"As I have stated, I do not."

"That just doesn't seem right to me," La Forge said in a tone that belied his frustration. He was fumbling for the words and he knew the logical answer to the question he wanted to ask, so why did articulating that question seem so difficult? "Do you miss the chip, Data?" he asked finally.

The android's head cocked to one side in his typical expression of thoughtfulness. "I understand what you are attempting to say, Geordi, but no, I do not miss my emotions. Rather, without them, I am following a new sense of purpose."

This caught the engineer by surprise. "Really? In what way?"

"My quest to better understand humanity was driven in part because I operated under the axiom that such information was required if I were to create my own emotional subroutines. I now know that creating such subroutines would result only in redundancy, as they already exist within the chip. Since the chip may be reinstalled someday, it appears that my energy and abilities would better serve the ship were I not pursuing goals of a personal nature."

The blunt statement stunned La Forge. "But Data, that very pursuit is what makes you *you*. No one expects you to give up part of yourself, regardless of whether you have that chip."

"I understand that," Data replied, "but such efforts now seem unnecessary to my duties aboard the *Enterprise*."

"Data," La Forge said, unsure how to proceed from here, "I . . . I don't know what to say to that." He shifted in his seat, suddenly uncomfortable with the direction this conversation had taken. "What about playing the violin or painting or acting out on the holodeck?" La Forge asked. "Are you saying that you don't care about any of that anymore?"

He allowed his gaze to wander about Data's quarters, seeing the mementos and other items the android had collected over the years. Placed carefully on a small table was the violin he had learned to play years ago, even going so far as to participate in numerous impromptu concerts performed with other *Enterprise* crew members who played other musical instruments. A display case mounted on one wall held the various medals and awards Data had earned during his Starfleet career. One bookshelf held a few treasured volumes: *The Collected Works of William Shakespeare,* which had been a gift from Captain Picard; *The Dream of the Fire* by K'Ratak, given to him by Worf; and *I, Robot,* a work of twentieth-century speculative fiction that La Forge himself had offered as a present some years ago.

Did nothing in the room offer an emotional connection any longer? Had all of these once-treasured items lost their meaning and value for Data? La Forge wondered what else his friend might have lost through the simple act of surrendering his emotion chip. Did Data believe that all the things he had once done for fun, or at least for the cataloguing of those sensory deviations that might approximate fun, no longer held any interest for him?

"I do not require or even desire recreation or hobbies as I once did," the android said flatly. After a moment, he added, "However, I do recognize the benefits of companionship and spending time participating in common activities of interest. If you would like, I will accompany you to the activity of your choice."

"Uh, sure, Data," La Forge said as he grappled with the sensation that he had just lost one of his best friends. He found himself trying to remember his old methods of introducing Data to intrinsically human experiences, but then again, that was when the android wanted to embrace such opportunities. Now that he seemed rather aloof to it all, where should Geordi start?

"Maybe we could try the holodeck?" he suggested. "I helped Lieutenant Osborne load a whole batch of new programs before we left Earth, including a couple of Sherlock Holmes mysteries written just last year."

"An excellent suggestion," Data said as he rose from his seat. "That should prove most entertaining."

As he followed his friend out into the corridor, however, La Forge was already beginning to have his doubts.

Chapter Seven

To: Dr. Yerbi Fandau, Surgeon General
        Headquarters, Starfleet Medical Services
        Division
        San Francisco, Earth
From: Dr. Beverly Crusher, Chief Medical Officer
        U.S.S. Enterprise-NCC-1701-E

Dear Yerbi,

I was pleasantly surprised on my return to the *Enterprise* to find your communiqué waiting for me. It was a gracious way for you to follow up our meeting, especially knowing how busy you must be these days. I also appreciate your sending along the monograph by Dr. zh'Costeth on Andorian toxic encephalopathy that we discussed, as I have been following her research for some time.

Please forgive the delay in my response. Truth

be told, I had not at all anticipated hearing from you so quickly given all the preparations you must be making. It should not surprise you that I still am grappling with the news of your decision to retire. While I'll miss your leadership and professional counsel, I hope you know that no one is as happy for you as I am that you feel ready to step away from your duties and enjoy life. Can I admit to being a little jealous of your plans to join Glinn and her children on Beta Trianguli III? Embrace every opportunity to enjoy your family, my friend. I know how much they mean to you.

Also, I must admit to being very flattered by your now formal offer for me to succeed you as Surgeon General. This especially is gratifying in light of your personal recommendation being approved by the Federation Council. I credit so much of my interest in curative medicine and xenobiological research to the invaluable mentoring I have received by your hand over the years. Knowing that you would entrust me to continue the practices and policies you have instituted during your tenure is an honor indeed.

When we last spoke, we laughed about the twists our lives often take when we least expect them. Had my desire to heed the call of practicing medicine in the field not led me back to the *Enterprise* after only a year at Starfleet Medical, I might still be serving in the very position you now are asking me to resume. That year taught me much about the bureaucratic side of medicine, something you know I continue to regard as a necessary evil. I do, however, want you to know that I understand and appreciate how the position can provide me the best of both worlds, if only I allow it. I could reintroduce myself to the inner circle of leadership at Starfleet Medical while following my own research pursuits. I also find very appealing the aspects of guiding other physicians and researchers in their various projects. To me, that's like having all the fun of being a teacher without the burden of having to grade term papers.

I realize that such an offer cannot remain on the table for long, but please know that I am giving serious consideration to it. As soon as time permits, I promise to contact you to discuss the matter further.

Again, thank you. Once more, you have proven yourself as an unwavering advocate and a treasured friend.

Sincerely,
Beverly

Reading her letter for the fifth time, Beverly Crusher found her finger wavering over her data padd, hesitating to send it.

It would have been easier to simply record a visual message to Dr. Fandau, but that seemed so informal, considering the subject matter of his correspondence. An actual written letter lent a credence to his request that a visual recording lacked.

With that in mind, she had still deferred writing the

letter as long as she could, and even then she had agonized over her choice of every word in uncounted drafts. Now she lingered over her actions yet again.

She believed her sincerity showed in her writing, as she had devoted a substantial amount of time to considering Dr. Fandau's offer. Being asked to once again lead Starfleet Medical, at this point in her career, would allow her much latitude in the pursuit of her personal goals. It would put her back on Earth, a place where Wesley might need her to be should his time with the Travelers come to an end. It would give her some stability in her career that her life aboard a starship could not provide. No one really would fault her for accepting the offer, coming as it had from an old friend and trusted mentor. It was not as if she were asking to be assigned to another ship, after all, even though she wished that Yerbi's timing could have been better.

Why do I feel like a deserter?

Crusher had always considered physicians as the first persons expected to act in a time of crisis. In all her career, she never had hesitated to scoop up a medikit and rush to an emergency situation, or failed to insure that sickbay was prepared to treat one or dozens of injuries at a moment's notice. She strived to be a calm presence and an efficient, capable healer no matter what the challenge or working conditions.

And yet now, when the political pressure being directed at the *Enterprise* seemed tuned to its highest intensity in her experience, at a time when the crew— Jean-Luc Picard in particular—might very well need her most, she was here, alone in her office and thinking about leaving the ship. For the first time in years, she was questioning herself and felt her confidence in her own decision-making skills faltering.

Why now? And why does it feel like I'm the only senior officer looking to get out?

The pneumatic hiss of the sickbay doors followed by a pained moan drew Crusher from her reverie and she bolted from her seat, already forgetting the padd displaying the still unsent letter. She raced into the main sickbay area to find a pair of crew members, each wearing exercise fatigues. She recognized Ensign Jarek Maxson from the ship's security division, a tall and muscular human male, cradling a woman in his arms.

"Lieutenant Perim?" she said as she got her first look at the woman's face. Perim had been serving on the *Enterprise* as a conn officer for the past few years and was also one of the ship's handful of Trill crew members. Taking some of the load of the lieutenant's weight from Ensign Maxson, Crusher asked, "What happened?"

"It's my knee, Doctor," Perim replied, the discomfort evident in her voice as she spoke. "I hope I didn't blow it out again."

With Maxson's help, Crusher eased Perim onto a diagnostic bed, its array of biosensors automatically activating as the injured officer attempted to adjust herself to a more comfortable position. Drawing a breath through gritted teeth, Perim groaned. "Damm it!"

Crusher produced a medical tricorder from the pocket of her smock and stepped around the bed to stand next to Maxson. He said nothing, but Crusher saw his expression of concern as he watched. She also noticed that his face was covered in sweat and grime.

Pulling the tricorder's separate peripheral scanner

free, she activated the unit and waved it over Perim's right leg. "I'm afraid it is your knee again," the doctor said a moment later, reviewing the tricorder's scan readings. "Been hiking the Tenaran ice cliffs again?"

Maxson answered, "Today, it was Half Dome."

"Well, tomorrow, it's a nice, safe, boring chair," said Crusher, allowing a smile in the hope it would ease some of Perim's concern. She traded her tricorder for a hypospray and dosed Perim with enough terakine to cut her pain. The doctor expected the standard analgesic to work quickly, given that the dose did not need to be metered with benzocyatizine, as would be the case for a joined Trill.

Crusher was thankful that none of the Trill currently assigned to the *Enterprise* carried the symbionts that distinguished the species as unique among Federation members. While the biological concepts relating to Trill humanoid hosts and vermiform symbionts fascinated her, particularly in the years after her very personal encounter with Ambassador Odan, the doctor was well aware that the risks associated with any emergency medical treatment escalated steeply for both Trill beings in a symbiotic relationship.

Perim closed her eyes and breathed deeply as Crusher watched the medicine take effect. A few moments later, the Trill opened her eyes and smiled a bit. "Much better. Thanks, Doctor."

"I can repair the damage easily enough," Crusher said, "but we should probably talk about this. Would you like to do it now or later?"

"Now's as good as time as any," Perim replied, then turned to Maxson. "Jarek, I'm fine. Go on and finish the hike. We still have the holodeck booked for another hour, I'd bet."

"Well, only if you're sure you don't need anything," the ensign said, his concerned expression relaxing only slightly.

"Go," Perim said, smiling as she waved him away. After he had gone, she said to Crusher, "I think this upset him more than it did me."

"I have to wonder," the doctor said, "what's more hazardous? Hiking in the holodeck or hanging around with Ensign Maxson?"

"But he's so cute," Perim said, laughing. "Doctor, it's just a fluke he was with me again when I got hurt. He's not a *bondo* or anything."

"A *bondo?*"

"Oh, a . . . what's the word," Perim said to clarify. "You know, um, a jinx."

"Got it," Crusher said, nodding as she worked to suppress a grin. The time for being a friend was over, and now she had to play the part of concerned physician. "So, Kell, here we are, looking at your third ligament problem in as many months. I think you know the drill by now. Plan on spending the rest of the day under a bioregenerative field for your knee, but the reality is that it's time to consider a bioim—"

"Please, Doctor, don't say it," Perim said, cutting her off and affecting a playful wince.

"A bioimplant replacement for your knee," Crusher finished, raising the volume of her voice while maintaining a tone of compassion. "I know you're hesitant, but there's no reason to keep putting it off. Your ligaments are not responding to the regeneration treatments as we'd hoped." She had to hide her amused expression as she watched Perim fidget on the table, sighing deeply and closing her eyes.

"Maybe if I stopped pushing myself," the Trill said. "I could give up the hikes for . . . well, I don't know, cooking classes?"

Crusher laughed softly, recognizing the lieutenant's humor as a good-natured attempt to deal with a diagnosis she obviously did not want to hear. "Kell, you're an active, physically fit young woman, and medically we have the treatment available for you to stay that way. Besides, in our business, the last thing you want is a body that could fail you when you least expect it."

Looking away as if to consider the doctor's words, Perim finally nodded a moment later. "I know you're right, really I do. I just hate the idea of surgery, or of having some kind of artificial component to replace a part of my body."

Crusher left the diagnostic bed long enough to wheel a stool and a field emitter to Perim's side. She swung the arm of the emitter to position it over the lieutenant's injured knee and, touching a small input pad, activated a soft-blue-colored beam that washed over the reclining woman's leg.

"It's a pretty simple procedure, Kell. I could schedule it today and in a few days, you'll never know the difference."

"But Dr. Crusher, I *will* know the difference," Perim said, the first hint of anger lacing her words. "It'll be something inside of me that is not *me*. I know that sounds stupid, but I can't help myself. I've been that way all of my life."

"It's not stupid," Crusher said, focusing her attention more on the emitter than on her patient. "I guess it just seems a bit . . . unusual . . ."

Perim filled in the pause herself. "For a Trill, you mean? That's what you wanted to say."

The doctor sheepishly admitted to herself that it was exactly what she wanted to say, or at least how she automatically completed the statement in her mind. "Yes," she admitted with a tinge of regret. "Yes, Kell, it is, and now it's me being the stupid one. I'm sorry."

"It's all right, Doctor," the lieutenant replied, sighing as the words were spoken. "It's nothing I haven't been asked about before."

Several moments passed as the two women sat in silence, the normally unobtrusive sounds of the sickbay's medical monitors and the hum of the starship's engines now quite audible to Crusher. How was it that she never noticed the omnipresent background noises except when she was searching for words that might help navigate an awkward moment in conversation? She busied herself adjusting the regenerative field's emitter a bit before Perim finally spoke again.

"You don't know this," she began, "but I was almost joined once."

The admission caught Crusher off guard. So far as she knew, nothing about this was included in Perim's personnel file. Then again, there was no reason for such information to be recorded, was there?

Returning the lieutenant's gaze, she replied in a soft voice, "I didn't know. May I ask what happened?"

"It's not a long story," Perim said. "My parents were never joined, but it was a dream that my mother had for each of us. I was perfectly happy without all of the stress of dealing with the Symbiosis Commission. I got good scorings in school, I played a lot of *wusher* and parrises

squares, things were fine. Then one day, these two people came to the door to take me for testing. My mother
had submitted my application to the commission and I
didn't even know it."

"And you were surprised?" Crusher asked.

"I shouldn't have been, but I guess looking back it all
was a bit of a shock." Shaking her head, Perim continued, "And I was gone for weeks to take more tests until I
finally went before the evaluation board for consideration."

"What happened?"

Perim smiled a bit. "They said I had qualified, but I declined." Crusher felt her jaw drop a bit as Perim paused. "It
embarrassed our whole family, and . . . well, things have
never been the same with my mother, but I walked away."

"That does surprise me, Kell," the doctor said. "I
thought approvals to join were few and very coveted."

Perim paused, mulling over Crusher's statement a bit
before answering. "Imagine yourself without arms or legs
or any real means of getting around at all beyond the
perimeter of a pool in a cave. You discover that other beings exist who can take you out of the pool, beyond the
cave, into the warmth of the sun and anywhere in the
galaxy. Then imagine those other beings as the only means
for you to sense more intensely everything in your environment, and I mean *everything* . . . food, music, a cool breeze
from the ocean, the touch of a man. You're not just depen-
dent on those beings, but actually addicted to them through
the intense bonding that you share. You cling to that connection, define your life around it, and guard it jealously."

Crusher nodded as she listened. It was not hard for her
to imagine what Perim was relating. Commander Riker

had offered similar descriptions in the days after he had carried Ambassador Odan's Trill symboint.

"So, Doctor," Perim continued, "in that case, wouldn't you do everything in your power to preserve your connection with your host? Fight to the death? Maybe tempt your host with a new ability to draw upon a greater knowledge or wisdom? And just maybe, over the generations, might you convince your host that carrying you around was something desirable, a privilege or even an *honor* for you?"

Finding herself without words, Crusher was unsure as to whether the blank expression she was certain was on her face would either puzzle or amuse Perim.

For generations, the people of Earth had challenged their belief systems with discussions of how the biological abilities of nonhumans affected their own ethical thinking constructs. In her days at the Academy, she and other medical students regularly posited the true impact on human experience of a Vulcan mind-meld or a Denobulan mating scheme or a Deltan oath of celibacy. Crusher certainly was no stranger to the bioethical implications of any symbiotic relationship, including but not limited to the dominant species of Trill.

"It's not as though I'm the only Trill who feels this way," Perim said.

"Oh, uh, of course not," Crusher said, stammering a bit. "It's just that I've never talked about this with a Trill before." In fact, such discussions typically took place among peers, fellow physicians and researchers, and generally *human* ones. This was a first for Beverly Crusher to hear a near damning of the Trill cultural system from a member of the species herself.

"Tell me, Doctor, have you ever discussed the physiological impact of suppressing emotions with a Vulcan before?"

"Well, yes, I have," Crusher replied.

"And I'm willing to bet that you've talked with Captain Picard at length about the rationale and justifications of the Borg collective?"

Crusher actually felt herself flinch at that question. She and Captain Picard had spoken at length about the Borg on numerous occasions, though usually it was in the context of his own traumatic experiences with them. In the months following his abduction and transformation into Locutus, it had been very difficult for Picard to discuss the incident and what he had been feeling. The intervening years had eased that pain somewhat, but Crusher knew that the captain might never fully come to terms with what had happened to him.

Unsure whether she appreciated what she perceived as a loaded question, the doctor nevertheless nodded in response. "Yes, of course I've talked with him."

"Well then," Perim said, "anytime you want to talk about Trills, just pull up a chair. Maybe we can broaden each other's horizons a bit. Besides, the more time I talk, the less time I have to tear myself up in the holodeck."

Smiling, Crusher nodded as she rose from her seat. "I just might take you up on that, Kell. You've given me something new to think about, and that's my favorite part of this job."

"Then you must really like it here on a starship," the Trill said as she lay back on the diagnostic bed. "I've learned something or found something new to think about just about every day since I came aboard."

Saying nothing as she made her way back to her office, Crusher stopped short when her gaze fell upon the still-activated padd lying atop her desk. With it came everything she had been thinking about and putting off and agonizing over for the past several days.

Damm it.

Perim was right. She did like it here on the *Enterprise,* but she had liked it at the Arvada III colony and in San Francisco and on Delos IV and other places she once called home.

They were also places she had left behind.

Standing alone in her private refuge, protected from the eyes of her staff or Kell Perim or anyone else who might enter sickbay, Beverly Crusher shook her head and sighed in exasperation.

I guess making the decision just got harder.

Chapter Eight

"LIEUTENANT?"

Lost in thought, Christine Vale was startled by the forceful voice coming from her right. Looking up, she saw Lieutenant Taurik, one of the *Enterprise*'s junior engineers, standing next to her. In the subdued lighting of the dining facility, the Vulcan's green-tinged skin looked even paler than usual, and his black hair seemed to absorb some of the room's ambient light.

"I'm sorry," Vale said as she reached for her glass of juice, as untouched as the rest of the meal she had prepared in one of the dining hall's replicators. It was a pitiful attempt to cover up the fact that she had allowed her mind to wander, one she knew the engineer probably saw through easily. Sighing in resignation, she shook her head. "I guess I sort of drifted away there for a minute. I hope you weren't standing there long."

Taurik replied, "Precisely one minute and forty-three seconds." His expression never wavered as he added, "I had begun to wonder if you had fallen asleep or perhaps suffered some form of hearing loss."

Vale chuckled at that. Few Vulcans understood humor, at least in the manner that humans embraced it, and fewer still actually employed it themselves. Taurik was an exception to that unwritten rule, his stoic nature being ideal for the deadpan manner he used to deliver his attempts at humor. By Vulcan standards, the engineer was practically jovial.

Holding a tray of his own, Taurik said, "I hope I am not interrupting you, but I was wondering whether I might speak to you for a few moments." Vale indicated the empty chair across from her and the engineer sat down. His tray held a single bowl containing what her nose told her was *plomeek* soup, a Vulcan dish.

"What's on your mind?" Vale asked, watching with some surprise as the engineer seemed to search for the appropriate words.

"Though you and I are of equal rank," he said, "as security chief, you are cognizant of things others of us are not. I was wondering whether you had noticed anything out of the ordinary in the behavior of the senior staff. I am speaking specifically of Commander La Forge."

An odd question coming from a Vulcan, Vale thought, *even Taurik.* Perhaps all the time he had spent among humans had rubbed off on him in other ways. "How do you mean?"

Straightening in his seat, Taurik replied, "I have heard some of the other engineers talking, and they all seem to agree that the commander has not 'been himself lately,' as one put it. I admit that while I do not understand the full range of human emotions, I believe I am familiar enough with his personality to know when there is a . . . deviation."

Vale cocked an eyebrow at that. "A deviation," she repeated, nodding after a moment. "Well, we've all had a lot on our minds lately. He could just be tired. I'm sure he'd be open to talking about it if one of his people thought it was affecting his duties in some way."

Taurik shook his head. "No, it is nothing like that. My interpretation of the others' comments is that they are troubled about his well-being. I would be remiss if I did not say I shared their concern." Pausing a moment, he added, "I apologize if I am overstepping my bounds, but it has been my experience that humans often work out their problems by talking about them to someone else."

"Thinking of a career change, Taurik?" Vale asked, grinning. "Counselor Troi might have something to say about you muscling in on her turf." She almost laughed at the shock that momentarily clouded the Vulcan's expression. It was fleeting and Taurik regained his control almost instantly, but there had been no mistaking his reaction. Even as he opened his mouth to defend himself, the security chief raised her hand. "I'm kidding. Look, this whole affair with Starfleet and the captain has us all a little frustrated, probably because there's really not anything we can do about it. I've tried to keep it from affecting my work, and I'm sure Commander La Forge has too, but he deserves to know if you or someone else under his command is troubled. I think it speaks well of you and the others to be concerned. Have you tried talking to him about it?"

"I have not," he replied, "but perhaps you are correct in that I should approach him."

Vale nodded in approval. As Taurik had already said, discussing a problem with someone else helped to resolve the issue. At the very least, it sometimes made the problem seem as though it was not insurmountable.

Truth be told, she had not yet discussed with anyone else her own feelings over Starfleet's decision to send the *Enterprise* on this latest mission or the manner in which they had treated Captain Picard. Displaying anger over how the entire affair had unfolded did not seem to be the right avenue to take, even though she could easily have argued the justification for such an emotion. Disappointment, perhaps? Yes, that seemed more appropriate.

Her thoughts were interrupted by the pleasant aroma of Taurik's *plomeek* soup as the Vulcan brought a spoonful to his mouth and sipped it. The action caused her stomach to grumble, reminding her that her own meal remained largely untouched.

"Tell me something, Taurik," she said after eating a few bites. "What made you request a transfer back to the *Enterprise?*"

The Vulcan replied, "I had not yet had the opportunity to serve aboard a *Sovereign*-class vessel, and felt such an assignment would provide an opportunity to enhance my skills and experience. That the *Enterprise*-E was the first such vessel in need of replacement engineers was fortunate happenstance. I am most pleased to be a part of Commander La Forge's team once again."

Vale recalled from her review of Taurik's service record when he had transferred aboard that he had been posted to the *Enterprise*-D after graduating from Starfleet Academy. Following that vessel's destruction, he was one of several crew members to be transferred to other assignments. In his case, it was to the Utopia Planitia shipyards orbiting Mars. When the Dominion War started, he joined the crew of the *U.S.S. Ilan Ramon,* where he remained throughout the conflict. His transfer to the *Enterprise*-E had come only two months before the incident with the *Juno.*

Unable to suppress a humorless smile, Vale said, "Given what's happened, I bet you're regretting that decision now, huh?"

"Regret?" Taurik asked. "Our current mission will provide the entire engineering staff an uncommon opportunity to expand our skills, without the benefit of Starfleet repair facilities. It will be a most interesting challenge."

Vale could not argue with that. Part of her welcomed the coming mission, for at its heart was the embodiment of why she had entered Starfleet in the first place. It seemed like forever since they had been given a mission of pure exploration, and now they were traveling to a part of space never before visited for just that purpose. Under any other circumstances, the promise of discovery would be exciting.

Instead, thanks to the way Starfleet had seen fit to give them their new assignment, the entire undertaking left a sour taste in her mouth.

"Lieutenant," Taurik said, "before the *Enterprise* departed on this mission, Starfleet extended an offer of transfer to another assignment to any member of the crew who might want it. If I may ask: Do you regret not taking advantage of that opportunity?"

"No," Vale replied without hesitation. Though Starfleet had seemed to focus its attention, and its ire, on Captain Picard with regard to the *Juno* incident and the fallout with the Ontailians, practically the entire crew had felt that scrutiny in one fashion or another. Rumors had run rampant that remaining on the *Enterprise* in the wake of the affair was an almost certain deathblow to one's career.

Nearly two dozen members of the ship's complement had elected to accept transfers to other vessels or stations, but her check of the personnel files for those individuals revealed that most of them had been assigned to the ship for only a short time to begin with. Perhaps they had not been aboard long enough to appreciate fully the sense of family displayed by those who had served here for a much longer time. Maybe there were those in the upper ranks of Starfleet who had lost their faith in Picard, but most who had served under him for years still trusted him without reservation. Even though she herself had been aboard the ship for a short time compared with others, she still felt a sense of belonging unmatched by any of her previous postings.

"I've only been the security chief here for a couple of years," she said, "but I see no reason to leave now." In truth, she had not given the decision a moment's thought. In her view, there were no other captains in Starfleet, and no other crews for that matter, with whom she wanted to serve. Looking around the dining room and seeing the dozen or so crew members sitting at other tables, recognizing each of them even though they were assigned to departments throughout the ship, only reinforced her feelings: For better or worse, the *Enterprise* was still the place to be.

She might not like where they were going, or why, but if she had to go, then she was happy to do so aboard this ship and alongside this crew. Besides, if she knew Picard as well as she should even after her arguably short tour of duty, it went without saying that the captain would find a way to turn their current setback into an opportunity for redemption.

And there's no way I'm going to miss having a ringside seat for that.

Chapter Nine

SETTING HIS PADD DOWN on the table before him, Will Riker raised his arms over his head, interlocked his fingers, and reached for the ceiling, welcoming the sensation as his back muscles flexed and stretched. That small motion, along with a deep cleansing of breath, helped clear his head and worked to shake off the fatigue that had been building steadily all afternoon.

Oh yeah, he chided himself. *I feel like two slips of latinum, all right.*

The task of reconfiguring the crew's duty rosters, to allow for ample free time as requested by Captain Picard while keeping the most qualified officers on hand across the day, had proven anything but simple. Even with the input of the department heads, it seemed to be taking forever. He wanted it done, though, so here he sat as he had for the past several hours, hunched over his data padd. He had forsaken his quarters for a seat in one of the *Enterprise*'s dining lounges, but refused to break for anything more than a mug of *raktajino*—or had it been two?—until he was finished.

Tuning out any distractions from the comings and goings of crew members, he found himself pushing to complete the assignment in short order, just as he had done with all of his tasks during the last few days. Not that Riker viewed himself as typically lackadaisical when it came to his orders; on the contrary, he strived to be efficient and precise, not merely to please himself but to set a standard for the rest of the crew on how Captain Picard should be followed.

Riker stepped up his pace now because he felt that loyalty had been compromised, and not by any member of the *Enterprise* crew. No, it had been wounded by the elite of Starfleet Command, and that, more than anything, angered him.

For two-thirds of his Starfleet career, he had served as Jean-Luc Picard's first officer. During that time, Riker had watched his captain make life-or-death decisions and lead fragile diplomatic negotiations, all while continuing to revel in the wonder of the unknown.

Time and again, Riker had been invited to leave Picard's side and assume a command of his own. Each time, he had declined, feeling that he still had more to learn, and more to contribute, right here. His place, he continued to believe, was on the *Enterprise.*

He had tried to rationalize Starfleet's viewpoint, arguing with himself that his understanding of Picard was something he had honed through years of experience. Many Starfleet admirals obviously did not share that perception, most likely only gleaning a fraction of it from reviewing mission reports or hearing apocryphal stories at strategy sessions. Consequently, they failed to appreciate or really even comprehend just how fortunate the Federation was to have Picard as one of its representatives. Otherwise, the first officer decided, they would not be doling out to the *Enterprise* captain the most menial of responsibilities and effectively putting him out to pasture, sending him to graze in the galaxy's open fields as did the Alaskan caribou Riker had watched in his youth.

It's no way to treat any captain, much less my *captain.*

Sighing loudly, Riker tossed his padd onto the table. Leaning back in his chair, he said, "Computer, dim lighting in this area to forty percent."

As the illumination in the portion of the lounge he currently occupied grew softer and more relaxing, he heard a voice call out in mock disapproval. "That's not very conducive to getting any work done, you know."

Looking up at the new voice, one that most definitely did not belong to the ship's computer, Riker sat upright and smiled at the new arrival. "Hello, Deanna. I didn't see you come in."

Deanna Troi returned the smile, her dark hair framing her soft features. As she drew closer, Riker was sure he detected the faintest hint of the Risian perfume she liked to wear on occasion. It was a pleasing scent, which was why he had purchased the perfume for her in the first place.

"You seem fairly engrossed there," she said. "Still working out the rosters?"

"You guessed it," he said, gesturing for her to take a nearby seat. "I might've been done sooner, but I'm trying to rig things for everyone to make the most out of this relaxation time prescribed by the captain. I'm adjusting the three shifts into four and rotating them so that everyone has opportunities for downtime at varied hours of the day."

Troi smirked as she settled into a chair at Riker's right. "Sounds complicated."

"You'd know if you'd been working on your assignment as well."

"Oh, but I have," she said. "It's done and filed for your review."

His eyebrow rising suspiciously, Riker retrieved his padd. A few touches brought Troi's proposed duty-roster alterations to its screen. "Well . . . damn, Deanna, this is pretty sharp."

"I found it easier to cut required postings in each department and extend the three shifts by two hours each. That allows for twenty-hour breaks while offering the duty-time variations you are suggesting."

"And it gives people even more time off than I'd calculated," Riker said, nodding appreciatively. "Excellent work, Counselor."

"It's nothing we haven't discussed before," she said, her expression turning to one of understanding. "You would have hit on it, too, were you not so preoccupied."

"I'm not that preoccupied."

Troi offered a slight smile. "Will, even a non-Betazoid could sense that you're not all here right now."

Never could fool you, could I?

Reaching out, she placed one hand on Riker's forearm. The simple touch caused him to relax muscles in his neck and shoulders for the first time in what seemed like days. "I've asked before and I'll ask again," she said. "Are you ready to talk about it?"

Frowning, Riker began to turn away, but her presence

had already succeeded in disarming him as efficiently as ever. He knew there was no one else on the ship—hell, in his life—to whom he would rather vent his feelings and frustrations at that moment. Still, he hesitated as he questioned whether she was seeking connection with him as his ship's counselor, his fellow officer, his friend, or his *Imzadi*.

Maybe it doesn't matter right now.

"Deanna," he said, "this whole situation can't be sitting well with you, either. What would I say that you don't already know?"

"I'm not seeking information, Will," she said, her voice continuing to soothe the edge on his nerves. "Just talk to me. If it'll help, I could use someone to talk to myself."

Nodding at that, Riker finally felt himself beginning to relax, the full effect of Deanna's presence asserting itself as it always had. "I'm not worried so much about my feelings over what's happened, but I am worried about Captain Picard. It might help me to know how *he* feels. What are you sensing from him?"

"He's hurting," Troi said, meeting his gaze. "It's as if he's mourning, in a way, for the way things used to be. I sense some embarrassment, as though he feels he's let the entire crew down or tarnished our reputations by his actions and decisions."

"Captain Picard has nothing to be embarrassed about," Riker countered. "This whole mess is so wrong for so many reasons." He realized his voice had risen as he spoke the last words, carrying across the lounge and attracting the attention of officers seated at other tables. Clearing his throat, he affected a weak smile to Troi. "Sorry."

"The captain doesn't seem to harbor any ill will against Starfleet or his superior officers," Troi said. "He understands this is the way things have to be. The captain would sacrifice his standing and reputation for any of us, Will. It's not a shock that he would do so for the Ontailians as well. I've never seen him place a boundary on his respect for any race or culture."

Riker nodded. "Well, no argument there."

"I think he just needs time to sort this all out for himself," Troi said. "Hopefully he'll eventually feel comfortable discussing the matter with me."

Smiling, Riker said, "You do have an uncanny ability to get people to talk."

"You, sir," Troi said, adding a touch of a purr to her voice, "are merely more susceptible to the power of suggestion than most."

"Now, hold on," Riker said, holding up both hands with an air of mock defensiveness, "Consider the source, here. When it comes to you, I . . ."

A voice over his combadge interrupted his train of thought. *"Commander Riker, you have a priority subspace transmission on an encoded channel."*

Tapping his communicator, the first officer replied, "Riker here. Who's the message from?"

"According to this," said the voice, which Riker recognized as belonging to the beta-shift tactical officer, Lieutenant Hines, *"it's from the Federation ambassador to Qo'noS. Shall I route it to your quarters?"*

Riker looked at Troi, raising his eyebrows and adopting a low tone of voice. "I guess news travels fast." He scanned the lounge and saw an unoccupied table with a computer terminal sitting atop it. "Lieutenant, route it down here, please. Riker out."

"I'll catch up with you later then," Troi said as she rose from her seat.

"Stick around," he replied, moving to the other table. "You know I'll only repeat it all to you over dinner."

"Oh, so now it's dinner we're having?"

Riker grinned as he sat down at the computer station and spun the terminal's flat-panel screen to face them both. He tapped a control and a moment later was rewarded with an image of Worf, dressed in his ambassadorial robes, filling the screen.

"Hello, Worf," Riker said to his former shipmate. "This is a surprise. Deanna is with me, too, so watch that language of yours."

"So I see, Commander." Worf's expression, as usual, showed no signs of amusement in response to Riker's remark. *"You both appear well."*

"Thanks, Worf," Troi said. "It's good to see you, too."

Riker asked, "And how goes your assignment?"

The Klingon's shoulders rose and fell with a protracted sigh. *"It presents its share of . . . challenges. Dare I pose the same question to you?"*

"Oh, we're doing just fine," Riker replied, not bothering to edit any frustration from his voice. "We're well on our way to where no one has bothered to go before."

"I am aware of the nature of your mission," Worf said. *"It would have been more appropriately handled by a ship other than the* Enterprise."

"Your powers of assessment are as sharp as always," Riker said. "It's a step up from all of us being sent to our rooms without supper."

The first officer saw his friend's expression cloud over, making him appear even more dour than usual. *"I confess that I am concerned for the captain's well-being,"* he said.

"We all are," Troi replied. "I believe that he's coping as best he can under the circumstances, and that he's drawing strength from the support of his friends." Smiling, she added, "He might appreciate hearing from you sometime soon."

Shaking his head, Worf said, *"When I was forced to accept discommendation from the Empire, the captain stood at my side and helped my family regain its standing. I promise you that I will do all in my power to support him in this time as he did for me."*

"I never thought otherwise, Worf," Riker replied, smiling. "It never hurts to have a few friends in high places."

"Indeed," the Klingon said. *"The right person in the right position is sometimes all it takes to turn a tide of opinion, after all."*

As his friend's eyes bored into him even across the vast distance separating them, Riker felt any reply he might have made die in his throat. There was something powerful behind Worf's words, something the first officer could not quite identify.

Apparently sensing the awkward pause, Troi said, "Please keep in touch, Worf. It's always good to hear from you."

"I shall," the ambassador replied, a smile forming or the first time on his usually intimidating features. *"I wish you good luck in the Dokaal sector. Worf out."*

As the Klingon's image was replaced with the familiar starred oval symbolizing the United Federation of Planets, Riker played his friend's remarks over in his mind once again. Was Worf suggesting that he contact another starship commander to help stir some goodwill for Picard among the ranks? Was he of the mind that, to the right person, a leak of the facts regarding the demon-ship incident would work in the captain's favor?

Or, was it something else? Something more personal?

Prior to Worf's departure from Deep Space 9 for the Federation embassy on Qo'noS, Riker had contacted his friend to wish him well. During that conversation, as he beheld his former shipmate and the new direction his life was about to take, Riker remembered thinking about his own career and the choices he had made.

At one time on the fast track for command, Riker had been offered a ship of his own on three separate occasions. He had carefully considered each appointment, but in the end had declined them all and chosen instead to remain on the *Enterprise.* Even though he had garnered a distinguished service record while assigned as executive officer of the *U.S.S. Hood,* when the first offer for promotion was presented, he had opted to serve under Jean-Luc Picard. A tour of duty as first officer of the Federation flagship was not an opportunity to be dismissed lightly, after all.

He had spent more than a decade as Picard's second-in-command, far longer than would be considered normal for an officer of his age and accomplishments. He had seen men and women, younger than himself, continue to climb the career ladder, progressing to captaincies of their own. With that in mind, why had he not taken advantage of the offers presented to him and advanced his career along the accepted lines?

The answer, odd as it might be, was simple. None of

the ships Riker had been offered was the *Enterprise.* They did not hold lineages and histories as storied as the vessel on which he currently served.

His decision to remain as Picard's first officer was the wisest move he could have made, so far as Riker himself was concerned. He truly believed that the value of all he had learned during the ensuing years under Picard's mentorship far surpassed even the experiences he would have acquired as captain of his own vessel. In Riker's eyes, there was no finer leader in Starfleet, and no one more deserving of his unflagging respect and support.

Still, had the time finally come for Riker to move on? Had Worf, with his mysterious words, suggested that the best way he could continue to serve Picard, to say nothing of Riker himself, would be to finally accept promotion and appointment to a vessel of his own?

How did we get to thinking about this, he wondered. These were thoughts that had not occupied his mind in . . . well, longer than he could remember.

"Will?" Troi asked, obviously sensing his unease. Blinking rapidly, Riker looked up to see the counselor staring at him from across the dining table. "Is something wrong?"

He shook his head to clear away the remaining wisps of his reverie. "No, no. I'm fine. Just lost in thought." Flashing what he hoped was an encouraging smile, he added, "Don't worry. I'm just tired, is all."

"Are you hungry, too?" Troi asked, the question enough to cause his stomach to grumble in response.

"Yes," he admitted, "for food and for company."

Troi's eyes met his and she smiled. "Good. Then we're in the right place."

Chapter Ten

Translated from the personal journal of Hjatyn:

I HAVE TRIED on several occasions to craft this entry, failing miserably with each of my previous attempts. Much has happened since I was last able to record my thoughts in anything approaching an ordered manner. Even as I write this, I am still finding it difficult to accept the reality of our situation.

After watching the crisis build over the course of nearly an entire cycle, those of us living among the asteroids could only stand by as our homeworld entered its death throes. Huddled in our quarters, Beeliq and I sought solace in one another's embrace, watching in silence as the news feeds overflowed with images of horrific destruction. People begged for help and for the quakes to end. Some even prayed for the end to come just so that the suffering would stop. They cried for release and I wept as well, for it was all I could do for them.

Having continued to increase in number and force, seemingly with each passing day, the quakes' destructive power was nearly rivaled by the other effects they unleashed across the planet. Enormous tidal waves slammed into coastal and island communities, wiping away most if not all evidence of civilization. Avalanches of rock and snow caused similar devastation in mountain areas. People stranded in remote regions had no hope of rescue as emergency service providers, already bogged down by the problems facing them in the more heavily populated areas, worked frantically to assist the growing number of victims.

Law and order had deteriorated in the face of the calamity, replaced by anarchy as people took matters into their own hands. Whether trying to flee the cities for the relative safety of the outlying regions or taking to the streets in search of food or medical assistance, citizens and law-enforcement officers clashed in ever-increasing incidents of civil unrest. This chaos only served to further hamper an already overburdened emergency response force, which in turn caused even more discord among the populace. In short order, both sides had seized one another, forming a deadly embrace from which there was no escape.

And what of those fortunate enough to flee the planet? Though the final tally has not been made public, it did not require much effort to figure out that a mere four or five thousand people could have been safely transported from Dokaal using every available space vessel. Once the order for evacuation was given, ships traveled back and forth in a constant convoy, each trip taking weeks. Upon their arrival, evacuees were transferred to various outposts throughout the colonies in an attempt to spread the additional burden as equitably and efficiently as possible.

Then, it happened.

Our first indication came when the news feeds began to stop, not all at once and not immediately. Some journalists were able to report massive quake activity before their signal was lost. Others simply ceased transmission in mid-report, taken by apparent surprise. Regardless of how it happened, one by one, each of the broadcasts vanished in a storm of static.

The communications center for the mining colonies informed viewers that they were attempting to regain the lost signals from our home planet, but they knew, just as we did, what had really happened.

Any lingering doubt was quickly erased by the images transmitted by one of the last ships to flee the planet, escaping with its final group of evacuees mere hours before the final cataclysmic event.

The initial pictures of our homeworld sent to us by that last ship were reminiscent of those transmitted by the first travelers courageous enough to leave the confines of our planet. Just as it appeared in those low-quality views I remember from my youth, the planet was a beacon of peace and prosperity, of life and potential, as well as an anchor for those brave enough to venture into the vast unknown.

All of that was soon shattered as our world came apart.

It is an image forever burned into my memory. Captured with haunting clarity, the transmission from the rescue vessel dispassionately broadcast our world's final moments and the simultaneous deaths of the uncounted people that could not be saved. At first the planet seemed to collapse in on itself before splintering into billions of fragments, slung outward in all directions along with magma from the molten core. The core itself, now freed from the tremendous pressure at the heart of the planet, vaporized as it succumbed to the sudden vacuum, creating a kaleidoscopic display that only served to punctuate the awesome destructive power that had been unleashed.

Dokaal was gone.

In the immediate aftermath of the catastrophe, I considered those left behind to be the fortunate ones. At least for them, the suffering was over and they could rest. For those of us left behind, our battles were just beginning, with our first priority being simple survival.

Faced with the sudden influx of several thousand new inhabitants, adjustments have to be made to support them, to say nothing of the thousands of colonists already living among the asteroids. For the newcomers, their abrupt arrival means that they will have to undergo an accelerated regimen of inoculations in order to survive the omnipresent radiation surrounding the asteroid field. Without the medications, which in essence alter a person's body chemistry at the cellular level, no one can survive here. For workers normally assigned to the colonies, the series of injections is carried out during an acclimation period prior to their arrival, but the survivors of Dokaal do not have that luxury.

The challenges extend to our facilities, as well. Designed for short-duration assignments after which crews were rotated back to Dokaal, our outposts are not capable of sustaining us indefinitely without the massive enhancement of our support systems. Such efforts already were under way practically from the moment the emergency situation on our homeworld was revealed. Knowing we would soon be without the benefit of the regular logistical aid we typically enjoyed from Dokaal, supply shipments were stepped up in addition to the transfer of those selected for evacuation. Despite all that preparation, much work still remains.

Things once taken for granted, such as the availability of food and drinking water, replacement supplies and components required to maintain the colony's support systems—even the expectation of privacy—are just some of the first things that have been impacted by the emergency measures enacted following the disaster. Power usage already has been redistributed throughout the colonies in order to conserve resources. Two, sometimes three families are being forced to share quarters originally intended for a single group. The living areas occupied by those without families, already cramped and utilitarian in nature, have been reconfigured to support twice the number for which they were designed.

One advantage of living in an asteroid field is that there is no shortage of key resources. The mining colonies' ore-processing plants and other factories are ideally suited to converting raw material into finished products used to construct new outpost facilities and maintain our current structures as required by the community. Indeed, they had already been doing so since long before my birth. In addition to easing the burden of supporting our expanded population, it also offers constructive, meaningful work for a people whose entire existence had been predicated on toiling to provide for others.

Still, the work to make the best of our dire situation is being hampered on many fronts. Throughout the colonies, administrators and security forces are facing panic and uncertainty in the midst of the rapidly unfolding situation. Some of the colonists are inciting riots, and there have even been reports of a few deaths. I know the unrest is born of fear rather than anger, but that does not lessen its severity.

People are too scared to place their trust in the colony leaders, who are now the sole arbiters of organized civilization remaining to us. They are woefully unprepared for the new responsibilities that have been thrust upon them.

One step in the right direction, however, is a plan put forth by the administrators to better communicate with the rest of our people. Each colony's habitation section is to select a representative, who will in turn act as a liaison between their group and the administration, communicating information back to their respective group as well as giving voice to concerns and grievances filed by the citizenry. Beeliq has already volunteered to act as the representative for our group. With this and other initiatives being put forth by the administration as well as the people themselves, we might eventually achieve some semblance of routine or perhaps even something approaching normalcy.

Still, I believe that our survival will be an unending struggle.

Chapter Eleven

"BRIDGE TO CAPTAIN PICARD." The voice of Commander Riker filtered through the intercom into Picard's ready room. *"We're approaching the Dokaalan system, sir."*

Looking up from the book he was reading, Picard smiled as he replied to the intercom. "Thank you, Number One. I'm on my way." After nearly four weeks of uneventful travel, the *Enterprise* had arrived. Now they could finally get to work.

Feeling the rush of anticipation at his first officer's report, Picard smiled as he closed the book in his hands and carefully laid the tome on his desk. Layered with adventure, intrigue, and a cast of characters that engaged him in the same way as the classical literature he preferred, the book had never failed to put him at ease on the rare occasions he could lose himself in its pages. Written nearly a century earlier and though clearly labeled as a work of fiction, it purported to be the "real story" of Earth's first encounter with the Vulcans.

Except, of course, he mused with a smile, *that it didn't happen that way at all.*

Commander Riker, with his penchant for the curious when selecting gifts, had replicated a copy of the novel for Picard as a birthday present shortly after the *Enterprise*'s encounter with Zefram Cochrane in the twenty-first century. Given his and the crew's covert involvement with the legendary man's historic initial warp-speed flight as well as humanity's first officially recorded encounter with an alien species, the book was a particularly whimsical gift. Though he did not normally partake of popular fiction for his leisure reading, Picard had nevertheless found the story to be so engrossing that he had reread the book several times in the years since first receiving it.

When done well, he decided, *fictional first contact is almost as exhilarating as the real thing.*

Picard exited his ready room and stepped onto the bridge to hear Commander Riker issuing the order to slow to impulse power. As the ship dropped out of warp space, the captain turned his attention to the main viewer and saw the multicolored streaks of light revert to distant points of light against the black tapestry that was the space surrounding the *Enterprise.* Even after all these years, he never tired of that sight.

"Report," he prompted as he crossed the bridge, stopping in his habitual place between and just behind the forward conn and ops positions.

Rising from the command chair in deference to the captain, Riker said, "We've just entered the system, sir. Long-range scans show no signs of other vessel activity anywhere in the area, but that's not saying much."

"Explain," Picard said, frowning at the report.

Dayton Ward & Kevin Dilmore

Turning in his chair at the ops position, Data said, "Our sensors are encountering a great deal of interference which appears to be caused by low-level radiation emanating from the massive asteroid field orbiting this system's sun between the sixth and seventh planets. The radiation is a by-product of various minerals and ores comprising the bulk of the asteroids. It is an effect that will worsen as we move farther into the system."

According to information gleaned from the probe recovered by the Vulcan ship in 2151, the asteroid belt had played an integral part in the Dokaalan people's economy, with all manner of minerals and other raw materials being extracted for various uses. A great portion of the people's limited interplanetary spaceflight capability had been devoted to a burgeoning mining industry, with dozens of freighters and personnel transports supporting a network of colonies operating among the asteroids.

"Is the radiation a danger to us?" Counselor Troi asked, rising from her own station and stepping forward until she stood next to Picard.

From the engineering station at the rear of the bridge, La Forge replied, "I don't think so, Counselor. Even in a reduced state, our deflector shields should be more than enough to protect us. I'll know more once we've finished analyzing our readings and after I've consulted with Dr. Crusher. As for the sensors, I've already got my people working on retuning them to offset the radiation's effects. We won't be at full capacity, but at least we won't be blind."

Satisfied with that, Picard turned his attention back to the main viewer, where a faint gray and brown band was just becoming visible on the screen. The asteroid field, he presumed, watching the swath of rubble and who knew what else continuing to grow and expand as the *Enterprise* traveled deeper into the Dokaalan system.

"Considering the extent to which the Dokaalan relied on the asteroid field," he said, "their physiology must have possessed a natural resistance to the radiation." Looking to Data, he said, "Commander, the message recorded by the Dokaalan first minister stated that as many people as possible would be evacuated to the mining colonies situated among the asteroids. Have you detected anything that might indicate the presence of such settlements?"

Shaking his head, the android replied, "Not as yet, sir. With our compromised sensors, we will have to move deeper into the system before we can hope for reliable readings."

"Do you still think we might find something, Captain?" Troi asked.

"I honestly have no idea," Picard replied. "At the very least, we might find some remnants of their civilization, some clue as to what actually happened after the probes were launched and how survivors, if there were any, might have coped." Smiling slightly, he added, "We may as well make the most of our opportunity to examine all the possibilities. Wouldn't you agree, Counselor?"

Picard's orders for this assignment had not been terribly specific, owing in no small part, he suspected, to the nature of their issuance. Admiral Nechayev had sent him and the *Enterprise* to the Dokaalan system as a means of keeping them out of the spotlight for a time. The mission itself was simple, yet lengthy in duration, and Nechayev had therefore left the details to Picard. It comforted him to know that despite all that had happened, the admiral still trusted him to exercise his judgment, regardless of the task he was assigned.

Hours before they entered the region, long-range sensors had determined that the fourth planet, once the home of the Dokaalan people, had in fact been destroyed. Its debris had expanded in all directions to form a smaller, less dense asteroid field than the one blocking the *Enterprise*'s path through the system. Essentially, their mission was completed, at least according to the letter of Nechayev's instructions.

However, the vagueness of the admiral's orders meant, to Picard at least, that he had a good deal of latitude in which to work. Why not exercise it, and see what else there was to learn here? Perhaps they could determine what actually caused the Dokaalan planet's destruction.

Moving to his command chair, Picard said, "Mr. Data, will you be able to negotiate the asteroid field even with reduced sensor capability?"

The android nodded. "Our navigational sensors and deflectors do not seem to be impeded by the radiation to the same degree as our defensive shields. It should be possible to augment their power sufficiently to provide the data I will need to guide the ship. However, I would recommend proceeding through the field with maneuvering thrusters only."

"I don't suppose you'd want to take the helm, sir?" Riker asked, a mischievous glint in his eye. "As I recall, you have a knack for this sort of thing."

It had been more than a decade since the *Enterprise*-D happened across a Promellian battle cruiser, derelict for centuries and drifting within an asteroid field not altogether different from the one they were currently approaching. It was soon discovered that a network of energy-draining devices had captured the ancient vessel and those same traps were threatening to ensnare the *Enterprise.* La Forge devised a plan using minimal power to maneuver the ship out of danger, and Picard himself piloted the vessel free of the trap.

Smiling at the memory the first officer's question evoked, Picard tugged down on his uniform tunic and settled himself more comfortably in his chair. "I think I'll allow Mr. Data the pleasure this time, Number One." Looking to the tactical station, he said, "Lieutenant Vale, please dispatch my latest status report to Admiral Nechayev." The admiral would be reading the report even before the *Enterprise* finished navigating the asteroid field, he guessed, thanks to the network of relay buoys deployed by the starship during the journey here from Federation space.

"Aye, sir," Vale replied. "Sending the message now."

At the ops station, Data finished entering a sequence of commands before turning to look over his shoulder. "I have plotted a preliminary course through the field, Captain, though I will almost certainly have to modify our heading while en route. It will take approximately nine hours to complete the crossing and will require me to assume control of the conn station as well as my own." Looking to Lieutenant Perim seated at the station to his right, he said, "No offense intended toward your own abilities, Lieutenant."

"None taken, Commander," Perim replied. "Are you sure there's nothing I can do to help?"

The android shook his head. "No, but thank you." He tapped a new series of commands to his console, and the ops panel before Perim's promptly went dark.

To the conn officer, Picard said, "You are relieved for the time being, Lieutenant." With a smile he added, "Take some time and rest that knee of yours. Dr. Crusher will be happy with both of us for that."

Smiling as she rose from her station, Perim nodded to the captain and said, "I'll be sure to inform her that she has you to thank, sir," before heading for the turbolift set into the bridge's starboard bulkhead.

The orders given, there was precious little else for the captain to do as his officers returned their attention to their various duties. Sitting quietly and observing the activity taking place around him, he reflected that it was almost possible to forget the reasons behind their being sent here in the first place.

Almost, he thought, *but not quite.*

"Now entering the asteroid field," Data reported without turning from his station. Having reprogrammed his own console in order to interface with both ops and conn functionality, the android was now using one hand each to control both operations. "Disengaging impulse drive and activating maneuvering thrusters."

On the main viewscreen, the effects of the radiation given off by the asteroids were beginning to assert themselves. The usually crisp display rendered by the viewer's imaging processor was now grainy and filled with static, jumping and wavering as lines crisscrossed the screen.

"Mr. La Forge," Picard said, "what is the status of your sensor modifications?"

Behind him on the bridge's upper level, the engineer replied, "Still working on it, Captain. The radiation levels are increasing at a faster rate than we anticipated, and it's overloading some of our sensor relays. I may have to reroute power from nonessential systems to compensate."

"At your discretion, Commander."

Beyond the haze of interference on the screen, the boundary of the asteroid field was now visible. Uncounted masses of rock, varying in size and shape, now dominated the image on the screen. Some of the asteroids appeared small enough to fit comfortably within the confines of the *Enterprise* bridge, while still others could themselves be small moons.

Then the image on the viewer cleared, and all the captain could see was a single, massive asteroid filling the screen.

"Data!" he snapped.

The android was already reacting to the looming threat faster than any living being could, his fingers a literal blur across the ops panel. On the viewscreen, the mammoth chunk of rock lurched to the left as the *Enterprise* swerved to starboard, shifting on its axis to avoid collision. Though Picard knew the ship's inertial dampening fields would guard against him being tossed about during the evasive maneuvers, he still gripped the armrests of his chair in an instinctive effort to hold on.

As the giant asteroid slipped away along the ship's port side, Picard wondered if the expression on his own face matched the look of relief on Riker's.

"No offense, sir," the first officer said, attempting to muster some of his trademark good-natured bravado, "but I'm really glad you let Data take the helm this time around."

True to his word, Data took just under nine hours to guide the *Enterprise* through the vast asteroid field, using the ship's maneuvering thrusters to alternate between their maximum speed and a slow crawl. Rather than subject himself to the tension merely watching the crossing would engender, Picard had instead opted for the solitude of his ready room. While he was able to relax somewhat within the room's soothing confines, attempting to read or even catch an hour or two of sleep had proven impossible. He was actually thankful when the call finally came.

"Data to Captain Picard," the android's voice said over the intercom, *"we are nearing the inner boundary of the asteroid field."*

"Thank you, Commander," Picard replied. As he exited his ready room a few moments later, he noted that Riker and the majority of the alpha-shift bridge crew had returned to their duty stations as well.

"Despite a few more close calls," Riker reported, "it looks like we made it through without any problems."

"Excellent work, Mr. Data," Picard said as he took his seat in the command chair. "Mr. La Forge, have you had any further success with the sensors?" He noted as he asked that the image on the main viewer had improved dramatically since he had last been on the bridge. While there was still static around the edges of the screen, the center of the picture was reasonably clear as it depicted the asteroid field now surrounding the ship.

"We're better off than we were, Captain," the engineer replied, "but still not one hundred percent. The radiation put out by the asteroids is too much for us to filter completely. As long as we're in the system, we'll have trouble with sensors and shields, as well as the phasers and the tractor beam and even the transporters. I've got my people working on it, but there's only so much we'll be able to do."

Picard nodded, unhappy with the report yet knowing that La Forge and his engineering staff were doing their level best to find solutions to the problems caused by the asteroid field.

"Captain," Lieutenant Vale called out from the tactical station, "our sensors are picking up low-level power readings from multiple sources. I'm attempting to ascertain locations now."

"Ships?" Picard asked.

"I'm not sure, sir," the security chief replied, "but if I had to guess, I'd say no. The power readings are inconsistent with any propulsion system I'm familiar with."

Riker turned in his seat to face the tactical station. "What about life signs?"

"Our scans are still being blocked to a large degree," Vale replied, "but we're detecting faint readings. Looks like somebody's home somewhere, sir."

Picard felt a surge of excitement at that. Someone was alive out here among the rocks. Were they descendants of the Dokaalan survivors, or merely others who had found the mineral-rich asteroid field to be of value?

"Mr. Data," he said, "coordinate with Lieutenant Vale and plot a course to investigate the power readings she's detected. Let's start in that fashion while we familiarize ourselves with the area."

"Captain," Vale suddenly called out, "I'm picking up a signal. It's on a very low frequency, and it's so weak I almost missed it."

"Is it being directed toward us?" Riker asked.

The lieutenant shook her head. "I don't think so, sir.

I'm processing it through the universal translator now." Without further prompting, she keyed in another set of instructions, and static erupted from the intercom system. Picard flinched at the abrupt explosion of noise, but he thought he could hear words spread intermittently among the racket. Vale adjusted the volume so that it was tolerable, and several seconds passed as she worked to clear the channel and enhance the message.

Her efforts were rewarded moments later as the static abated and a male voice broke through. The audio was distorted, but the message was clear.

"This is Outpost Takir. Help us!"

Chapter Twelve

PICARD ROSE from his chair, stepping forward until he stood directly behind the conn and ops consoles, as though the movement might bring him closer to the person pleading for aid.

"Our reactor coolant tank has ruptured, and our environmental system has failed. Send any available transports for evacuation!"

Picard's eyes locked on the viewscreen and the uncounted asteroids drifting all around the ship, as if he might locate the caller by sight alone. Somewhere out there, among all the tumbling and drifting rock, someone needed their help. Turning to Vale, he asked, "Can you locate them?"

The security chief did not look up as she replied, "Triangulating now, sir." After several moments spent adjusting and studying her console, she added, "I think I've isolated the source of the transmission. I'm reading a concentration of life-forms approximately three thousand kilometers from our present position."

"Relay that information to Commander Data's station," Picard ordered. "Data, lay in an intercept course and engage at our fastest safe speed."

Data keyed the instructions into his console and said, "Course laid in, Captain. Estimated time to rendezvous is four point seven minutes."

"Sensor readings are clearing, sir," Vale said. "The signal is coming from what looks like a sizable outpost constructed on the surface of a large asteroid. I'm picking up nearly four hundred life-forms there."

Digesting this new information, Picard asked, "Can you determine the extent of the damage they've suffered?"

"There are power fluctuations in what appears to be a fusion reactor core, consistent with a breach or leak. It might have been caused by a structural failure of some kind."

That meant the possibility of radiation-related injuries, Picard knew. "Notify Dr. Crusher so her team can prepare. We'll transport all survivors to the cargo bays for initial triage." Even if every single person on the mining outpost was in need of medical attention, the ship's cargo storage areas would provide more than sufficient room to accommodate them all, at least for the time being.

At the engineering station, La Forge said, "From what I can tell, Captain, they've got maybe a few hours, if that."

With preparations to receive the outpost victims under way, the captain could feel the energy of the people around him as they set to work, an almost palpable tingle on his skin. It was infectious, for he felt his own pulse beginning to quicken in anticipation of the task that lay ahead and the idea that after so many weeks of monotonous travel, they were finally going to do something useful.

Still, he knew that actually getting any victims to the ship still presented a bit of a problem. "What's the status of the transporters?"

The engineer turned from his console with a resigned expression, a feeling even seemingly communicated by the man's artificial eyes. "Sorry, Captain, but we're still having trouble tuning them to filter out the ambient radiation. Even with portable pattern enhancers, using them to transport people would be very risky."

It was not what he wanted to hear, but Picard also knew that it was useless to waste any more time concerning himself with an option currently unavailable to him.

Moving to the upper deck and the rear bridge stations, Riker said, "Geordi, could we maneuver close enough with shuttles to dock with an airlock or some other form of entry to the outpost?"

He watched the engineer scroll through screens of sensor data before freezing the image on one display monitor. As he moved closer to Riker and La Forge and studied the screen, Picard saw what looked to be a cylindrical protrusion extending from one rectangular section of the outpost structure.

"This is an external access point," La Forge said, "probably a docking port, the only one I can find. Our own airlocks won't match up perfectly, but we might be able to erect forcefields around the entrance." Turning in his chair, he added, "Captain, the radiation will affect any focused energy source we activate outside the ship. Even a forcefield will be risky."

"Is there any way you can compensate?" Picard asked.

The engineer shrugged. "If we move close enough to extend our shields to cover that section of the outpost, it might provide some additional protection. But the shields will already be compromised by the radiation before we extend them. Maintaining shield integrity could cause them to overload."

"We'll have to coordinate maneuvering shuttles to and from that docking port," Riker said, shaking his head. "And even then we can only take a handful of people at a time."

"Moving all those people is going to take a hell of a lot longer than a few hours," La Forge replied, "and that's if we even have that long."

Listening to his people, Picard was already ruling out the option of relying on shuttles. With only four full-sized shuttlecraft and eight smaller shuttlepods aboard, even using the new captain's yacht to assist in the evacuation would take entirely too long.

"Can we move the *Enterprise* herself close enough to link up?" he asked.

"We can do it using one of the docking ports along deck ten, sir," the engineer said, "but we'd have the same potential problems with our forcefields."

Picard nodded. "Continue your scans, Geordi. See if you can determine whether we can shut down the reactor." To Riker he said, "We'll move the *Enterprise* into position for direct docking. Number One, coordinate with Lieutenant Vale to handle security concerns for getting evacuees to the cargo bays."

Riker nodded. "Aye, sir."

As the first officer moved to put a hasty evacuation plan into motion, Picard returned to the bridge's lower level. "Lieutenant Vale, open a channel to the mining outpost."

When the security chief nodded to him and reported that the frequency was open, he said to the intercom, "This is Captain Jean-Luc Picard of the Federation Starship *Enterprise.* We have received your distress call and are moving to assist you. Please acknowledge if you are able."

There was a pause, and Picard flinched at the sharp crackle of static bursting through the com-system speakers before a bewildered male voice responded. *"Hello? Who is this? Where are you?"* To Picard, it sounded like the same person who had been transmitting the original distress message.

He said, "We are strangers here, but we are moving to help you. Please stand by."

"You mean . . . you mean you're not *from the colony? Then where did you . . . ?"*

Trying to keep the situation under some semblance of control, Picard cut him off. "We will be happy to answer all your questions once you are safely evacuated. Our ship is moving to link up with one of your external docking ports, and we will move you all to our ship. Are you able to organize your people for the transfer?"

Rather than a direct response, his ears were assaulted by multiple voices, all yelling within range of the audio pickup and all of them panicked.

"It's coming toward us!"

"Look at it!"

"Dokaa has damned us!"

"It's huge!"

Gesturing for the audio to be muted, Picard turned to Riker. "Number One, we need to act before the situation over there deteriorates any further. Are you ready?"

Looking up from where he and Vale were coordinating their plans, the first officer nodded. "I think so captain. We can at least get started, and adapt as necessary."

Picard nodded in approval. "Make it so."

This is almost too easy, Christine Vale warned herself. *Not that I'm complaining.*

Trying hard not to contemplate the narrow, utilitarian tunnel that was all that protected her from the vacuum of space, Vale instead focused her attention on the evacuation that was now well under way. That was fine with her, for the faster they could get the rest of the beleaguered miners off this godforsaken rock and safely aboard the *Enterprise,* the happier she would be.

Her duties had not given her the opportunity to inspect much beyond the airlock access passageway, but even a quick look at that had been enough to give her the basic lay of the land. The Dokaalan level of technology looked equivalent to Earth's during the late twenty-first century at the advent of the first long-duration colonies on the moon and Mars. The corridors here were cold, most likely due to insufficient insulation, and the air was stale thanks to the outpost's inoperative life-support system. The gravity also was lighter, only one-sixth that of Earth. Vale and her team were able to move about easily enough, but it required an extra bit of attention to keep from bounding around, so the lesser gravity wouldn't take them by surprise.

The tunnel and the chamber beyond were surprisingly clean and appeared well maintained. Vale had expected more clutter or other evidence of a people who had lived for an extended period of time within the confines of a habitat not intended for such use. This told the security chief that the Dokaalan had adapted to their situation with remarkable success and composure. These people would have amazing stories to tell, she knew, and Vale was looking forward to hearing them.

What do you say we get them out of here first?

Her thoughts were interrupted by the signal of her combadge followed by the voice of Lieutenant Jim Peart, her deputy chief of security. *"Group three is aboard, Lieutenant."* Static still corrupted the communications link, even though the two officers were separated at most by a hundred meters. *"So far the forcefield is holding. Want to send another group?"*

"Absolutely," Vale replied. "I'm sending them over now, Jim. Stand by to receive." Nodding to Melorr, the Bolian ensign she had placed in charge of the team at the docking-port hatch, she gave him the signal to commence transferring the fourth group of evacuees to the *Enterprise.* In response, Melorr opened the hatch to the access tunnel that connected to the rest of the complex and began to usher members of the next group forward. Vale had insisted on keeping the hatch closed in the event the forcefield protecting the airlock failed.

No sense taking any chances, she thought. *Not now.*

It had been a masterly feat of flying, as was usual for Data, to maneuver the mammoth starship into position to link up with the damaged mining outpost via its lone external docking port. That accomplished, Commander La Forge and his group of engineers had next rigged a supplementary power supply to the emergency forcefield generator for the airlock now connecting the ship to the mining outpost.

Even though the two hatches could not connect, owing to variations in their design, the forcefield acted to create a seal around the gap. La Forge had also taken the extra precaution of setting up a portable generator on the outpost's side of the airlock to augment the energy barrier. Though not entirely comfortable with these little feats of mechanical wizardry, Vale figured she could deal with them long enough to accomplish her current task.

"Thank you," a female Dokaalan said to her as she passed, part of the fourth group of evacuees being transferred to the ship. "You are a gift from Dokaa."

Understandably panicked by their situation, the Dokaalan miners had expressed only momentary concern upon meeting the strange beings who had come to their rescue. There was also the possibility that they were still a bit cowed by the appearance of the *Enterprise* beyond the windows of the outpost. Vale idly wondered if any of them might be fearful of a superior alien force coming to conquer their civilization.

Commander Riker had handled the initial contact procedures, where it had been learned that the people living both here and elsewhere within the asteroid field were indeed descendants of those who had survived the catastrophe that had claimed the Dokaalan's home planet generations ago. According to the miner who had acted as spokesperson for the group inhabiting the damaged outpost, there were even survivors of the original disaster still living among the population.

Vale's first thought at the revelation was that this race must have an incredibly prolonged life span, rivaling even other long-lived races like the Vulcans and perhaps even the Trill symbionts. The amazing trials they would have faced in the aftermath of such colossal tragedy boggled the security chief's mind.

Riker had done his best to put the miners at ease, his experience in such matters far exceeding Vale's. That addressed, the first officer had escorted the person in charge of the miners back to the ship, where he would meet with Captain Picard—after Dr. Crusher had examined him, of course. That left Vale and her security team in charge of the remainder of the operation.

Things had been made much easier thanks to the Dokaalan themselves. While she was sure these people would have countless questions, most of them at least had the presence of mind to hold them until the evacuation could be completed.

They can't be strangers to adversity, she reminded herself, *or the need to react quickly to a situation.*

Just like the image of First Minister Zahanzei from the centuries-old probe's recorded distress message, the Dokaalan Vale and her team found on the outpost were essentially humanoid in appearance. Their light blue skin was several shades lighter than the first minister as depicted on the visual recording, undoubtedly an effect of having lived for years inside cramped artificial structures and insulated from the natural light of the Dokaalan sun. Still, their skin and lack of hair made them look vaguely Bolian in appearance, but it was there that the resemblance ended. They were much taller and slight of build, and their skulls were shaped differently. Vale had to wonder how such large, lanky frames lent themselves to the rigors of subsurface mining.

That's probably the least of their worries, she thought. Descendants of those who escaped the disaster that had claimed their home planet, these people seemed to have tackled the challenge of surviving for centuries out here among the asteroids. Judging by the evidence all around her, the Dokaalan had hammered out an existence from the very lifeless rock that at one time had most likely been viewed as nothing more than a massive storehouse of resources. Now, that same rock had evolved to be all that separated these people from possible oblivion.

"Lieutenant Vale," Peart's voice called out over her combadge, *"group four is evacuating now. No problems so far."*

"Acknowledged," she replied, nodding in satisfaction. *Yes,* she thought, *nice and easy. I could get used to this.*

Chapter Thirteen

"DR. CRUSHER? Dr. *Crusher?*"

Beverly Crusher turned away from the prostrate form before her and looked for the source of the voice calling her name from somewhere in the depths of cargo bay four.

"Over here!" she called out.

"Another group is coming," the voice replied, which Crusher now recognized as belonging to Alyssa Ogawa, her typically unshakable head nurse and a valued member of the *Enterprise* medical staff for more than a decade. Still, even she sounded as though she might be rattled at the prospect of more injured boarding the starship.

Sighing, Crusher shook her head at the news. The cargo bay had been turned into an emergency field hospital, helping to screen roughly one hundred Dokaalan requiring varying degrees of treatment. However, the evacuees were coming at a rate that she knew threatened to overwhelm the ship's medical personnel, or at least overrun the physical space of the large room. Other cargo bays were being converted and would be ready soon, but that did not aid her immediate situation.

There's nothing you can do about that, she reminded herself. *So worry about the problems you* can *fix.*

Brushing a lock of red hair from her face, Crusher moved to the next emergency treatment bed and activated its array of diagnostic sensors. The Dokaalan lying on the small bed was having difficulty breathing and was holding his abdomen, though there did not appear to be a great deal of blood. An internal injury, most likely.

"Temperature is 29.4 degrees Celsius," she said. "Is that even normal for you?" She was not surprised when the Dokaalan merely looked at her in confusion, and she patted him gently on the arm. "Don't worry," she offered in her best bedside-manner voice, "we're going to take good care of you."

"Dr. Crusher," Ogawa called out again. "The next group is arriving."

Without looking up from her work, Crusher replied, "Resume triage protocols and I'll be right there." Ogawa and the rest of the medical staff were more than capable of assessing injuries and quickly assigning treatment priorities in emergencies, even while under attack. Still, coordinating triage involving beings heretofore unknown to Federation medical science would have tested the mettle of even Starfleet's best physicians.

Using the peripheral scanner from her medical tricorder to examine the young man—she assumed he was young, anyway—Crusher compared the unit's readings with those of the dozens of patients she had already treated. This was most definitely not the way she preferred to practice medicine, knowing that everything they were doing to help these people was, for the moment at least, based purely on instinct.

While she and the rest of the medical staff continued their efforts down here, data about Dokaalan physiology was streaming constantly into the ship's computer with each patient they examined. Once the analysis of that data started to yield results, she would be able to determine what pharmaceuticals might be medically effective in stabilizing her new patients and easing their pain. For the moment, however, she was depending entirely on her own abilities, experience gleaned from years of treating new and exotic alien species, and a generous helping of good luck.

I guess it was too much to ask that the probe carried data files on Dokaalan anatomy and physiology.

Studying her tricorder's readings, Crusher now knew that her initial diagnosis of the wounded Dokaalan was correct. The sound of the patient's labored breathing was unmistakable. A lung had collapsed and what looked to be the equivalent of the spleen in a human had been lacerated. Those, at least, were injuries she understood and which could be treated quickly, here and now.

Retrieving a hypospray from her medikit, she set it to deliver a mild sedative that would let the Dokaalan sleep through his pain. The effects were immediate as she saw her patient's pale blue features relax.

He struggled to speak. "Th-th . . . thank . . . youuu. . . ."

"Of course," she said, leaning in as the Dokaalan closed his eyes again. "Be still, now."

Crusher gave silent thanks for the only advantage she truly enjoyed at this moment: a crumbling communications barrier. The Dokaalan probe's recording and other data files stored in its small onboard computer had provided enough of a language sample that Federation linguists were able to construct a competent protocol for the ship's universal-translation subroutines. Those programs were getting a workout now and being given the opportunity to improve with each passing moment as they sifted though the reedy, nasal tones of Dokaalan vocalizations and extrapolated them into a semblance of Federation Standard.

She did not need any of that, however, as she saw the smile on the Dokaalan's face before he slipped into unconsciousness, his anxieties eased at least a small bit at the realization that he was among friends.

As she gave the necessary treatment instructions to an assisting medic, she grabbed her gear and made her way toward the triage operation's makeshift staging area. Stepping past the small line of cargo containers that had been arranged to mark off the staging area, Crusher felt a sudden tug on her entire body, her legs wobbling in momentary disorientation.

Forgot about that, she realized as her legs took the extra second to reacquaint themselves to carrying her full weight. To accommodate the recovering Dokaalan, artificial gravity throughout the main section of the cargo bay's triage area had been reconfigured for one-sixth that of Earth, while remaining normal in the staging area so as not to disrupt the workings of the rescue teams and medical staff. Therefore, transitioning to and from the separate gravity fields always came as a bit of a shock.

At least we didn't have to change the air mix, too.

As she steadied herself and resumed her pace to the

entrance of the bay, she saw the first of what appeared to be dozens of Dokaalan shuffling through the hatch, some not under their own power. As they entered the bay, they passed through a series of arches that had been jury-rigged to act as emergency bioscanners. The sensors were in turn providing preliminary readings that aided the medics with their initial diagnoses.

Denizens of the outpost seemed so far to be adults of two genders, Crusher noted, with none of them appearing particularly youthful or elderly. By their attire and demeanor, it was obvious that these people were used to living in nothing resembling the lap of luxury.

"Anything unusual?" Crusher asked Ogawa, who was busily tapping information into a padd.

The nurse's normally well-groomed hair was disheveled. She looked up and shook her head. "A few injuries, but unless someone's keeping something from us, these are all greens."

Following triage guidelines, medics were grouping the Dokaalan by the extent of their injuries and coding them by color: green for evacuees needing no treatment and who could be quickly moved to temporary berthing areas, yellow for those who suffered from injuries that did not threaten their lives, red for those who would die without immediate treatment—and black. Crusher had coded three Dokaalan as black so far, and that was three too many so far as she was concerned.

"Sounds great, Alyssa," Crusher said. "We could use the break. Make sure you get some rest and something to drink before the next group comes. You look like you need it."

"We all may need it," Ogawa said over her shoulder as

she started toward the row of emergency bioscanner arches. "According to Lieutenant Vale and Commander Riker, we've only seen about a third of the Dokaalan on the outpost."

Crusher turned away to hide her grimace. It would not do for her subordinates to see her frustration at the current situation. Instead they had to see that she was in control and would continue to work no matter the difficulties that lay ahead. The Dokaalan were counting on them, after all.

She was moving from the reception area to inspect the status of their medical supplies when she saw Dr. Tropp, one of her three fellow physicians on board the *Enterprise.* "Hello, Doctor," she offered as he approached.

"Dr. Crusher," the Denobulan replied, holding up a dermal regenerator. "While treating our guests I have discovered that our regenerators aren't working as efficiently as I would like. I am trying to take advantage of our slight lull to see if I can recalibrate one of them, but I admit to having little success."

Since his arrival on the *Enterprise,* Tropp had shown an unwavering drive in his practice of medicine, and she quickly had come to appreciate his opinions and diagnoses. Additionally, he had demonstrated a keen interest in working with the younger and newer members of her team. Tropp seemed to enjoy functioning as the *Enterprise* medical staff's own continuing-education program, something that she welcomed considering that his people had served as biologists and healers even on the earliest of Earth's deep-space exploration vessels.

"I appreciate what you're trying to do, Tropp," she said, "but it might not even be possible to accelerate their healing. Let's hold off on that now, and focus instead on stabilizing the wounded."

"Oh, I heartily agree, Doctor," Tropp replied. "I'm just trying to anticipate what we might see later, given the circum—"

"Hey! We need some help here!"

Both doctors turned at the sound of the voice. Craning to see past the lines of Dokaalan at the bioscanning arches, Crusher spotted a pair of Starfleet crewmen ferrying between them what appeared to be a tarp—supporting a body. As the two physicians sprinted across the deck toward the new arrivals, she caught sight of another such makeshift stretcher, this one carried by a Dokaalan and an *Enterprise* crewman. Crusher peered into the tarp and saw that just what Tropp had anticipated was starting to come to pass.

"What happened?" Crusher asked as she activated her tricorder.

"Coolant pipes ruptured," said one of the rescuers. "These two got doused with the stuff. There were others, but . . ."

"I understand," Crusher said as she got a better look at the extent of the victims' burns. Swaths of their pale blue skin had turned a pallid gray. Wounds that should have been bleeding were cauterized. One of the Dokaalan was shuddering noiselessly, while the other was deathly still.

Tropp appeared at Crusher's side with the steering pads for an antigrav gurney in each hand. "Use these," he instructed as he passed the pads to a pair of medics. "It will help ease the pain from the burns." As the two victims were maneuvered onto the gurneys, the Denobulan produced his own tricorder and scooped out its hand-held scanner.

"I cannot tell whether these are chemical burns or scaldings," he said as waved the scanner over one of the Dokaalan. "They may be both. Are there open beds in the red area?"

"Forget that," Crusher said. "We can't handle this down here." She tapped her combadge. "Crusher to sickbay. Activate emergency medical hologram."

A second later, a cool, reserved voice responded through her communicator. *"Please state the nature of the medical emergency."*

"This is Dr. Crusher," she said as she tapped commands into her tricorder. "I'm in cargo bay four leading a triage team, and I'm transferring the medical information for two patients that are being taken to you now. I need you to prepare sickbay for use as a burn unit. I need . . ."

"Wouldn't it be simpler to beam them directly to sickbay?" the hologram asked.

"Transporters are not cleared for use," she said. "Please just listen and don't second-guess me."

"Affirmative," came the hologram's crisp reply.

"Thank you," she snapped, trying to remind herself that the EMH was a valuable asset in situations such as this, when time was of the essence. The holographic doctor could instantly access the ship's medical database and retrieve all the information on the Dokaalan, allowing him to begin work immediately. Further, he would be able to work indefinitely without the need for rest, a unique advantage considering the extensive and likely time-consuming treatment he was about to provide to the three inbound patients.

Unlike many starship medical officers, who had opted for more advanced versions of the emergency medical hologram, Crusher had decided to keep the Mark I model EMH program after a test period to evaluate its successor. Though the newer Mark II version was unquestionably a superior product of computer software engineering, she had grown accustomed to the Mark I's personality and felt it better served her as well as her medical staff and, ultimately, the rest of the *Enterprise* crew.

That's not to say its bedside-manner subroutines still couldn't stand some additional adjustments, she thought.

"I need you to prepare beds as dermaline gel baths for burn treatment. Attune the support frames to monitor for signs of infection and also to continuously cycle the gel for debriding." She paused, unsure that the course of treatment even would work on the lanky beings.

"I am aware of the protocols, Doctor," said the EMH. *"Is there anything else?"*

"Yes, you can reduce the gravity in sickbay to one-sixth normal," Crusher said. "Dr. Tropp and a nursing team are on their way with the patients. I want you to make their stay as comfortable as possible." She actually thought she heard the EMH huff before responding.

"I'm a doctor, not a concierge."

Crusher bit her lip to stay an equally terse reply, then said, "I know you'll do your best. Crusher out."

As she helped a pair of nurses maneuver the gurneys toward the closest turbolift, Crusher's attention was drawn back to the scene of organized chaos unfolding around her. Seeing the steadily growing number of

Dokaalan patients as well as *Enterprise* medical staff as every other crew member who had heeded her call for extra assistance working to maintain order and continue to the triage process, she could not help the silent plea that screamed in her mind.

Now, if we can just do our *best. . . .*

Chapter Fourteen

GEORDI LA FORGE HAD WORKED on a variety of machinery over the years, from the latest in Starfleet engineering concepts to unique specimens of alien technology. Thanks to a bizarre set of circumstances, he had even traveled through time to the twenty-first century and assisted the great Zefram Cochrane in preparing the man's prototype warp-capable vessel for its maiden voyage. Given his wide range of experiences, it was a rare occasion when the *Enterprise*'s chief engineer encountered a problem he could not solve eventually.

And it was those instances, such as the one he faced right now, that tended to frustrate him.

"What a mess," he said aloud, though there was no one else around to hear him. "We'd be better off jettisoning the whole thing and building a new reactor from scratch." Shaking his head, La Forge deactivated his tricorder and returned the unit to the holster on his waist, wiping sweat from his brow as he did so. It was hot down here, a by-product of the overworked reactor and its malfunctioning coolant system.

The engineer took another look about the cramped room, the control center for the mining outpost's main power reactor situated in a sealed chamber hundreds of meters below the surface of the asteroid upon which the complex had been constructed. He was seeking any clue, any hint that he might have missed which could help him and his team to bring the malfunctioning reactor under control.

Like the rest of the outpost, the control room was sparse in its construction and crammed from deck to ceiling with all manner of control consoles, tool lockers, and storage containers. Its most prominent feature was the large electronic status board mounted to the wall at the room's far end, which reminded La Forge of the large master situation monitor in the *Enterprise*'s engineering section.

As for the remainder of the room, the bulkheads were composed of metal plating riveted and welded together, and La Forge could see crude join lines and other indicators of hasty repairs completed without the luxury of always having the correct replacement component or even the proper tool for the job.

The reactor itself, while possessing key differences from others he had seen, appeared to La Forge to be similar enough to those used to power the first manned interplanetary spacecraft from Earth in the early twenty-first century. Those power systems had been based on the concept of fusing deuterium and tritium with helium to create high-energy plasma that was in turn channeled by electromagnetic coils to generate thrust. The principle employed by the Dokaalan was similar, at least in this system's original design, though it appeared to have been adapted to work using minerals found in abundance among the asteroids. Even more remarkable was that the Dokaalan engineers had apparently devised a process that was free from potentially harmful residual waste such as neutron radiation, a dangerous by-product of the early Earth fusion reactors. All in all, it was an impressive piece of technical craftsmanship.

Not unexpected, La Forge conceded, *considering the only tools and materials these people have are what they can fashion for themselves.* Under the circumstances, the overall maintenance of the equipment he had inspected since arriving on the outpost was well above what he had expected to find.

Hearing footsteps behind him, La Forge turned to see Lieutenant Taurik and one of the Dokaalan specialists, a short yet stocky specimen named Rysatam, approaching the control center from the reactor room's main floor. As with the rest of the engineers sent from the *Enterprise,* the Vulcan was dressed in a tan utility jumpsuit ideal for the type of climbing and crawling activities the away team could be expected to perform during their investigation of the outpost's power center.

"What have you got, Taurik?" La Forge asked.

Holding up his tricorder, the junior engineer replied, "According to my analysis, Commander, the reactor's cooling system can be repaired, but I do not believe we can do so in the time remaining to us."

Frowning at the report, La Forge said, "Maybe we can rig up some kind of bypass and hook in a substitute cooling unit." The *Enterprise* stored such devices, which normally were used to regulate the operating temperature of mobile power generators employed by temporary settlements on newly established colonies. He judged that one or two of those would be more than sufficient to handle the cooling needs of the ailing Dokaalan reactor.

"That is not all," Taurik continued. "My scans show that several of the reactor's key components have melted or malfunctioned due to the excessive internal heat. If left alone, the reactor will continue to generate energy at uncontrolled levels until it overheats and explodes."

"What about switching to backup systems?" La Forge asked.

Standing next to Taurik, Rysatam replied, "The systems that allow us to switch from main to secondary power are among those damaged. Our automated connections are severed and the manual overrides are fused."

The chief engineer shook his head. "So there's no way to shut it off." He had arrived at a comparable conclusion after his initial inspection of the reactor systems, but he was hoping that one of the Dokaalan engineers or a member of his own team might provide another option after a more thorough examination of the problem.

"I am afraid not," Rysatam replied, his expression sullen. Like the other Dokaalan workers the away team had met upon entering the outpost, he had quickly overcome any anxiety at meeting visitors from space and eagerly embraced the *Enterprise* engineers, hopeful that the new arrivals might offer a solution to their problem that was beyond their own technical expertise.

Sorry to disappoint you, friend, La Forge mused, the thought laced with frustration at his team's apparent inability to provide that magical solution. *Well, this certainly didn't take long.*

Turning to Rysatam, Taurik said, "There is nothing

more to be done here. Prepare your people for evacuation to the upper level. You will be escorted to our ship with the rest of the outpost residents."

The Dokaalan nodded gratefully. "Very well." Looking to La Forge once more, he added, "Do not feel bad, my friend. The situation was dire well before your arrival. We will adjust to the loss of equipment and matériel as we have in the past, but because you are here, many people will be saved who would have certainly perished without your assistance."

Not wishing to spoil Rysatam's goodwill, La Forge smiled as he wiped more perspiration from his brow. "I suppose you're right. That is the most important thing, after all."

As Rysatam turned to gather his people for the move back to the outpost's main level and Taurik notified the rest of the away team to gather their gear and head out, the chief engineer tapped his combadge. "La Forge to Vale."

"Vale here," the voice of the security chief replied a moment later. *"What's the story down there, Commander?"*

"The reactor's a hopeless case," La Forge replied. "With the coolant gone, some of the key mechanisms have melted, including the ones that would have let us shut the damn thing down. There's nothing we can do to keep it from overheating." The temperature in the room was continuing to climb, another sign that the situation was worsening, at least if the sweat running down his back was any indication.

"How much time do we have?" Vale asked. La Forge knew she was in the midst of coordinating the evacuation of all four hundred colonists from the out-

post, so any information he could provide her would be helpful.

At his prompting, Taurik replied, "Approximately thirty-six point four minutes, Lieutenant."

"We might be able to bleed off some of the pressure that's building," La Forge added, "but we'd only be delaying the inevitable. We need to get those people out of here, Christine."

"We're working on it, Commander. Vale out." The connection severed, leaving the two *Enterprise* engineers alone in the sweltering reactor control room. Looking around, La Forge realized that the temperature of the reactor had risen to the point that his ocular implants could pick up the waves of heat emanating from its outer shell. They did not have much time, he knew.

"I guess that's all we can do, Taurik," La Forge said. "Let's get our people and head back topside."

"Commander, a moment if I may," the lieutenant said. Pausing a moment, as if to insure that no one else could overhear them, Taurik activated his tricorder and tapped a command sequence into the unit's small control pad. "During my analysis of the reactor I discovered an anomaly." He held the tricorder so that La Forge could see its compact display screen. "I detected evidence of structural fatigue in this control valve on the coolant system's flow regulator, but according to my scans, that is inconsistent with the age of the component in question."

"A faulty part, maybe?" La Forge offered. "Wouldn't be the first time a replacement part was defective, here or anywhere else."

Shaking his head, Taurik replied, "Were it the single valve I might be tempted to agree. However, I discovered similar indications in three other valves, each of which is an integral component in its respective part of the overall system. Further, the signs of fatigue would appear to be older than the valves themselves."

"That might still be explained by a defect in manufacturing," the chief engineer countered, but even as he said the words they rang hollow in his ears. What Taurik had shown him simply made no sense, given their surroundings. Like everything else he had seen in the mining outpost, evidence of meticulous care was visible everywhere, from the lack of dirt and grime on the surface of equipment to the cleanliness of the floors and walls and the absence of trash or detritus that might be expected to accumulate over a lengthy period. The Dokaalan obviously had learned early on that with only themselves to rely upon, the need for proper maintenance and diligence was essential, particularly with those systems charged with keeping them alive.

So what had happened to the coolant system?

His thoughts were interrupted by the sound of an alarm wailing outside the control center. It was quickly followed by several indicators on the room's main status board, all of them illuminating an attention-grabbing crimson red.

"Uh-oh," La Forge said as, one after another, more of the indicators flared to life. "I think we've got another problem."

Closing out the communication with Commander La Forge, Vale exhaled audibly.

Nothing's ever easy, is it?

Working with his team of engineers as well as a few Dokaalan technical specialists, La Forge had hoped to bring the rapidly overheating power generator under control. The outpost engineers had argued it as an impossible task, but La Forge wanted to take a shot at the problem himself with the equipment and technology at his disposal, which far exceeded that of the Dokaalan.

It had not been enough, apparently.

Thirty-eight minutes remained to them, according to Taurik's estimate. That was probably right on the money, considering the Vulcan's predilection for accuracy. It should be plenty of time, barring any unforeseen circumstances.

Most of the fourth group of evacuees had made the move to the *Enterprise,* with the fifth complement already standing by and awaiting their turn. Her security detachment had organized the miners into eight groups of fifty, with the most seriously injured to be transferred first. Those requiring immediate medical attention were already being treated by Dr. Crusher and her medical teams. To this point, Vale's quickly developed evacuation plan had worked just as she had hoped.

From what she could see now, though, things were no longer proceeding as smoothly as they had been only moments earlier. Ensign Melorr and his team looked to be working harder to keep the miners orderly and positioned for their transfer.

"What's the problem here?" she asked in her most authoritative security chief voice, mindful once again of the lower gravity as well as the need to keep herself beyond the reach of any of the miners as she stepped closer.

"This is taking too long," replied one Dokaalan. "The reactor will overload soon. Why are you keeping us here?"

Vale noted that the miner sounded more fearful than angry, and she briefly considered trying to explain the effects of the radiation emitted by the very minerals these people extracted from the asteroids. She figured they might comprehend the basic concept of forcefields, tractor beams, and perhaps even transporters, but she had no desire to stand on a ticking bomb discussing the details of current Federation technology or the problems it was experiencing here. There would be time enough for that later.

She hoped.

"There are safety concerns with evacuating so many of you," she said, hoping the simple explanation would be enough. "We can't do this without your cooperation, so I'm going to ask that you maintain your places and wait for instructions from my people. Rest assured that all of you will be evacuated to our ship and have your injuries tended to."

It was too much to hope that her words would completely ease the miners' worries, but Vale was pleasantly surprised when the anxious Dokaalan appeared to relax somewhat.

"The probes," someone else said from behind her, and Vale turned to see a female Dokaalan regarding her with what the security chief believed to be a quizzical expression. "You found one of our probes, did you not?"

Smiling, Vale nodded. "Two of them, actually, though many, many years passed between finding the first and the second." She caught herself before saying too much. After all, she didn't want to incite any more negative feelings by revealing that centuries had passed before Starfleet or the Federation had decided to send a ship to investigate the Dokaalan's plea for help.

That'd sure make them feel better, wouldn't it?

"Melorr," she called out, "get ready to send the next group." Tapping her combadge, she said, "Vale to Peart. We're sending the next . . ."

The rest of the sentence died in her throat as she felt the metal deck plating shudder beneath her feet.

"What the hell was that?" Melorr asked. There was no mistaking the nervousness in the Bolian's voice, and his emotion was mirrored in the faces of the Dokaalan miners. Some of them were moving from the orderly lines established by the security team and were pressing toward the airlock and the tunnel leading to the *Enterprise.*

The answer came from her combadge in the voice of the ship's chief engineer. *"La Forge to Vale. The reactor cooling system is shot. Get those people out of here now!"*

"What happened?" Vale asked, at the same time giving Melorr the signal to start moving the remaining miners out.

"It was cycling nothing but air after the coolant tank ruptured," La Forge replied, *"and I couldn't bleed off enough pressure. According to our calculations, the reactor will go in about ten minutes. The chamber it's in might be enough to contain the explosion, but I don't know what it might do to the surrounding rock. I'd rather not stick around to find out."*

Vale heard the engineer breathing hard as he talked, as though he was running. More than likely he and his team were scrambling to get back here. Turning around, she saw that her security people were frantically ushering the miners through the airlock and into the tunnel. By her count there were still more than two hundred people left to evacuate.

"Let's keep it moving," she called out, trying to keep her voice steady and confident. "We don't have much time."

Then time ran out as somewhere below her, too far away to see yet close enough for her to feel the effect, something exploded.

Vale threw out her arms, desperately grabbing for any kind of handhold as the deck pitched and disappeared from beneath her feet. Her hands closed around empty air and she slammed into the nearby bulkhead. Even with the reduced gravity, the impact was enough to make stars erupt in her vision and force the air from her lungs.

Groaning in pain as she slid to the floor, Vale realized the deck was still shaking underneath her. She was bounced along the unforgiving metal plating as she scrambled for something to grasp, finally clutching a safety railing mounted to the bulkhead. All around her, Dokaalan miners and the members of her security team were in similar straits, having been tossed about by the force of the explosion erupting from the depths of the outpost. Then the lights went out, only to be replaced seconds later by dimmer emergency lighting spaced at regular intervals down the length of the passageway.

The reactor, she thought, but had it overloaded faster than Commander La Forge had predicted? Had he and his team been able to make it out in time?

Before she could reach for her combadge in an attempt to contact the engineer, the corridor trembled around her once more. This time the motion was accompanied by an alarm klaxon wailing in the confined passageway.

"Breach!" someone yelled before Vale recognized the sound of air escaping through what could only be a tear in the metal plating forming the corridor around them. Where was it coming from?

Then the hiss became a howl as, less than ten meters away, the tunnel leading to the *Enterprise* disappeared along with the twenty or more Dokaalan who had been standing in it.

Chapter Fifteen

"Detach from the airlock! Now!"

The order came too late as, despite the *Enterprise*'s inertial dampening field, Picard felt the starship roll with the asteroid. The massive hunk of rock shifted on its axis in response to the outpost reactor's detonation, taking the mining outpost and anything attached with it. While he was sure his ship could handle the stress of the sudden movement, the same could not be said for the more primitive structure of the outpost, let alone the fragile conduit connecting them.

His worst fear was realized an instant later as, displayed on the main viewer for all to see, the transfer tunnel sheared away, ripped from its moorings as easily as a banana might be peeled of its skin.

"The outpost has sustained a massive breach," Data reported from the ops position. "They are suffering atmospheric decompression."

The damned reactor had overloaded faster than anticipated, Picard realized. What had happened to cause the accelerated results? Where were La Forge and the rest of the away team?

Then there was no more time for such thoughts as something on the main viewer caught the captain's attention. Horrified, he watched as the metal cylinder that had been the tunnel spiraled away from the mining outpost. Falling apart as it did so, its disintegration revealed dozens of bodies flailing in the vacuum, people who had been in the tunnel when disaster struck. At least one appeared to be wearing a Starfleet uniform.

"Picard to transporter room one," Picard said as he tapped his combadge, "lock transporters on the people outside the ship and beam them to cargo bay four." He knew that Commander Riker was coordinating the influx of new arrivals from there, and that Dr. Crusher and her medical team were already on site, treating the wounded Dokaalan miners who had safely made the evacuation from the outpost.

"Captain," said the voice of T'Bonz, the transporter chief currently on duty, *"that will require our shields to be lowered, and transporters are still being recalibrated by the engineering staff. They have not been certified for humanoid transport."*

"I'm aware of the risks, Chief," Picard snapped. What choice did he have? Those people were dead if he stood by and did nothing. "Lock on and transport, *now.*"

"Aye, sir," came the Vulcan's cool reply. *"Energizing."*

Knowing the interval of time required for a successful transporter cycle to complete, Picard silently counted off the seconds before prompting, "Bridge to cargo bay four. What is the status of the new arrivals?"

The lack of an immediate response filled his heart with dread, a feeling cemented a moment later when the voice of Commander Riker came through the intercom.

"Twenty-seven people have just materialized here, sir." There was another distressing pause before the first officer continued, and when he did Picard could hear the barely controlled trembling in his voice. *"I'm afraid none of them survived."*

Silence engulfed the bridge, broken only by the sounds of control consoles and computer interfaces dutifully processing their various instructions. Picard could only close his eyes and shake his head in momentary despair.

He had gambled, and lost.

It was not the first time he had given orders that resulted in the deaths of others, be they enemy combatants, members of his own crew or, on rare and horrifying occasions, even innocent bystanders. In all of those instances he was able, sooner or later, to divorce personal feelings from his command responsibilities. He knew that, after a time, even the pain he was feeling now would also pass.

Soon, he knew, *but not now, and deservedly so.*

"Thank you, Number One," he said after a moment, struggling to keep his own voice level. "Please keep me apprised of any new developments." As the connection severed, he stared at the viewscreen and the rapidly expanding cloud of debris cast off from the ruptured outpost airlock.

"Captain," he heard Troi say from behind him. Her voice trailed off, but he could tell from the inflection behind the single word that she wanted to say something to him about the tragedy that had just occurred.

That he had caused.

"Not now, Counselor." There would be time enough to examine and criticize his incorrect decision later. Now, somewhere beyond that turmoil depicted with cold indifference on the bridge's main viewscreen, people were still in danger. His people.

"Open a channel to the away team," he said. He had to know what was happening over there.

Still holding the guardrail, Vale managed to wrap her left arm around it and clasp her hands together before she felt herself pulled off her feet as the rapidly escaping atmosphere dragged at her body. Screams of terror echoed in the corridor as people were dragged through the air toward the jagged metal maw which was all that remained of the transfer tunnel on the other side of the airlock.

Hanging on for dear life, she had been powerless to do anything except watch as Ensign Melorr succeeded in securing his own hold on the airlock hatch's control lever, only to be struck by the flailing body of a Dokaalan miner. Both of them vanished through the open hatch, swallowed by the dark airless void.

They had been so close! Fewer than half of the miners remained to be evacuated when the tunnel had ruptured. Some of them had been lost to the hull breach but many were still here, holding on to anything that would support them.

The air was still rushing to flee the confines of the corridor, telling Vale that no emergency hatches or bulkheads had closed deeper inside the complex. How much time did they have before this entire section of the outpost was completely without oxygen? No more than a minute, she guessed. Probably less.

"Enterprise *to away team!*" the voice of Captain Picard called from her combadge, but even his commanding tone was nearly lost amid the screaming wind. *"Lieutenant Vale, are you all right?"*

Vale ignored the call as she decided on a course of action. Her eyes already ached, the moisture in them beginning to freeze from the rapidly dropping temperature inside the corridor. Her pulse pounded in her ears and her lungs cried out for more oxygen. She had at most a handful of seconds left, and for certain only a single chance.

The hatch.

Twisting herself around so that she was now facing headfirst toward the open airlock, Vale released her hold on the guardrail. She immediately felt herself pushed toward the hatch by the force of the rushing atmosphere. Darkness beckoned beyond the open doorway, but she focused instead on the section of bulkhead just to the left of the hatchway. That, and the lever which would seal the hatch shut, the same lever that Melorr had grasped in a frantic yet futile bid for survival.

She felt the fingers of her left hand swipe across the cold metal of the bulkhead plating, sliding along its surface until they contacted the rough metal of the lever. Closing her grip around the protrusion, Vale swung her body back toward the wall, this time absorbing the impact with the soles of her boots. Now she was anchored to the bulkhead by a two-handed death grip on the control lever.

Already growing fatigued from the lack of oxygen, Vale ignored her increasingly blurry vision. She drew one final deep breath from the dwindling atmosphere around her before heaving down on the lever with all her remaining strength.

The lever slid down, and her effort was rewarded with the whine of the motors controlling the hatch as the reinforced metal door cycled shut. Only once it had closed completely, stopping the frantic flight of air from the corridor, did Vale release her grip on the lever and allow the outpost's reduced gravity to pull her to the deck.

Okay, let's hope we don't have to do that again anytime soon.

"Is everyone okay?" she called out, hearing her own raspy voice and realizing for the first time that her throat was parched, another effect of the sudden decompression. Voices shouted from farther down the corridor, and only then did Vale realize that someone had opened the other hatch, the one leading back into the main part of the outpost. Looking in that direction, Vale was happy to see so many faces, mentally patting herself on the head for her decision to keep that door closed during the evacuation process. With the exception of those nearest to the airlock when the tunnel had breached, it looked as though most of the remaining Dokaalan miners had survived.

The lucky ones, she mused.

"Enterprise *to away team,*" Captain Picard's voice called out again from her combadge. *"Report your status if you are able. Do you require medical assistance?"*

The security chief tapped her communicator. "Vale here, Captain. I need a minute, sir. We're still picking ourselves up off the deck over here." Turning to look back up the corridor, she called out, "Alpha team, report."

A male human and a female Andorian wearing Starfleet uniforms, two of her four-person team, emerged from around the corner at the corridor intersection. Both of them looked haggard, no doubt as beat up and relieved to still be alive as she.

"We're missing six of the miners, Lieutenant," Ensign Zelev th'Chun reported, pausing a moment to wipe blood from a cut along her forehead. "The others have a variety of bruises and lacerations, along with a few broken bones. Nothing serious, though."

Standing next to Zelev, Ensign McPherson regarded Vale with an expression of dread. "What about Melorr . . . and Graham?"

"I saw Melorr fall through the airlock," Vale replied. "Graham was escorting the last group of evacuees to the ship when everything went to hell." She shook her head. "I don't see how he could have . . . I'm sorry."

McPherson and Graham had been teammates since the former's arrival aboard the *Enterprise* nearly five months earlier. Vale had paired them after it had become apparent during training exercises that the two worked exceedingly well together. Such cohesiveness and trust were vital components in developing an effective security team, but they also meant that the pain ran even deeper than normal when a member of that team was lost.

Placing a hand on the young ensign's shoulder, she said, "It's hard, I know. We'll pay our respects to Melorr and Graham when the time's appropriate, but right now we've still got the rest of these evacuees to get to safety."

She indicated the remaining Dokaalan miners who stood quietly a discreet distance down the corridor, regarding the Starfleet officers with expressions of pain and empathy. These people also had just lost friends and perhaps family members, but Vale was sure this was not the first time they had faced tragedy.

Maybe our being here will bring them some unexpected joy, Vale thought grimly as her people turned their attentions back to the task at hand, *but so far we haven't given them much to be thankful for.*

Chapter Sixteen

WITH THE RESCUE and recovery operation now in the cleanup stages, Picard allowed himself a moment of respite. Dr. Crusher already was providing preliminary reports that with the exception of a handful of cases, most of the wounded Dokaalan miners would recover from their injuries.

Leaving Data in charge on the bridge until Commander Riker's return, the captain retreated to the sanctuary of his ready room. He waited until the doors closed before dropping onto the small sofa positioned across from his desk. Here, tucked away from the uncounted details that required his attention, he closed his eyes and finally tried to release the frustration he had been keeping at bay. Only now could he purge the emotions he had contained while standing before those he commanded.

His solitude was short-lived, however, interrupted by the subdued melody of the door chime.

"Come," he said, suspecting who would be there. His

suspicion was confirmed as the doors parted to reveal Deanna Troi.

"Captain, we need to talk."

Picard scowled in response. "This is hardly the time, Counselor."

Standing before him, her hands on her hips and studying him with dark eyes that had always seen so effectively through his reserved veneer, Troi waited in silence. Picard knew she would do so until he acquiesced to her wishes—or the star in this system went nova, whichever came first.

"Please, sit down," he said finally, offering her the other half of the sofa. For a moment he said nothing else, instead closing his eyes and trying to lose himself in the soothing, ever-present hum of the *Enterprise*'s engines.

When that failed him, he opened his eyes, realizing that Troi had spent that time studying his face before saying anything. "I sense your anger at what happened. Anger, guilt, and uncertainty that you acted correctly."

"You're damned right I'm angry," Picard replied, more harshly than he had intended. In a softer voice he continued, "I knew the transporters were a risk, but I gave the order anyway. Those people would have died if I hadn't tried, but there's a part of me that's already questioning the decision. Did I act too quickly? Was there another option I could have considered?"

"And was there?"

Picard shook his head. "No. Anything else would have taken too much time. Still, twenty-seven people died and I can't help second-guessing myself."

"I think we both know that your feelings are misplaced," Troi said after a moment. "By doing nothing, you would have automatically sentenced those people to death, and it's not in your nature to simply stand by and allow something like that to happen. You were compelled to act, and in a split second you made a life-or-death decision."

Exhaling audibly, Picard replied, "There's nothing grand about deciding on the only course of action available to you, Counselor."

"No, but it takes courage to actually take that action, especially when you know that you might fail. Anyone can make easy choices, Captain, but it's the true leaders who act on the difficult ones."

Picard smiled at that. It was not a verbatim quote from one of the many leadership texts he had read while a student at Starfleet Academy, but it was close enough. He had no doubt that those same words, in some fashion or another, appeared in one or more of the volumes Troi had been required to study during her own training. After all, it made sense that a counselor would have to be familiar with the many factors that molded a leader if he or she was to provide thoughtful counsel to such individuals, did it not?

"However," she continued, "I've seen you make hard decisions many times before, even when it entailed loss of life. Now, though, I sense something deeper about the frustration you're feeling."

Nodding, Picard smiled grimly. "Observant as always, Counselor." Rising from the sofa, the captain moved to the replicator set into the wall on the other side of the room. "Tea, Earl Grey, hot." When Troi shook her head at the offer of something to drink, he retrieved the cup and saucer that materialized before him and returned to his seat. Troi sat in silence, patiently waiting as he stirred the steaming beverage and took a tentative first sip. He knew that she would give him all the time he needed to reveal what was on his mind.

"It's important to me that this mission be successful in every way," he said finally. "Not for my own sake, mind you, but for that of the ship and the crew. Starfleet needs to see that they've made a mistake, and not because they elected to send us all the way out here. After all, contacting new civilizations is why I joined Starfleet in the first place. There's no shame in being assigned a mission such as this, but I need for those in charge to understand that treating it as a punishment is wrong."

"Admiral Nechayev doesn't feel that way," Troi countered. "She sees this as an opportunity for us to redeem ourselves in the eyes of Starfleet."

"And that's precisely the problem," Picard said, setting his cup down on the table next to the sofa, the tea having abruptly lost its taste for him. "The crew shouldn't have to redeem themselves for anything." Sighing, he continued, "But there's nothing to be done about that now. All that's left is to make sure that the crew carries out this assignment, and the ones after it, in their usual exemplary manner. That includes me, and I can't afford to make mistakes like the one I did today."

He saw Troi opening her mouth to respond and held up a hand to stop her. "I know we've already discussed that, Counselor, and I will get past today's events in time, but so many people are questioning whether I'm still capable of making the correct decision at the right time. On top of that, they've got me questioning myself."

"Captain, it's perfectly normal to question any decision, particularly the difficult ones," Troi replied. "Leaders especially are obligated to examine their choices. In my opinion, it's no different from what you've always done. That's a good thing."

Deep down, Picard knew that to be true, but it was still gratifying to hear such thoughts voiced by another. It went a long way toward easing the frustration and remorse he carried, as well as returning his focus to the mission that still lay before him.

If there was one thing Christine Vale hated more than a mission that had gone bad, it was the debriefing session that took place afterward.

"We were unable to retrieve the people caught in the decompression when the hull breached," Captain Picard said from where he sat at the head of the table in the observation lounge. "Twenty-five of the Dokaalan died as a result of exposure." Looking to Vale, he added, "Ensign Melorr and Ensign Graham were also lost. I'm sorry, Lieutenant."

Vale had prepared herself for the worst even after hearing that the *Enterprise* had attempted to recover everyone blown into space from the outpost airlock. The grim news was still painful to hear, especially considering everything the away team had been through. It had not taken long for word to get around about Captain Picard's daring yet disastrous attempt to rescue the decompression victims. Vale believed the captain had acted decisively and correctly, despite the results.

"Still," Picard continued, "you and your team did an exceptional job under very trying circumstances. Well done, Lieutenant."

After working his way back to the airlock, La Forge had coordinated with engineers on the *Enterprise* to reestablish a forcefield-protected conduit between the ship and the mining outpost. Thought not as stable as the original setup the chief engineer had devised, thanks to the damaged section of tunnel leading from the outpost, the jury-rigging had held long enough for Vale and her team to evacuate the remaining miners. They were all in the capable hands of Dr. Crusher and her medical staff, being treated in one of the seven cargo bays that had been reconfigured to provide the Dokaalan's reduced gravity requirements.

"The surviving Dokaalan have asked that we accommodate their request for a gathering in accordance with their beliefs," Picard said. "They have invited us to attend and wish to include a memorial for Ensign Melorr and Ensign Graham as well, to honor their sacrifice."

That made Vale smile a bit. Despite the dreadful circumstances surrounding their first meeting, the Dokaalan were making the effort to show gratitude for the efforts of the *Enterprise* crew on their behalf.

Seated to Picard's right at the table, Riker said, "In the meantime, we've sent a message to their main colony and center of authority with word that we've rescued their people. They haven't responded to our hail, but sensors show three small ships navigating the asteroid field in our direction."

"Any weapons?" Vale asked.

Leaning forward in his chair, La Forge replied, "Nothing our sensors picked up. Their technology is about two centuries behind us in most respects, even farther back in others. Unless they've got old-style nuclear warheads strapped to their ships and they somehow manage to fire one through our shields, I'd say we're pretty safe."

Vale nodded in relief at the report, noting as she did so that the engineer's right hand still was encased in a portable dermal regenerator. The device was working to restore skin tissue he had lost after inadvertently grabbing on to a pipe routing hot water through one of the mining outpost's lowermost sections. Like Vale herself, La Forge had managed to convince Dr. Crusher not to keep them in sickbay if at all possible. With so many things happening aboard the ship at the moment, neither the head of security nor the chief engineer could afford to be out of action for any longer than was absolutely necessary.

"Mr. La Forge," Picard said, "were you able to determine a cause for the reactor's malfunction?"

La Forge replied, "To be honest, I'm confused, Captain, for several reasons. First, the condition of several of the reactor's key components suggests that it was due to improper maintenance or maybe even negligence."

Waving one hand in the direction of the lounge windows and the asteroid field beyond, Riker countered, "They've been living out here among these asteroids for over two hundred years. Maybe the reactor was just old and they'd run out of spare parts to keep it running properly? It could have just been a matter of time before the thing blew."

"That could be," the engineer said, "but compared to the rest of the place, it just doesn't make sense. That outpost was as well maintained as any starbase I've seen. There's something else, too. Based on the condition of the reactor when we found it and after figuring out the rate of heat and pressure buildup, Taurik was able to calculate how much time we had left before it overloaded, but it went early. Almost seven minutes early. While I don't doubt that I could have made a mistake with those calculations, I don't think Taurik could."

Vale agreed. After all, Vulcans possessed far greater mental discipline than humans, particularly in the areas of mathematics and the memorization and recall of a wealth of information. Computing complex formulas without benefit of computer assistance presented as much difficulty to the typical Vulcan as remembering her security access code was for Vale.

Okay, bad example.

"Was there some sort of other systems failure you hadn't anticipated?" Picard asked.

"Nothing we detected, Captain. So far as we know, we had enough time to get the rest of those people off safely."

Her brow creasing in concern and not liking where her gut was taking her, Vale asked, "Are you suggesting this wasn't an accident, Commander?"

Sighing, the engineer frowned and shook his head. "I really don't know what to think. If these people have been out here all this time, then the only way they could've made it this far is by working together and trusting each other."

"There may be internal political or other machinations at work within this community of which we are not aware," Picard said. "For all we know, they may have splintered into factions and are openly at war with one another. We'll have to proceed with due caution until we make contact with their representatives of authority and learn more."

Nodding in agreement, Picard turned his attention back to Vale. "Lieutenant, have your people reported any problems with the Dokaalan miners we rescued?"

"No, sir," Vale replied. "So far everything's been un-eventful. The Dokaalan have been surprisingly receptive, both to the care provided by Dr. Crusher and her team as well as to us, in general, I mean."

She had not participated in many first-contact situations, but on each of those rare occasions the party being contacted had always expressed wonder and, yes, even awe at meeting a race of beings from another world. While the Dokaalan miners had responded with some of that same amazement, relief at being rescued had quickly eclipsed those initial reactions.

Now that they were safe aboard ship, however, the miners' questions were starting to spill forth about who their benefactors were, where they came from, how far they had traveled, and so on. It was actually quite uplifting to see the happiness on the faces of the Dokaalan. She hoped the rest of the community would be as receptive to the *Enterprise*'s arrival as this group had been.

"Bridge to Captain Picard," Data's voice interrupted the conference via the ship's intercom, *"the three Dokaalan vessels are approaching our position. Estimated time to rendezvous is three point six minutes."*

"Thank you, Commander," Picard replied as he rose from his chair. "I'm on my way." To the officers assembled around the conference table he said, "Meeting adjourned. Thank you all. Number One and Lieutenant Vale with me, please."

Here we go, Vale thought as she fell in behind Commander Riker and headed for the bridge. As she moved to her tactical station, she looked to the main viewscreen and saw three ships arranged in a tight triangular formation with each of the vessels on the same horizontal plane. She guessed the configuration to be effective for navigating the asteroid field.

As for the ships themselves, they were spare and utilitarian in design, essentially rectangular in shape with a pair of engine bells mounted at their rear. With the viewer's current magnification and resolution Vale could actually see the rivets holding the hull plates together. What looked to be a cockpit was the most prominent feature of each vessel's front, and she could also see people moving inside the transparent canopies.

"Hail them, Lieutenant," Picard ordered.

Vale entered the necessary commands and replied, "Channel open, sir."

A moment later, the image on the viewer changed from the three ships to that of an aged Dokaalan. Standing stoop-shouldered, his withered and pale blue skin etched with uncounted wrinkles, he was dressed in regal robes, richly colored in maroon and gold, which hung loosely from his emaciated frame.

"My name is Jean-Luc Picard," the captain said, "of the Federation Starship *Enterprise*. We come in peace on a mission of exploration."

The Dokaalan's features brightened at the introduction. *"So it is true then. Our message from long ago has at last been answered."* Bowing formally to Picard, he added, *"Greetings. I am Hjatyn, first minister to the people of Dokaa."*

Chapter Seventeen

Translated from the personal journal of Hjatyn:

FOR THE FIRST TIME in many years, my hand is shaking as I write this. I am actually nervous!

I know that my upcoming inauguration as first minister should be a time of celebration, not discomfort. Were Beeliq here, she would surely tell me the same thing.

While I have served the people of Dokaal in many capacities during my life, this is by far the most important position I have ever entered. In another time and place, a first minister would have commanded prestige and even celebrity, but those times are long gone. Now it is above all else a position of immense trust and, perhaps more importantly, of hope.

As I have written in these pages before, I did not set out to be a leader, at least not in any official capacity. I realize that my role as a teacher placed me in a position of leadership, but that was in the context of molding young minds with the knowledge they would need to succeed in their own lives. Though I had always believed that to be a noble goal, I never held any illusions that my influence would extend much beyond those few precious hours in the classroom.

That all changed when Dokaal was destroyed, of course. One of the first things realized by those of us who escaped the tragedy was that in almost every way, life as we knew it had ended just as it had for those we were forced to leave behind. If we were to have any chance of survival, we would be required to examine every aspect of our existence and make whatever alterations were required for the greater good.

As for myself, I have my wife to thank for my change in thinking.

The constant growth and change within the colonies brought with it all manner of challenges. New communities formed among the different settlements, some based on the various nation-states that once comprised Dokaal as well as other factions created out of the necessity to share resources and facilities. Beeliq wasted no time wading into the quagmire that was to become the new guiding force of our people, taking on the role of liaison for our group. Her former position as assistant to our colony's administrator gave her a voice already known to those bearing the mantle of leadership, and she used it to great advantage. Every day, she and her peers worked to insure that the citizens and their concerns did not become lost in the ongoing shuffle merely to survive out here. She took the concerns of the people she represented directly to the seats of power, lobbying for better living conditions and better use of our resources.

When colony procedures called for the selection of new group liaisons, my wife was chosen time and again, usually as the result of a nearly unanimous vote. Even when she contracted her illness and her health began to deteriorate, she refused to step down from the position I and others had entrusted to her. I tried to help her as best I could by assisting her in carrying out her responsibilities, and along the way I managed to learn the ins and outs of the constantly evolving politics of our new society while earning the confidence of those my wife represented.

It was a confidence that was sorely tested when Beeliq's illness finally took her from me. Though she had left a void that could never be filled, not only in my life but in our community as well, many felt it appropriate for me to carry on in my wife's stead. I was hesitant, unconvinced that I would be able to perform at the same level as she had, but the faith of those she had once led ultimately overcame my uncertainty.

I am grateful for that support, which has remained resolute over the years as I found myself taking on even more duties and rising to higher levels in the new government. Without that trust and confidence, I would never have been able to advance from representative to a member of the Zahanzei Council, to say nothing of the office I am about to enter today.

Were she here, I have no doubt that Beeliq would be the one about to assume this most awesome of responsibilities. Fate has conspired to prevent that from happening, instead leaving me to take on the work for which my wife seemed destined. I can only hope that, as I pledge to exercise my new authority to the best of my ability and with the well-being of all my fellow Dokaalan as my foremost priority, her strength and passion will continue to guide me.

Chapter Eighteen

WATCHING THE ELDER Dokaalan wander the full course of sickbay for what must have been his tenth time, Beverly Crusher felt a bit of a vicarious thrill. She had experienced a similar rush decades ago when a layover at a space station or planet allowed her to turn her young son loose in a toy store. She could not help but smile with some pride as her visitor puzzled over a diagnostic bed, turned a hypospray over and over in his long blue fingers, or showed a flash of utter amazement over the variety of equipment at her disposal.

He had made his way around her domain for the better part of an hour, checking on her—now their—handful of Dokaalan patients, and only occasionally breaking the silence with a question. Crusher stood by, keeping a professional distance while letting him silently drink in as much of the environment as he desired. The Dokaalan healer's reactions were not unlike her first inspection of a starship's medical facilities, and she let herself just enjoy this experience enough for both of them.

In response to the toll the *Enterprise*'s normal gravity would have taken on the Dokaalan's body, Crusher had asked engineering to provide her with an antigravity work sled. Designed for use by maintenance workers operating within the ship's network of turboshafts, the chair was capable of carrying a person and an extensive toolkit. It also made for a more than passable wheelchair, which the Dokaalan healer had quickly learned to operate before spending the ensuing hour driving around sickbay.

"Dr. Crusher?"

Looking up from the diagnostic monitor positioned above the patient she was examining, she replied, "Yes, Healer Nentafa?"

The tall, hairless Dokaalan moved the antigrav chair closer. "Forgive me, I must seem a nuisance to you."

Crusher waved the notion away. "Hardly," she said, still very thankful that a physician had been among the Dokaalan delegation that greeted the *Enterprise* following their rescue mission to the mining outpost. Within an hour of his arrival, Nentafa had assessed her diagnoses on more than three dozen of the wounded and even corrected her on a few of them. Advising her staff, he had helped to make short work of cases that had stumped Crusher, ones that she feared would turn for the worse despite her best efforts. Thanks to him, the bulk of the outpost survivors had already been released from treatment and sent back to the cargo bays to await transfer to the Dokaalan's central habitat and the *Enterprise*'s sickbay had seen its patient numbers dwindle down to the five Dokaalan currently occupying beds, those most seriously burned or otherwise injured.

"You are most gracious, Doctor," Nentafa said. "I was wondering how you are insuring my people get the nutrients they need while they are unconscious."

Before she could respond, a medical scanner monitoring one of the Dokaalan beeped for Crusher's attention. Walking over to the patient's bed, she tapped the unit's keypad to silence the alert.

"We administer a nutritional supplement by hypospray on a regular schedule," she said a moment later. "Our computer analysis of your people's physiology helped us determine what vitamins and compounds needed to be replenished each day, so we formulated the supplement accordingly." Studying her patient's diagnostic readout, she noted that he was slightly feverish and adjusted the Dokaalan's antibiotic dosage and fluid intake accordingly.

"Ah . . . of course," Nentafa said, hesitating as if lost in thought. "I cannot keep from thinking that had this situation been reversed and our people had been your rescuers, our resources would not have enabled us to be so helpful so rapidly. Allow me to be a bit . . . overwhelmed by it all."

"No need to explain," the doctor replied. "You're not the first to get a crash course in Federation technology like this. And, if I may, your people strike me as very resourceful and capable given your way of life. From what I understand, the Dokaalan have a lot to be proud of."

Nentafa smiled and said, "We do our best."

She followed as he turned his chair and made his way to another diagnostic bed, hoping to ease any concern he might have for the patients' recovery. While Crusher had

three fellow physicians on board as well as a complement of medical technicians and nurses on whom to rely,
she sensed that Nentafa thought himself as alone in his
responsibility for the more than four hundred Dokaalan
displaced from the outpost.

After helping *Enterprise* engineers to reconfigure the
cargo bays as living quarters for the Dokaalan temporar-
ily residing in them, and even suggesting changes in food
replicator programs to better meet their dietary needs,
Nentafa continued to move back and forth between the
cargo areas and sickbay, almost hovering over his patients. Crusher could not fault the Dokaalan healer for his
diligence, as she knew she would act in the same manner
if she faced similar circumstances. She hoped the
Dokaalan healer would be more at ease upon their arrival
at his people's central habitat complex, situated well
within the asteroid field the *Enterprise* now traversed.

Nentafa leaned over the bed, peering closely at burns
and wounds covering the limbs of an unconscious
Dokaalan suspended and bathed in dermaline gel. The
gel's pinkish hue lent the patient's skin an unnatural
color and tended to mute the unsightly nature of the injured flesh beneath it. "This is miraculous, Doctor. Her
skin appears to be mending at an unbelievable rate, and I
see no evidence of residual scar tissue."

"Dermaline is a wonderful aid to the healing process,"
Crusher replied, "and we've been having better luck with
everyone's dermal regeneration sessions than we hoped
initially. They seem to be progressing very well, and no,
there should be no scarring when we're done." Examining the patient's wounds, she was satisfied that their
healing was progressing normally. After checking the di-

agnostic readout above the patient's head, she added, "There's been some problem with fever and other lingering aftereffects, but nothing we can't treat easily enough."

"Well, all I can say is . . . praise Dokaa," the elder healer said. "There is no doubt in my mind that you were led to us by providence. For visitors to chance across us is indeed astonishing, but for someone with the knowledge and ability to come and save our people at a time of crisis is nothing short of divine."

"We're glad to be of service," she said, more than a bit uncomfortable at the gushing praise. "Besides, you haven't seen anything yet. If you get the chance to travel back with us, I'm sure the entire Federation will be ready to welcome you with open arms."

"I am so intrigued by the idea of your Federation," Nentafa replied, his voice seeming to shed some of its earlier weariness. "It includes how many races?"

"More than one hundred fifty planets and societies have allied with the Federation over the course of two centuries," Crusher said. "And we've made contact with hundreds of other races who are not members."

"I would think that everyone would like to be a member of your Federation," the Dokaalan said.

"You'd be surprised, then," Crusher said, smiling knowingly. "There are strict requirements that a society must meet to become a member as well, and it's not so amicable a galaxy we live in beyond the asteroids."

"Ah . . ." Nentafa's words trailed off for moment as he considered her words. "Our people learned quickly to set aside squabbles. It was necessary for our survival. We also learned to compromise, to make the best of every situation, to use every resource to its fullest and waste nothing, to follow direction and to make choices that sometimes seemed impossible."

"You became fighters," Crusher offered. "You learned how to battle against incredible odds. That's apparent in this sickbay today, Nentafa."

"You flatter us, Doctor," he said. "In our lives, we have known no other way."

She noticed Nentafa reaching up to massage the side of his head, closing his eyes as he did so. It was obvious to Crusher that the healer was feeling the effects of fatigue. Putting her hand on the healer's shoulder, she said, "Why don't you get some rest? My staff can monitor your people and report to you as often as you like."

"Rest?" Nentafa seemed to laugh at the notion. "How can I rest when I have such an unparalleled opportunity to learn right here before me?"

Almost as if on cue, the doors to sickbay slid open to admit Dr. Tropp and, two steps back, Data, each at a brisk pace. The Denobulan nodded curtly at the pair as he made his way to a supply cabinet. Data, seeming to do his best to appear courteous, mimicked the physician's head movement precisely, eliciting a quiet laugh from Crusher.

"Your interests are well timed, Nentafa," Crusher said, raising her voice enough to be heard by Tropp, "as our best instructor in all things medicinal just walked through the door."

She saw Tropp stop at the cabinet, his chin sinking to his chest with a sigh. "I appreciate your show of confidence in my abilities, Doctor." Indicating Data, he added, "But being in charge of this . . . er, student . . . while performing my other duties is taxing enough."

Wide-eyed to the point of seeming almost peppy, Data turned to speak to Crusher. "Dr. Tropp has been indulging my interests in learning more about the Dokaalan. He has allowed me to follow him and observe his treatment procedures, and I have asked my questions while he works."

"*Many* questions," Tropp said, nodding and using a polite smile to cover what Crusher imagined was a set of gritted teeth. "So if I might defer a discussion with Healer Nentafa to a time when I could devote my undivided attention to him?"

"Absolutely, Doctor," Crusher said as a thought crossed her mind. "In fact . . . maybe guiding Healer Nentafa would be a task better suited to Mr. Data."

"It would?" the android asked.

"Oh, my, it *would,*" Tropp practically shouted. "I think that's a tremendous idea!"

"Yes, Data," Crusher said, trying not to fumble her effort to give Tropp the break he obviously sought. "Nentafa has expressed a great deal of curiosity about the Federation, our level of technology, and the known races of our galaxy. Given your level of knowledge on all those topics, I think you would make the perfect tour guide."

"I would be happy to assist the healer in his research," the android replied, cocking his head a bit as he considered the offer, "if there is no objection from Doctor . . ."

Data turned to address the Denobulan, whose foot Crusher glimpsed in the corridor for an instant as the door to sickbay closed behind him.

". . . Tropp?" Data finished.

"He seemed to be in quite a hurry, Data," Crusher said. For a moment, she worried that Tropp's departure might offend the android in some way before remembering that for the first time in years, he no longer had a sense of pride to bruise.

Lucky him.

"So," she said, "would you like to help Nentafa in his studies? Along the way, he could tell you more about his people, so you'd be helping each other out."

"Certainly, Doctor." Turning to Nentafa, the android said, "Sir, would you care to begin in our stellar cartography department? I could plot out the worlds of the Federation for discussion in the order of their admission. Or, perhaps you might be interested in a visit to one of our holodecks, where I could show you reenactments of milestones in the history of the Federation. If that does not appeal to you, I could set up a comprehensive database review of known races, their physiological characteristics, and their important contributions to technology and culture."

It was a physical effort for Crusher not to laugh openly as she watched Nentafa's jaw drop and he tried to sort out the myriad of educational options being made available to him. Data was definitely cruising at his usual warp nine today, she decided, and the poor Dokaalan healer was about get the ride of his life.

"Partaking in all of that would seem to require a great effort," the healer said after a moment. "How in the name of Dokaa do you have time enough to manage it all?"

Stepping forward, Crusher said, "Data is a unique being, Nentafa. He's an android, and one of the most sophisticated examples of technology you're bound to encounter."

The Dokaalan drew a breath, his jaw open as he maneuvered the antigrav chair toward Data. Slowly, he reached out with one long-fingered hand to stroke the android's cheek, pressing two fingertips to it. "You are a machine?"

His head tilting to the right in his usual inquisitive manner, Data answered, "That is correct."

Nentafa's brow furrowed as he studied Data's face. "A sentient machine?" he asked.

"Yes," Data said. "I was created forty-three years ago by Dr. Noonien Soong at the Omicron Theta colony approximately eight thousand, two hundred and fifty-five light-years from our current position."

"Ah," Nentafa said, pulling his hand back. With a smile he added, "You, sir, will take some getting used to."

Data nodded. "Then, we have a lot to teach each other. Where would you like to begin?"

As the pair departed, Crusher noted the corners of Data's mouth curl upward into the beginnings of a smile as he studied the Dokaalan with the same scrutiny that was being focused on him. Was it curiosity, maybe even fascination? Despite the lack of his emotion chip, the android seemed to possess a spark of seemingly human interest that he had not exhibited for years, she realized.

It was a side of her friend she admitted to missing after all this time.

This may do them both a world of good, Crusher thought as she watched them go.

"Dr. Crusher?" she heard Nurse Ogawa say from behind her, and turned to see the other woman standing next to one of the Dokaalan patients.

"What is it, Alyssa?"

Pointing to the diagnostic panel above the patient's

head, Ogawa replied, "Her pulse is rapid and her temperature's rising again."

Crusher frowned at that. Again? It was the third time in four hours such a change in one of the patients' condition had occurred. On the previous three occasions, she had prescribed a mild sedative as treatment, which had resulted in correction of their symptoms.

"Check the others again," she said.

"Could it be an allergic reaction?" Ogawa asked.

The doctor shrugged. "Either that or an infection of some kind. We'll need to run some more tests to be sure, though." None of the previous tests had indicated the Dokaalan might react negatively to any medicines she might administer while treating their injuries. Had she missed something? In order to be sure, she would need to have the *Enterprise* computer evaluate all the medical data gathered about their guests from the beginning.

What did we miss? she wondered. *And what if their conditions get worse?*

Chapter Nineteen

PICARD HAD NEVER been prone to discomfort in low- or zero-gravity conditions. In fact, he always had enjoyed the feeling of weightlessness, taking to zero-g combat training at Starfleet Academy like a newborn horta to a granite quarry. So it was with no sense of apprehension whatsoever that the captain, accompanied by Commander Riker and Counselor Troi, stepped into the observation lounge's reduced gravity, which had been lowered for their guests' life-support requirements.

His spirits were also buoyed by the knowledge that what had begun as nothing more than a make-work assignment had, in less than a day, evolved into a wondrous opportunity to establish first contact with a new species. For a fleeting moment, Picard wished he could be a fly on the wall of Admiral Nechayev's office when she relayed his report to her peers. He smiled at the thought of the reactions it was likely to engender within the halls of Starfleet Command.

A group of five Dokaalan waited for them in the observation lounge, seated around the conference table. Hjatyn sat at the table's far end, flanked on each side by two companions dressed in robes similar to their leader's though somewhat less ornate than those he wore.

"First Minister Hjatyn," Picard began, nodding formally to the elderly Dokaalan who stood at the front of the five-person delegation, "I am Captain Picard. It is my privilege to welcome you aboard the *U.S.S. Enterprise.* Allow me to introduce my first officer, Commander William Riker, and my ship's counselor, Commander Deanna Troi. It was our intention to meet with you in your offices or some other location of your choosing, but we are honored that you traveled here to meet with us."

The Dokaalan replied, "This momentous occasion warrants more than our limited amenities can provide, Captain, as you will soon see for yourselves. In the meantime, it is our honor to visit such a magnificent ship. When I was informed of your arrival and your efforts to rescue my people, I knew I had to thank you personally. This is a tremendous day for all of my people."

It was praise that still felt undeserved to Picard, despite his earlier talk with Counselor Troi. "First Minister," he said, "though most of your people who were injured have been treated and released, my chief medical officer and her team are still monitoring a few whose injuries were more severe. However, I must offer my sincere apologies for the loss of your people during our rescue attempt. I regret the circumstances surrounding their deaths."

Bowing his head for a moment, when Hjatyn returned

his gaze to Picard a small smile graced the Dokaalan's features, and there was also moisture in the corners of his eyes. "While we mourn their loss," the minister said, "many more would have shared their fate if not for your actions. I also understand that two of your people were killed. We will honor their sacrifice in the same manner that we commemorate those of our people who have given their lives in the defense of others."

Nodding in agreement, Picard directed Riker and Troi to take a seat before moving to his customary place at the head of the conference table. "I have been informed that we will arrive at your colony's central complex within the hour," he said. After docking with the *Enterprise* to allow Hjatyn and his party to board, the minister's vessel remained linked with the starship as it navigated a new course through the asteroid field to the heart of the Dokaalan colonies. "In the meantime, I imagine that you have numerous questions for us, just as we have many for you."

His smile widening, Hjatyn replied, "Indeed we do, Captain, beginning with the obvious one: Where are you from, and how far have you traveled to find us?"

Picard did not doubt the Dokaalan would comprehend the staggering distances involved in traveling from the Federation to this area of space, or even in understanding the basic concept of the technology employed to make the journey, but there would be a time where discussing all of that would be more appropriate.

"We have come here on behalf of the United Federation of Planets," he said, "a shared society of many cultures from many different worlds who have joined together in the spirit of mutual cooperation." He indicated Troi. "Counselor Troi was born on a different planet than Commander Riker and myself, and my crew is comprised of representatives of many other member worlds, as well."

He noticed Hjatyn's warm expression falter a bit as the minister said, "While my enthusiasm at your arrival is unbridled, Captain, I also hope you will understand my need to be cautious. Several of my aides advised against this meeting, offering instead the need to be suspicious of your motives." He held out his thin arms, indicating the conference room and, by extension, the rest of the *Enterprise.* "One look at this vessel is enough to tell me that, were you so inclined, you could conquer our people with minimal effort. Therefore, I must ask what your intentions are now that you are here."

Picard recalled the reports submitted by Lieutenant Vale and Dr. Crusher regarding some Dokaalan's reactions to learning the identities of their unexpected benefactors. While some of the miners rescued by the *Enterprise* were most receptive to their new visitors, many more had expressed doubt, suspicion, and even fear.

With that in mind, he replied, "Some of the people we rescued from your outpost have expressed concern that we may be here as invaders, and I hope that I can put that worry quickly to rest. We have traveled a great distance to see what is here, and we do so in peace. There is much more here than we expected or even hoped to find, and my crew and I are most anxious to learn all that you can teach us. However, should you ask us to leave and never return, then we will do just that."

Noting the palpable silence as Hjatyn seemed to ponder his words, Picard glanced to Riker and saw the subtle change in his first officer's expression. He too was worried that everything that had come so far had happened for naught. The look in Counselor Troi's eyes seemed to mirror Riker's but Picard could not be sure. Was she sensing Hjatyn's unease?

He forced his own features to remain fixed as he waited for the Dokaalan's response. In truth, the *Enterprise* already had completed the mission as set out by Admiral Nechayev. Still, he would be saddened if understandable yet misplaced xenophobia guided the first minister's decision and prevented him and his crew from making the most of this opportunity.

Thankfully, it did not come to that.

"It seems to me, Captain," Hjatyn said after a moment, "that given the resources at your command, were you of a mind to harm us you would have done so already, and not bothered with the compassionate action of rescuing my people. My instincts tell me that you are telling the truth." Smiling, he added, "Besides, did we not invite you here, after a fashion? I am told that you discovered two of the three unmanned space vessels my people dispatched prior to our world's destruction."

Picard nodded. "Yes we did, though the story surrounding their separate discoveries is a lengthy one. Suffice it to say that the first probe was found long ago, but it was determined that the available technology and resources were insufficient to reach your planet in time." Choosing his next words as carefully as possible, he added, "With that in mind, those in positions of leadership at the time deemed other priorities to be in greater need of attention. Several events, some with long-lasting repercussions that were both positive and negative, transpired in the period soon after the probe's discovery. I'm afraid to say that the matter was soon forgotten, at least until the second probe was found only a short time ago."

"I think I understand what you mean, Captain," Hjatyn replied. "To be honest, I am not even sure if anyone involved with the probes' construction or their launch from Dokaal survived the catastrophe. Most people today have either forgotten about the probes or never learned about them. As you said, other concerns became more important after a time."

It's certainly understandable, Picard thought. From the reports Vale and Crusher had given, most of the miners rescued from the outpost possessed no knowledge of the probes. Perhaps the story had been relegated to myth, or simply forgotten in the face of struggling for mere survival.

"What is amazing," Hjatyn said, "is that someone has found one of the devices only now, after all this time. Even more astonishing is that it was still in a condition which allowed you to hear the plea of our people." Smiling, he added, "I think I am beginning to appreciate just how far you have come to find us, Captain."

"It seems that your people already had an appreciation for the vastness of space before your world was destroyed," Troi said. "After all, the probes were equipped with engines that allowed them to travel faster than light. Did you have a space exploration program in development prior to the disaster?"

Hjatyn replied, "Of a sort, yes, though it never progressed to the point of manned flights beyond the boundaries of our solar system. Several science and engineering specialists who escaped the catastrophe tried to re-create and even build upon the technology lost with our planet, but their attempts were unsuccessful. Oh, they were able to develop a prototype engine, two actually, and a plan was even put in motion to send two ships away from our system in search of other life. They were launched on separate trajectories and each succeeded in leaving our system.

"According to messages we received, tragically, the crews of both ships died during their flight from unknown causes. At the time, our scientists theorized that traveling faster than light was somehow harmful to living beings, and the technology was abandoned." Indicating the *Enterprise* officers with open arms, the minister added, "Obviously, that was a mistaken conclusion, or perhaps it is only correct with respect to the Dokaalan. Either way, it is unfortunate for us." The elderly leader smiled at that, and Picard found himself warmed by the expression of emotion. Yes, he decided, despite the earlier tragedy, a good thing had happened here today.

Leaning forward in his seat, Riker said, "I imagine you had your hands full as it was. According to some of the people we rescued, you've had to make do with what are essentially temporary facilities since your planet was destroyed. That you've managed to survive this long is remarkable."

"Necessity has always proven to be a fine motivator, Commander Riker," Hjatyn replied. "When Dokaal exploded, we were faced with sustaining not only the existing mining contingents but several thousand evacuees as well. We had to reallocate our limited resources to accommodate our increased numbers. Many of our original outposts still exist, though they have been pressed into service for far longer than their original designers ever intended. They are in constant need of repair, and many lives have been lost due to accidents or structural failure. Such incidents have become more common in recent years, which is why there has been a concerted effort to construct new facilities, such as the central habitat and control complex that now serves as the heart of our community." Shrugging, the aged Dokaalan added, "Though our level of technology is primitive compared to yours, I think you will be most impressed by the ingenuity of my people."

"Of that I have no doubt, First Minister," Picard said. According to the analysis provided by Data and La Forge, Dokaalan technology in many respects was on par with that of Earth during the late twenty-first century. Had they continued with their research into faster-than-light travel, or perhaps been inspired by the presence of an extraterrestrial race as humans had once been, that comparison might have even been closer. "In my travels I have learned that there is always something to be learned. Also, once I notify the Federation of your situation here, I'm sure there will be no trouble obtaining aid for your people."

To the captain's surprise, Hjatyn seemed for a fleeting moment to be troubled by the proposition. It was only a flicker in the elderly leader's eyes, one which he covered quickly enough. "We have always been a self-sufficient people, Captain, even before our planet was destroyed. I am not sure the idea of long-term outside assistance will be palatable to them."

Before Picard could further any debate, the minister held up a frail hand. "However, there will be time enough to discuss such a kind and intriguing offer." The captain and his officers stood in deference to the leader as he rose from his own chair. "Forgive me, Captain, but at my age I grow fatigued easily. With your permission, I will return to my vessel. There are still many preparations required to give you and your crew a proper reception, after all."

"As you wish, First Minister," Picard said, putting on his best diplomatic smile to cover the momentary unease he had felt. "We can meet again at your convenience."

"Excellent," Hjatyn replied. "I am so looking forward to introducing you to the rest of my people, Captain. I hope that you will want to meet them and see all that they have accomplished, just as I hope to see more of this breathtaking vessel and meet your crew."

"I'm sure we can see to that," Picard replied.

The Dokaalan leader nodded in satisfaction. "Though we must certainly pause to remember those who have fallen, this will still be a wondrous occasion for celebration."

After asking Commander Riker to escort the Dokaalan delegation back to their ship, Picard waited until the doors to the lounge had closed and he was alone with Troi before turning to her. "Counselor, would I be mistaken if I said I thought Hjatyn seemed a bit uncomfortable during the meeting? Did you sense any duplicity or deliberate withholding of information on his part?"

Troi nodded. "His mind is incredibly focused, Captain, but he was holding back something. He could simply be acting with caution, as I did sense his relief when you accepted his request to end the meeting. It's possible he still views us as a threat, but that type of reaction is normal in first-contact situations. Such an event is often unsettling, after all, even when the exchange is welcomed by the contacted party. I've detected similar anxiety in some of the miners we rescued, though many more are enthusiastic at meeting us."

Frowning, Picard considered the counselor's words. He had participated in enough first-contact missions to be familiar with the type of trepidation she described, but that did not soothe the gut feeling he had experienced while observing Hjatyn during the meeting. Was there something more than simple fear there?

"These people haven't had the benefit of a normal civilization for a long time," he said, still trying to rationalize his own misgivings. "After being on their own for so many years and succeeding in marvelous fashion despite the odds against them, it seems natural to me that they would apprehensive with any change in their routine, be it good or bad." Picard knew from practical experience that feelings such as the Dokaalan seemed to be displaying, justified or not, could injure relations with a new species to such an extent that years might be required to repair the damage.

I certainly did not travel this far for that to happen, he thought.

"Considering how long it took us to get here," he said, "I am not in a terrible rush to leave just yet. With that in mind, we will simply have to work that much harder to alleviate their worries."

As he rose from his chair and headed back to the bridge, however, Picard could not shake the feeling that there was something more going on here.

Getting paranoid in your old age, Captain?

The thought teased him. Could some sort of residual bitterness, brought about by the circumstances that had brought them here in the first place, be making him overly cautious and causing him to second-guess every action? Perhaps.

Then again, perhaps not.

Chapter Twenty

As IT HAD for more than a day, the image on the bridge's main viewer featured uncounted asteroids drifting past the screen's edges. It also depicted the two Dokaalan ships that had accompanied Hjatyn's vessel to the *Enterprise,* guiding the starship through the dense field.

Picard noticed that the screen's resolution appeared to be sharper than it had been for most of the time since their arrival. Much of the static and grain that had become almost a fixture of the system's visual imaging was gone. "Mr. La Forge, I take it that your attempts to improve our sensor readings have been successful?"

"To varying degrees, Captain," the engineer replied from his console at the rear of the bridge. "We don't have the range we're used to, but up close I've managed to filter out most of the interference. We might still have some problems if we get too close to a large source of radiation, like one of the bigger asteroids, but we'd have to be a lot closer than I think either one of us would want to be."

"According to my readings," Vale said from the tactical station, "that might be just what we're in for. I'm picking up a massive asteroid that appears to be along the course we're navigating, and if this is right, I'm also detecting more than sixty thousand life signs there."

"Sixty thousand?" Riker repeated. "That has to be one hell of a big rock."

Vale replied, "Initial measurements show the asteroid as being fourteen point eight kilometers across at its widest point."

"Considering the level of their technology," the first officer said, "that's a pretty bold achievement. It took nearly a century before that many people were living on our first lunar colony."

"And these people didn't have the Vulcans looking over their shoulders the whole time, either," La Forge added. "Today we've got more than fifty million people living on the moon. Imagine where the Dokaalan might be after the same period of time."

Though Picard knew the chief engineer made the comment in jest, it was true that much of humanity's drive to succeed in the decades following first contact with the Vulcans was due in no small part to a desire to show their mysterious benefactors what human ambition and ingenuity could accomplish simply if given the chance. As a student of history born and living in the twenty-fourth century, he benefited from the hindsight of those who had recorded the events for posterity. He understood the Vulcans' reasons for not interfering in Earth's development and maturation into a peaceful society. Things were markedly different for the people living during those tumultuous years, however, trying to forge a better world from the ashes of the one their ancestors had nearly succeeded in destroying. Long after enthusiasm and determination had been exhausted, feelings of resentment and frustration toward the Vulcans often fueled the passion of those who laid the groundwork for the society enjoyed by Federation citizens today.

He imagined a similar attitude taking hold among the Dokaalan people. Although engendered more by a basic survival instincts rather than the influence of an outside party, the results would be the same. Facing bitter defeat, the Dokaalan had banded together and raised a collective fist in defiance of the universe itself, proclaiming that they would thrive regardless of the obstacles laid before them.

Picard was only beginning to smile at the rousing image the thought conjured when one equally awe-inspiring appeared on the main viewer.

"Would you look at that," La Forge said from behind him.

Dominating the image was what at first appeared to be a gigantic asteroid, dwarfing every other mass of rock visible on the screen. Despite its rough surface, which was peppered with craggy peaks and dark chasms, Picard thought he recognized a sort of symmetry to the massive body. In addition to its natural terrain features, he also noted the network of artificial constructs crisscrossing the surface. Large buildings sprouted from the rock, linked by a maze of connecting tunnels that wove around, over, and sometimes through the rolling mountains that formed the asteroid's topography.

"Wow," he heard La Forge say, and turned in response.

"What is it, Geordi?" Picard asked as he walked to the rear of the bridge, and the engineer waited that interval before continuing.

"You're not going to believe this," he said, indicating the upper right monitor at his station. "That isn't a single asteroid, Captain, but a whole bunch of them that have been brought together."

"What?" Riker said as he rose from his chair. "You mean they've actually pushed asteroids together to make one big rock?"

Turning in his seat at the ops station, Data said, "Theoretically, it is possible, Commander. Many hypotheses have been put forth examining the benefits of such a venture. In the late twentieth and early twenty-first centuries on Earth, several such plans were conceived that would utilize the asteroid belt between Mars and Jupiter, but it was ultimately deemed to be too dangerous and cost-prohibitive an undertaking, particularly when it was determined that the sum total of available material would equal less usable land mass than Earth's moon. Outposts were constructed in the belt in much the same way that the Dokaalan have done here, but plans to create a planet from the asteroid belt eventually were discarded altogether."

"Well, this is no theory," La Forge said. One of the engineering station's monitors depicted a computerized schematic of the asteroid, and the engineer pointed to a series of colored areas he had highlighted. "These are magnetic interlocks, embedded into different asteroids so that they're concealed as the rocks come together. Though the technology is much more primitive, it's not really that different than the system connecting the *Enterprise*'s saucer section with the secondary hull."

Turning back to the main viewer, now close enough that the ship's sensor readings were providing much more detail on the mammoth construct, Picard could plainly see the web of fissures spread out across the face of the rock. It would have been easy to dismiss them as nothing more than cracks, but now he could distinguish the lines of different asteroids, of all shapes and sizes, that had been brought together, the crevices between them looking like the outlines of individual pieces all working together to create a colossal three-dimensional puzzle.

"We've used asteroids as the foundation for starbases and observation outposts for centuries," he said, "and there have been several instances where a space vessel was fashioned within the hollowed-out interior of an asteroid, but the sheer audacity it must have taken to realize a project like this is amazing." Even though he was not skilled or knowledgeable in any of the technical disciplines required to create such a structure, Picard found himself anticipating the opportunity to inspect the colony habitat and to see just how these people had managed such a staggering feat of engineering.

Already envisioning how this development would look in his next report to Starfleet, the captain could not help being amused at the questions it likely would raise. Would there be second-guessing over the decision made two centuries ago not to send a ship to investigate the origin of that first Dokaalan probe, the one discovered by the Vulcan vessel? Picard figured the question was all too easy to answer. The assorted bickering and other minutiae that composed the livelihood of politicians and others constantly working to remain in power would overshadow the true story worth telling here: that of the Dokaalan people and their valiant struggle against the tremendous adversity Fate had seen fit to pit against them.

Just one more reason, he reminded himself, *to avoid politics altogether.*

The Dokaalan wasted no time transmitting boarding procedures to the *Enterprise,* after which Picard, accompanied by Data and Troi, transferred to the central habitat via shuttlecraft. While there had been assurances that the starship itself could safely link up with one of the complex's external docking ports, the captain had opted to keep the vessel mobile for the time being. His conversation with Troi following the first meeting with Hjatyn and his people was not forgotten, after all.

"Welcome to our home, Captain," Hjatyn said as Picard and his team stepped through the airlock. In the chamber beyond, the first minister waited with a contingent of eight Dokaalan, each dressed in robes similar to his own. "I present to you the Zahanzei Council, the duly elected ruling body of our society and named after the first minister who oversaw our people up until the time of our world's destruction."

After introducing the eight council members, Hjatyn indicated the chamber with outspread arms. "As you can see, we possess little, but everything we have we offer to you, our distinguished guests."

Like everything else Picard had seen of the mining colonies to this point, this facility appeared to be constructed in the same sparse manner and without any embellishments. Even though this was supposed to be the area of the station where the colony's government was headquartered, the chamber offered no decorative or frivolous accoutrements whatsoever. The bulkheads appeared to be of the same material as those used throughout the other mining outposts, with cylindrical tubing running near the ceiling that presumably protected wiring as well as water and coolant transferal. Everything in the room, from the furniture and computer workstations to the various storage containers arrayed around the perimeter of the room, spoke to the no-frills nature of Dokaalan existence.

"The pleasure is ours, First Minister," Picard replied before introducing Data to the Dokaalan delegation. "This is a most impressive facility." He opted not to make mention of the definite stale tang lacing the air, no doubt a byproduct of the colony's life-support recycling process.

Nodding, the Dokaalan leader said. "It is the result of many years of joint effort on the part of my people."

"Minister Hjatyn," Data began, "I have spent some time with one of your medical specialists, Nentafa. He told me about the construction of this habitat, but was unable to offer any information about the technical aspects of the project. According to our analysis, such a venture would have proven quite a challenge, given your present level of technology. I am therefore very curious as to how you went about it."

Picard thought the android's request, phrased in his usual straightforward manner and without any conscious attempt to insult, might still be interpreted as offensive by the Dokaalan. He was relieved when Hjatyn smiled warmly in response.

"It was indeed a test of our resolve, Commander Data. Building this new home pushed us to the limits of our resources and technical acumen, to say nothing of our resolve. I admit to being skeptical about the concept when it was first proposed, but the project turned out to be a defining moment for our people. It gave us a singular goal, a unified purpose if you will, of making life better for all of us. The costs were great, both in matériel and in the number of people who lost their lives during the course of construction, but the completed habitat is itself a memorial to everyone who sacrificed for the greater good."

"It is a marvelous accomplishment," Picard replied, "my engineers are most eager to learn more about it. I have to confess to being drawn in somewhat by their enthusiasm."

Hjatyn smiled again. "Of course, Captain. We will do our best to accommodate that curiosity, but something tells me your engineering staff will have no trouble comprehending our work. As it happens, our most learned minds have envisioned a future for us that is even grander in its scope." Gesturing for the *Enterprise* officers to follow him, he said, "Come, my friends, and be the first outsiders to see what awaits the Dokaalan people."

Data followed as the first minister shuffled his way across the room and toward one of three doors set into the chamber's rearmost bulkhead, but as Picard started after them he felt a gentle touch on his arm. He turned to see Troi glancing toward the Dokaalan delegation, obviously waiting for them to move out of earshot before speaking.

"What is it, Counselor?" he asked, continuing to walk slowly so as not to attract too much attention from their hosts.

"Something I sensed from Hjatyn," Troi replied. "He doesn't appear as guarded as before, but I still get the feeling he's hiding something. It's almost as though he's aware that we're suspicious and he's trying to overcompensate. He wants to appear more hospitable than he's comfortable with, hoping to put us at ease. Some of the council members have similar feelings, as well as the expected mix of hesitation and excitement provoked by a first-contact situation."

"But you're still not sensing any sort of threat or danger from them?" Picard asked.

"No, sir. As I said before, I think some of them, Hjatyn included, feel we are more a threat to them than the other way around."

"Very well, Counselor. Continue your observations."

Hastening their pace to catch up with the others, Picard and Troi entered the room beyond the reception chamber, which the captain recognized as some form of command center. Computer consoles and maps lined the walls, and workstations were situated in such a way that they faced a central large screen at the room's far end. The image on the screen was divided into two sections. One of the sections displayed a view of a planet as seen from low orbit, while the other showed scrolling series of computer code, including what the captain took to be complex mathematical equations.

Hjatyn pointed to the divided display. "What you are seeing is Ijuuka, the fifth planet of our system and one-time neighbor to Dokaal. While it is approximately the same size as our former planet, like the other worlds in our system its atmosphere is unable to sustain our people and possesses poisonous vegetation and no animal life.

We learned all of this in the early days of our space-exploration program, long before Dokaal was destroyed, when we sent unmanned reconnaissance probes to the other planets."

"First Minister," Data said, "have you considered constructing habitats similar to those you have here on one or more of the other planets?"

The Dokaalan leader nodded. "For a time after the loss of our world, we considered building such facilities and transplanting our community to one of the planets, but to what end? We would still be living within a contained environment, relying on an artificial world to protect us from the dangers that lay beyond the metal walls."

Turning from the screen to face the *Enterprise* officers, Hjatyn spread his arms. "While we have been successful at carving out a serviceable existence for ourselves, what my people lack is a true home, a world where they can roam freely, secure in the knowledge that the air they breathe is not the product of a machine requiring constant maintenance and repair." He indicated the image on the central screen once more. "We have decided that if such a world is not readily available to us, then we will make one."

The enormity of what he thought the minister was proposing actually made Picard's jaw drop. "Are you suggesting that . . . ?"

"Yes, Captain," Hjatyn said, cutting Picard off. "Ijuuka is the one planet in our system with the potential to provide that home to my people. We are therefore recreating it in Dokaal's image."

Chapter Twenty-one

Translated from the personal journal of Hjatyn:

THERE WAS ANOTHER accident yesterday.

Of all the duties I have had to perform since being elected first minister, notifying a family that a loved one has been lost remains the most painful. That I will have to carry out such a heartrending obligation fifteen times before the day is out weighs even heavier on my soul.

It is a responsibility I could entrust to one of my aides or perhaps one of the other council members, but I have never been one for delegating the unpleasant aspects of my position. I have always felt it important to remain in close contact with the people of our community, whether we are rejoicing in joint celebration or grieving in shared sorrow.

The number of accidental deaths during construction and repair operations around the colonies has been on the rise. This time it was due to a ruptured bulkhead while a maintenance crew was working inside one of our factory complexes. The explosive decompression caused by the structural failure also inflicted extensive damage to the delicate equipment housed in that section.

It feels wrong to even contemplate the harm to machinery, mere equipment that can be replaced, at the same time I am mourning the dreadful loss of life, but that way of thinking is also a necessary responsibility I bear. In addition to lamenting those who have been taken from us, I must also consider the well-being of those left behind. It is my duty to find out what happened and apply that knowledge in such a manner that it reduces the likelihood of such an incident happening again. To do anything less is to insure that those who sacrificed their lives did so in vain.

My engineering consultants have told me repeatedly that as our facilities age, despite our best efforts to maintain them, the likelihood of breakdowns or structural failures will continue to increase. It was based on their recommendations that I approved plans to construct new outpost buildings for use as habitation areas as well as for maintenance and support services.

There is no shortage of raw materials, thanks to the vast asteroid belt, but there is always the risk of injury or death to those workers subjecting themselves to the harsh environment of space with only their hardened excursion suits to protect them. That much has proven apparent on occasions too numerous to recount here.

Additionally, there is the inescapable fact that once the work is complete, we are really no better off than we were before. We will still be living inside artificial constructs, metal containers created to keep us alive but not designed in any way that allows us to truly live. Our efforts have gone toward building better cans in which to pack ourselves, hiding from the unforgiving environs of the space that surrounds us.

However, there are those who have strived for something more. The most gifted minds among us have proposed one bold idea after another in a constant quest to improve life for the entire community. I recall listening in both astonishment and skepticism as the first plans for the central habitat were presented to the council. The very idea of using our spacecraft to push asteroids together so that they might form one larger body seemed preposterous, regardless of the confidence the engineers held for the data supporting their theory. While even my limited grasp of the sciences was enough to tell me that the idea itself was hypothetically possible, my concerns for the safety of workers and our limited fleet of spaceships gave me pause.

Despite my misgivings, I soon became aware of the effect the intrepid scheme was having on the overall morale of the community. No longer satisfied to merely exist within the confines of the mining facilities, the people were energized by the idea of crafting a grand new home from the very rocks that had been their safe haven for so long. The sustained effort would provide a focal point of united purpose that went beyond simple survival. As their leader, I had no choice but to set aside my own uncertainty and allow the project to commence.

And what a glorious achievement it was! Though to this day I do not understand very much about the intermagnetic systems used to hold the asteroids together, I was able to appreciate the opportunities the magnificent accomplishment provided for us. The complex constructed upon this new asteroid was capable of housing nearly every member of the community, helping us to alleviate the strain on the mining outposts. This in turn gave us the opportunity to begin a more aggressive schedule of upgrading and replacing the existing facilities.

From a morale standpoint, I was finally able to relax the mandates restricting the growth in the colony's population. Until now a prime concern as we worked to find a balance between the conservation of our resources and the need to allow families to propagate, the creation of the central habitat saw the first newborns brought into our tiny world for nearly a generation, guaranteeing that the descendants of Dokaa would continue on even through these times of adversity.

As the years have passed, however, I and others have realized that even the central habitat is not enough. At its heart it is still a box, an artificial world made of metal and composite materials obtained from the rocks. It exists merely to serve us, possessing no heart or soul of its own. My people crave still more.

Those who were born here among the asteroids feel the yearning despite lacking a frame of reference with which to compare their desires. They are unable to give voice to their longings, but I and others who are old enough to have lived on our home planet can well sympathize with such feelings. I also miss the sensation of grass beneath my feet, of sunlight on my face, and breathing rich, full air that has not been recycled through an atmospheric regenerator. For a time I believed that such joys were long behind us, lost forever along with the world I had once called home.

None of the planets in our system are capable of providing such things, however, and our attempts to re-create the technology which allowed our spacecraft to travel faster than light have met with failure. There is nowhere else for us to go. Of that I have always been certain.

That is, until today.

I am still somewhat in awe of the sheer audacity of the latest proposal offered by our science ministry during the council's morning session. Creij, the leader of the ministry and our most revered scientific mind, has put forth the idea that one of the other planets can be transformed in such a manner that it will be capable of supporting our species. Needless to say, her presentation was at first met with stunned silence before the council chamber dissolved into a flurry of animated discussion.

I will admit freely that my first reaction to the idea was that it was preposterous at best and perhaps even an affront to Dokaa herself at worst. After all, is the creation or remaking of an entire world to suit our needs not on par with the acts performed by divine beings?

Still, Creij is confident of its chances for success. While she tried to describe her idea of designing and creating machinery that could mimic the actions of plant life, transforming the harsh, poisonous atmosphere of the target planet into one capable of sustaining us, I confess that even her simplified explanations left me confused. When she began to explain the concepts of introducing genetically engineered algae, lichens, and other chemical compounds to enrich the soil for the cultivation of vegetation including, eventually, the planting of various crops for food, my mind was hopelessly muddled.

And yet, I am fascinated by the idea.

Creij, in her usual affable manner, tried to put the matter into humorous perspective by reminding us that we would not have Dokaa's resources at our disposal. For such a feat to be accomplished by simple mortals, it is a strategy that will take generations and require the development of technology that does not yet exist. It would be an endeavor that far surpasses any other in the history of the Dokaalan.

Though I would almost certainly not live long enough to see the completion of such a mammoth undertaking, I am inspired by its potential. Later today I intend to put before the council a proposition that will allow Creij to perform the range of experiments she has requested to determine the viability of this concept. Even those will take years to conduct and, if they are successful, at that time we will be faced with an even larger choice.

I am sure that there are those who will doubt the feasibility of such a bold scheme and condemn it as a foolhardy waste of resources, but I am equally confident that it is an idea that will stir renewed hope and purpose in the majority of my people. I have no illusions that it will be an easy choice to make. Offering uncertainty in the face of that which is familiar has always been laced with risk.

Still, for the first time in generations we have been given a chance for real, lasting change that will give us new life. This project, if completed successfully, would usher in the rebirth of Dokaalan society on a level never before envisioned. How will such a choice weigh on our convictions?

Are we committed to a better life for ourselves and our progeny, or have we resigned ourselves to the existence we have shared these many years, content to remain occupants in a prison we created?

Chapter Twenty-two

"IT WAS A MANDATE of the council that the world selected for this project be completely devoid of life," said Creij, the Dokaalan introduced to the *Enterprise* officers as Hjatyn's science minister. Also the current director of the massive effort to transform the planet Ijuuka from an inhospitable world into a new home for the Dokaalan people, she had been tasked with explaining the endeavor to their visitors.

Like Hjatyn, Creij looked to be quite old to Picard, perhaps even close enough in age to have survived the destruction of Dokaal generations ago. That thought also made the *Enterprise* captain wonder about normal Dokaalan life spans, which seemed to be even greater than that of Vulcans.

Time enough to learn about that later, he reminded himself.

"This narrowed our choices to two candidates," Creij continued, "after which it was determined that Ijuuka was the better option. With our planet selected, we began the process of erecting massive atmospheric processors at fifty-six key locations around the planet. Just as we predicted, the process of converting the planet's atmosphere is a long and laborious one. It will be well into the next generation of our people before the air is fit to breathe. Still, preparations are under way for the next phases of the project, so that we can be ready when the time finally arrives."

"The Federation has been involved in several projects very similar to what you are attempting," Data said as Creij concluded her presentation. "From what I have seen, your level of achievement to this point is extraordinary, particularly given the limitations that you face."

Nodding, Creij replied, "It has produced a variety of ancillary benefits, as well. Developing new technology for the project has also resulted in the creation of many new tools, skills, and chemical compounds, to name but a few, that have found uses throughout the colony. Our standard of living has improved markedly in many other areas because of the work necessary to culminate this vision of ours."

Picard had listened with increasing admiration to the science minister's presentation. The atmospheric processors, already in place and operating for decades, had taken years to design and build. What had been accomplished so far was a stunning achievement, to say the least, and yet it would pale in comparison when the Dokaalan's ultimate goal was reached. The determination of these people, as personified by their leaders, was nothing less than inspiring.

"I am also impressed by your commitment to insuring that no innocent life is placed at risk by this effort," Picard said. "In doing so, you've already circumvented one of the larger issues taken into consideration when the Federation contemplates any terraforming effort."

"We have always been a people that attempted to live in harmony with our surroundings, Captain," Hjatyn said. "Though we did utilize the natural resources of our planet to aid in our progression as a civilization, we always endeavored to minimize the impact to the rest of the environment. In time we learned that a balance with nature could be achieved if only we made the effort to do so."

Picard nodded. "It is a belief we hold dear, as well." Of course, such awareness had not come easily. Humanity had instead taken generations to reach that level of understanding toward their own world, but the rewards that had come as a result of that realization were, to Picard at least, incalculable.

"I take it that a pursuit such as ours is commonplace in your society, Captain?" Creij asked.

"We have had some experience with the concept," the captain replied, "but I would not consider it a common practice, no." Though he was aware of the current effort to terraform the planet Venus in his own solar system, Picard knew of no other such projects currently under way.

Not intimately familiar with the concept of terraforming himself, the captain had read enough that he was able to hold his own in conversations on the subject. From what he did know, there had been several such projects completed just in the last few decades. Despite these successes, terraforming was still a significant undertaking even by the standards of twenty-fourth century Federation technology, and that was only if one measured the effort's technical aspects. "Long ago," he continued, "the Federation established the Terraform

Command, which is charged with overseeing all such projects and insuring that they are properly conducted."

He recalled the project on Velara III that had ended in near disaster almost fifteen years ago. The circumstances surrounding that incident had provided an unequivocal justification for the need to monitor such projects with a relentless scrutiny. In that instance, the supposedly uninhabited world had in fact been the home to a race of crystalline life-forms dwelling beneath the planet's surface. When the project called for raising the water table, that action threatened the existence of the planet's indigenous inhabitants.

Going forward at that point would have been devastating enough had it been done in ignorance, but the larger crime was that the project's director had known about the life-forms and yet elected to proceed anyway. Fortunately, Picard and his people had discovered the truth about Velara III and averted disaster, after which the project was abandoned and the planet quarantined by the Federation.

Though no one would ever openly admit it, Terraform Command had been established in the wake of the most formidable example of planetary reformation technology ever devised, Project Genesis. Even the name assigned to that astounding venture was still among the most closely guarded Federation secrets, and with good reason. Created more than a century ago, Genesis had been and still was the ultimate realization of transforming an uninhabitable planet into one capable of sustaining life, reducing the time needed to complete such a process from decades to mere hours.

It had taken little time for the usefulness of Genesis as a tool of aggression to become apparent. The notion that an enemy could pervert the promise of Genesis into a weapon of catastrophic and unmatched offensive power was one that had persisted for decades after the original designers' initial experiments. It was also a threat that had come to horrible fruition only recently, with the effects of the awesome technology still being felt across hundreds of worlds in one sector of the Alpha Quadrant.

Yet another example of our innovation getting ahead of our wisdom, Picard mused. It was because of incidents such as Velara III and the Genesis Wave that the Federation took a very hard stance on terraforming. While there could be no arguing the benefits of such technology if employed properly, there would always have to be defenses in place to guard against its misuse.

"First Minister," Picard said, "now that we are aware of your situation here, I would be more than happy to submit a report to my superiors detailing your efforts as well as my recommendation that we provide whatever assistance you may need, up to and including relocation. Starfleet can dispatch transport vessels capable of evacuating all of your people and transferring them to a planet ideally suited to your species. There are hundreds of worlds throughout the Federation where you would be welcomed, or we can find one that is uninhabited that you can settle on and make your own."

Hjatyn did not say anything immediately, apparently considering the suggestion for a moment before returning his gaze to Picard. "It is an interesting idea and a most generous offer, Captain. When we first learned that our world was doomed, the idea of attempting a large-scale evacuation was put forth. Our limited space-travel capabilities made that impossible, of course. Since then we have made our way as best we can despite the obstacles laid before us. The topic of relocation has been raised occasionally at council meetings, usually in the context of a miraculous rescue by visitors from another world." Smiling as he spoke the words, the Dokaalan added, "You must understand that those discussions were held with the belief that such circumstances would never actually occur. In any event, it is felt by many among my people that we should remain here and continue our attempts to make a new home as well as we are able."

"Captain," Data said, "I am sure that Terraform Command would be most interested in learning about the Dokaalan's efforts here." Turning to Hjatyn, he added, "They may even be able to suggest alternatives to your current methods that would take less time to complete."

Picard had no doubt that Terraform Command would take great interest in the Dokaalan's efforts here. Given their current state of technology, their goal of remaking Ijuuka to suit their needs was indeed formidable, if not impossible. Surely Hjatyn understood that, just as he had to recognize the extraordinary value of accepting Federation assistance.

To Picard's surprise, the aged leader held up a staying hand at that proposition, as well. "I have no doubt you could teach us about a great many things, Commander. However, it is important to our people that we complete this task ourselves."

"First Minister," Troi said, "your conviction is inspirational, as is that of your people, but there is no reason for you to continue this endeavor yourselves. The Federation will almost certainly be willing to help in any way you require while respecting your wishes."

Indicating the large display screen with its images of the Dokaalan's hoped-for new world, Hjatyn said, "Ijuuka will be as much a memorial to the millions lost when our world was destroyed as it will be a home for those of us left behind. For such an effort to have true meaning, it will have to be completed solely by us, and with the resources and skills we are able to fashion for ourselves."

A noble goal, Picard conceded, *to say nothing of a remarkable demonstration of these people's character.*

"I admire your principles, First Minister," he said, "and have no wish to intrude on them in any way. Please know that we stand ready to assist you should you change your mind."

Bowing his head respectfully, the Dokaalan leader replied, "For now, I think it best to continue as we have. I will not claim that what we are doing here is universally accepted. There are many who feel that the effort is insurmountable, given our requirement literally to envision and create the necessary technology at every turn. They believe that simply surviving out here on the colonies is difficult enough without expending resources remaking an entire world. Some have even gone so far as to accuse us of committing deliberate acts of aggression in order to frighten people into supporting the project."

"Such as the reactor explosion on the colony outpost," Data said. "Do they believe that to be a deliberate act of sabotage on the part of your government?"

Hjatyn replied, "We have received preliminary reports that suggest this, yes."

"Surely they don't have grounds for such accusations?" Picard asked.

His expression one of disapproval, Hjatyn replied, "Certainly not. I could never condone such action. In truth, it has always been our intention that anyone who wishes to stay here on the colonies be welcome to do so. After all, we will still have need of the resources mined from the asteroids even after the bulk of the population moves to Ijuuka." Shaking his head, he added, "However, it is very possible that an underground effort may be responsible for some of the incidents that have occurred recently, including the outpost accident."

The doors to the command center opened and Picard turned to see a Dokaalan, dressed in a simple beige-colored jumpsuit, enter and proceed directly toward Hjatyn, carrying a metallic rectangle perhaps twice the size of a standard Starfleet padd. The new arrival handed the object to the first minister. Picard noted with curiosity that the Dokaalan glanced twice in his direction, each time with what the captain regarded as a look of nervousness clouding his pale blue features.

Hjatyn studied the device for a moment before returning his attention to the *Enterprise* officers. "I am sorry, Captain, but the council and I have some business to address. Perhaps we can continue our conversation over dinner? We would be honored to have you and your staff as our guests this evening."

After following one of Hjatyn's assistants from the command center, Data said to Picard, "Captain, with your permission I would like to continue my research on the Dokaalan's terraforming efforts. Though they have refused our offer of assistance, we may still be able to provide suggestions for accelerating their processes using resources at their disposal."

The captain nodded. "Excellent idea, Mr. Data. Make it so."

As the android headed back for the docking port and the shuttlecraft they had used to travel from the *Enterprise,* Picard turned to Troi. "Anything new to report, Counselor?"

"While I believe they are sincere in wanting to finish the project for themselves, Hjatyn seemed unnerved by your suggestion of Federation assistance with the terraforming of Ijuuka. He was also uncomfortable discussing the possibility of sabotage within the colonies."

The captain frowned at that. "Do you think he or any of the others still harbor uncertainty about our motives?"

"It's possible," Troi replied. "There's definitely more to what's going on here than they've shared with us, but I can't say for certain that their intentions are malevolent."

Picard wanted to believe that Hjatyn was simply suffering from the pressures of his office. Guiding these people through such trying times would be a challenge for even the most gifted leader, after all. *A situation almost surely complicated by the arrival of visitors from another world,* he mused.

Still, he had learned long ago not to discount Counselor Troi's observations. Her ability to tap into the emotional state of an enemy had given him a tactical advantage on more occasions than he could count, and it gave him pause now. If there was something sinister taking place here, just out of their sight, Picard was certain they would discover it soon enough.

And that was what worried him.

Chapter Twenty-three

ALONG WITH HJATYN and the other seven council members, Creij took her place at the large table that was the most significant feature of the ruling body's meeting chamber.

As did nearly everything else in the room, the table's design reflected function rather than form. The bulkheads were bare metal plating just like every other wall in the colony, uncluttered for the most part by artwork or other embellishments for the sake of the room's occupants. Even the chairs used by the council members, salvaged from a passenger transport long since retired from service, were in need of new upholstery. Hjatyn, as always, had deferred such priorities in favor of focusing on the council's real responsibilities.

The chamber's sole capitulation to decoration was a painting that portrayed a sunrise as seen from Egiun, the botanical gardens that had once graced the center of Dokaal's capital city of Wyjaed. Rendered by one of the elder citizens who had survived the planet's destruction, it had been presented to the council as a gift upon the completion of the central habitat. Creij herself had always been enamored with the painting, for some reason seeking comfort in the tranquillity it depicted. Even though she had been born after the disaster, it was as though the scene reached out to her and offered a tenuous link to a world she had never known.

At the moment, however, even the painting could not soothe her anxiety.

"My friends," Hjatyn began as he settled himself into his seat, "this is a wondrous time for us, even without our new guests. Our people are counting on us for confidence and leadership, particularly now. We cannot afford to lapse in our duties, either together or as individuals. I am looking to each of you to continue displaying the same calm and poise you have demonstrated to this point. Do you not agree that this is the best course of action, for all our sakes?"

The other council members all voiced their approval, Creij included, but the anxiety she already felt only deepened when Hjatyn turned his attention to her.

"Creij," the first minister said, "you have been troubled of late, my friend. How can we help?"

It was true that she was worried, about Hjatyn. Creij was sure something was wrong with the first minister, though it was nothing she could easily explain and there seemed to be nothing empirical on which to base her suspicions. At first, she had been hesitant to mention anything, wondering if perhaps Hjatyn simply was feeling the pressures of his enormous responsibilities. The first minister had always taken more work upon himself than normally was required for a person in his position, reluctant to delegate even the most mundane of tasks to other council members or his cadre of assistants. While this sometimes had the effect of aggravating his fellow leaders, it was one of the many qualities that endeared him to the rest of the Dokaalan people.

Even before ascending to the Zahanzei Council as science minister and becoming one of its longest-serving members, Creij had been a friend of Hjatyn's for nearly all of her adult life. Among the first children born here on the colonies after the loss of Dokaal, Creij was one of the many who had looked to the council for guidance. As an adult, she had discovered a way to return that gift, using her natural affinity for interacting with people in order to help them find the strength to carry on with the Dokaalan's makeshift existence. It was a function she continued to perform even as she moved into public office, providing support and assurance for the citizens as well as fellow members of the council, including the first minister himself.

More than anyone, Creij believed she knew Hjatyn best, which was why she had finally decided to confront her friend with her concerns at the earliest opportunity.

She had just not expected that chance to come now.

As if sensing Creij's unease, Hjatyn asked, "Come now, surely you can unburden yourself to us. After all the times we have come to you for your wisdom and strength, it is only fair that we return the favor."

Nodding, Creij said, "I have sensed some things that worry me, yes. While I was at first fearful of these visitors, I now believe that they truly wish to help us. Many of the people feel the same way, but many more are expressing uneasiness, even distrust, toward the visitors. Those feelings are being reflected here among the council, and I fear that our divided positions will only serve to make matters worse."

"Come now," said Nidan, minister of security, another senior member who had served nearly as long as Creij himself, "are you suggesting we cast aside all thoughts of caution and welcome these newcomers with open arms? We cannot possibly know or understand their true motives after such a short time."

To Creij's right, Council Member Ryndai said, "As the first minister has already pointed out, if they are seeking something then they hardly need to engage in deception, to say nothing of making the effort to rescue the miners on Outpost Takir."

Nodding enthusiastically at her friend's words, Creij was heartened to hear someone else echo her feelings. She knew that others on the council felt the same way, and hoped that they would take advantage of this forum to air their views, as well.

Of course, not everyone felt the same way.

"Twenty-five people did die in the attempt," Nidan said.

"As did two of their own," Ryndai countered. "Are you suggesting they would sacrifice their own people to gain our trust as part of some elaborate ruse? I think you spend too much of your free time reading those mystery stories." The comment prompted several chuckles around the table, and even Nidan joined in.

"The point I am laboring to make," Nidan replied, "is that we know nothing about these people. We do not know what they are capable of, or how they value life. It may be commonplace for them to execute subordinates for the most inane of reasons. Obviously I hope that is not true, and that they are who they claim to be. I have

seen how uplifting their arrival has been for the populace, but I am saying we should remain cautious until we
learn more about them. Is that so unreasonable?"

Creij said, "Of course we should be careful, but not to
the point where we begin to alienate them. They have traveled a great distance to find us, and now that they are here
they have offered to help us realize our greatest goal since
we were forced to make a life here for ourselves. Should
we not at least consider what they can provide for us?"

She was convinced that what they had seen of the *Enterprise* was but a tantalizing preview of the vessel's remarkable capabilities, and she could not wait to see them
for herself. Though Captain Picard had graciously allowed
a schedule of guided tours of his vessel to anyone who
might be interested, Creij had not yet had the opportunity
to act on the gesture. *Soon enough,* she promised herself.

"But what is the price of that aid, Creij?" Hjatyn asked.
"Suppose we accept their help. What will they ask for in
return? Will we be willing or even able to give whatever
that might be? What if they present us with an ultimatum?
Perhaps they have powerful weapons on that ship of theirs,
just waiting to be used should we refuse their demands."

Ryndai said, "With all respect, First Minister, what
could we possibly have that they could not take by
force? We have seen enough of their technology to know
that they can destroy us without a second thought if they
so desire."

"There is something else to consider," Hjatyn said.
"What about our commitment to honor those lost on
Dokaal by creating our new home on our own?"

Shaking her head, Creij replied, "When we made that
pledge, did any of us truly consider the possibility of a

ship visiting us from the stars with the ability to help us in ways we could scarcely dare to imagine? I know that I did not, but they are here now. With their aid we would have a much better chance of completing the project successfully, and perhaps even faster than we originally planned."

At their present rate of progress, Creij knew that despite the best efforts of everyone on her reformation team, the conversion of Ijuuka into a habitable world would not be completed in her lifetime. With Federation assistance, there was the distinct possibility that, for the first time in her life, she would be able to walk on the surface of a real planet and breathe nonrecycled air with the rays of their sun warming her skin. Was it selfish of her to want that for herself? She did not believe that allowing Captain Picard and his people to contribute to the project would somehow cheapen what the Dokaalan were trying to accomplish here.

Her comments sparked several moments of debate, with the members doing their best to outtalk one another as they debated the positives and the negatives, before Hjatyn called the council back to order.

"It is obvious that we will have much to discuss in the days ahead," he said. "There is no need to rush into any decision." Looking to Creij, he added, "You have given me much to think about, my friend. While I am not yet completely comfortable with our guests, I feel better about them now than I did before listening to you. Once again your guidance has proven invaluable."

After determining that there was no further council business, Hjatyn adjourned the meeting. As the members moved to file out of the chamber and return to their various duties, Creij felt a hand on her shoulder. She turned to see Ryndai smiling at her.

"Do not worry, Creij," her friend said. "They will come around, but they must do so on their own. Hjatyn has always done what is best for us regardless of his own feelings. Soon even he will realize that these Federation people are a blessing from Dokaa." Taking a deep, satisfied breath, he added, "Just think, we may yet walk on Ijuuka."

"I hope you are right," Creij replied. "I understand his caution, but it is not normal for Hjatyn to be so resistant to any new idea. His open-mindedness has always been his hallmark as a leader."

Ryndai chuckled. "Do not judge him too harshly. After all, how many times has his leadership been tested in this manner?"

Unable to help herself, Creij returned the laughter as the pair began to make their way toward the door. Before they could exit the council chamber, however, she heard another voice from behind her.

"Creij, Ryndai." It was Nidan, and Creij saw from the look on his face that the security minister was evidently unhappy about something. "A moment if you please."

His own features clouding with concern, Ryndai asked, "What is it, Nidan? Are you still troubled?"

"I have a delicate matter to discuss with both of you," Nidan replied. Looking about the room as if afraid he might be overheard, Nidan gestured toward another door with his hand. "Perhaps it would be better if we speak in my office."

Creij exchanged confused looks with Ryndai. What was this about? Was there some pressing security situation that required their attention? Even if that were so, such matters were almost always discussed with the rest of the council.

They followed the security minister through the door separating the council chamber from the small room he used for his office. Like Nidan himself, the workspace was a picture of order and efficiency.

The only things that seemed out of place were the two security officers waiting in the room as the two council members stepped through the door.

"What is this about?" Creij asked as Nidan entered the room behind them and pressed a control that closed the door.

Instead of replying to her, the security minister instead turned to his two subordinates.

"Dispose of them quietly."

Chapter Twenty-four

"I'VE BEEN WATCHING their vital signs for six hours now, Jean-Luc. Any change we can induce with medication lasts thirty to forty minutes at most before their symptoms resurface. Damn."

Sitting behind her desk in her office, Beverly Crusher rubbed her brow in frustration. In her other hand she held her padd, which displayed the latest status report for the five remaining Dokaalan patients. According to the report, just like its predecessors, the patients' condition was worsening.

On her computer screen, the image of Captain Picard peered out at her from his ready room. *"But their physical injuries seem to be healing well?"*

"Our treatment of their burns, shrapnel wounds, bone breaks, and assorted bruises is all progressing as expected," Crusher replied. "Still, my people and I have been working nonstop trying to find some medicine or other therapy that will combat these persistent symptoms." She shook her head. "I have no idea what is going on."

Thanks to Nentafa, as well as the battery of initial scans and tests conducted during the prolonged triage effort following the evacuation of the mining outpost, the *Enterprise* computer had been able to analyze a whole host of medical information pertaining to her patients. Even with all of that, however, there was no denying the most current status report.

In addition to accelerated heart rate and heightened body temperature, metabolic rates were wildly inconsistent, cell reproduction had dropped, and neural activity throughout the body had become spastic. Readings that had been stable when the patients arrived in sickbay were showing signs of failure even though the areas of trauma were healing. It simply made no sense to her, and studying the figures over and over did not bring her any closer to an answer.

"From what you've told me," Picard said, *"the symptoms would seem to point to an allergic reaction or infection of some kind."*

Crusher nodded. "That's what we thought at first, too." She had made that determination with the help of Dr. Tropp and the Emergency Medical Hologram. They had tried every treatment regimen for such maladies that she could think of, exhausting the *Enterprise* medical files and her own comprehensive experience in the process. Nothing had worked. "We've even consulted with the Dokaalan medical specialists, but they're at a loss about this, too."

Now, she was running out of ideas.

Movement in the doorway to her office caught her attention and she looked up to see the EMH wave to her before returning to the patient he was overseeing. "I have to go now, Captain," she said to the image of Picard on her terminal. "I'll update you if there's any change in their condition."

"Good luck, Doctor," Picard said before the terminal went blank.

Emerging from her office, Crusher made her way across sickbay to where the five Dokaalan were being treated within the confines of a containment forcefield, erected to shield the patients from anything that might prove to be a contaminant to their internal systems. As she drew closer to the isolated area, she saw the EMH apply a hypospray to the neck of one of the two burn victims, the female named Jipta.

The hologram had agreed with her theory that some form of allergy was at work here. After suggesting that the duplication of the Dokaalan's natural environment in sickbay might offer some insight into their condition, he had configured the atmosphere in the isolated area to match precisely the Dokaalan's native environment as well as altered the gravity to equal that of their asteroid home. So far, none of the measures had produced any change in the patients' condition.

"What's up?" she asked as she stopped short of making contact with the containment field.

Without looking up from his patient, the EMH replied, "Cortical monitor readings showed that Jipta was starting to seize again. I administered another dose of melorazine to counter the seizure's effects, as well as a tri-ox compound to aid her breathing." Finished with his current task, he turned to face Crusher. "Other than the fact that their symptoms present themselves so quickly, their condition is very similar to that of someone suffering the final stages of Iverson's disease."

"All five of them?" she asked. That did not make sense. A rare chronic degeneration of muscular function, Iverson's disease was incurable and fatal to humans. To suggest that such a rare disease would manifest itself in a nonhuman was reason enough for alarm. But the idea that five such beings would fall prey to the same rare human ailment—at an extremely accelerated rate, no less—was just absurd.

Got any better ideas?

"Are you suggesting we begin enzymatic therapy?" she asked.

The EMH shook his head. "I am merely comparing her readings to those of Iverson's patients available in our records. She is the worst off so far, but I'm afraid the rest of them appear to be following the same trends."

Despite being enthusiastic at the potential for the EMH program and being the one responsible for its initial funding during her tenure at Starfleet Medical, Crusher had never been able to place her complete faith in the concept of a computer-generated physician. Her original reservations had mellowed over the years as the *Enterprise*'s EMH distinguished itself on several noteworthy occasions, including one emergency that had required life-or-death surgery despite the patient's cultural restrictions against invasive medical procedures.

The hologram had simply adjusted the solidity of its hands and medical instruments, thereby enabling itself to pass through the body of the patient and operate on his damaged heart without actually cutting through the skin and muscle tissue. It had been an exceptional bit of innovation on the artificial doctor's part, one that would have been impossible with a flesh-and-blood physician, and had gone a long way toward solidifying her trust in the EMH concept.

So, why not trust him now?

"Okay," Crusher said, pausing a moment to consider a new course of action. "Let's go ahead and run an inner nuncial series and a neuromuscular scan. Depending on the readings, maybe some enzymatic treatments are a good idea at that."

The holographic physician smirked a bit and said, "I am capable of the occasional 'good idea,' Doctor."

Crusher allowed herself a smile at that before hearing the sound of the doors opening. She turned to see Dr. Tropp guiding Healer Nentafa's antigrav worksled into sickbay.

"Hello, Dr. Crusher," the Dokaalan physician offered as Tropp directed the chair toward her. Crusher noted that the healer looked as though he was even more fatigued than the last time she had seen him.

"Nentafa, are you all right?" she asked.

The healer nodded. "A lack of sleep, Doctor," he said. "Understandable, given the circumstances." Pointing to where the EMH worked behind the containment field. "Has there been any improvement in their condition?"

"I'm afraid not," Crusher replied. "At the moment we're working from a theory that they're reacting to something in our environment, so we've isolated them for the time being and attempted to duplicate the conditions on your colonies as closely as possible."

"Those are thoughtful measures, Doctor," Nentafa said. "You have taken reasonable actions."

Shaking her head, Crusher said. "But they haven't responded to any of it. Instead they're just wasting away."

Tropp stepped closer to the containment field, his attention on the patients lying immobile within its confines. "Perhaps they're reacting to something that's lacking in the environment."

From within the isolated area, the EMH turned and said, "We've compensated for everything: gravity, atmosphere, nutrients, all of it."

"No, it has to be something we're not looking for," Crusher said, trying to organize the sudden rush of half-formed ideas and suspicions flooding her mind. "It's almost as if they aren't getting a vitamin they need, or a chemical, or . . ."

"Something illicit?" Tropp offered when she paused.

The thought had not occurred to her, but it was worth considering. Medical scans of the Dokaalan treated during the triage operation had not identified anything resembling an intoxicating or psychoactive substance present within any of the patients. Even after her staff repeated the tests once the *Enterprise* data banks were augmented with as much Dokaalan medical information as Nentafa and other healers could offer, nothing untoward had been found.

Had they missed something there, as well?

"You're thinking withdrawal?" Crusher asked.

"It's not beyond the realm of possibility," the Denobulan said, turning his head to cast a curious look at Nentafa.

"Oh, I assure you that is not the case," the healer said. "Even in times of desperation, our people have never squandered our resources on any sort of recreational drug. Medical and pharmaceutical supplies are closely monitored in order to prevent such unlawful use." He paused as he said that, and Crusher watched as the healer slumped in his chair and reached for his forehead.

"Nentafa?" she asked as she crossed toward him. "Are you all right?"

The Dokaalan responded by pitching forward, falling unconscious from the antigrav chair as he crumpled in a disjointed heap to the floor.

Retrieving her tricorder from her pocket, Crusher waved the device over the fallen healer. "Temperature rising, pulse racing." His pale blue skin was warm to the touch, and Crusher looked up at Tropp in shock. "He's showing the same symptoms as the others."

How is this happening?

With the help of Tropp and the EMH, Crusher maneuvered the elderly Dokaalan to another of the treatment beds. As she and her fellow physicians began the task of tending to their newest patient, her mind sought out any clues this might offer toward solving the larger problem they still faced.

"It has to be something here," she said, shaking her head at the now familiar, and useless, information being relayed by the diagnostic monitor over Nentafa's head. "Nothing else makes sense."

From the other side of the bed, Tropp said, "Perhaps we should move them to one of their own hospitals."

"That would be the equivalent to sending a modern-day heart patient to nineteenth-century Earth for transplant surgery," the EMH countered. "Their medical facilities are hopelessly primitive compared with ours."

"But even with our advanced technology," Tropp said, "we have been unable to treat them. If I understand Dr. Crusher correctly, removing them from the potentially dangerous environment of the *Enterprise* itself may have an effect on their condition."

Though he was nothing more than a highly sophisticated computer program, the EMH was now doing an exceptional imitation of an irate human being. "As I have already explained, we have duplicated their native environmental conditions to the smallest degree. It makes no sense that moving them would induce any change."

"It makes no sense that they're dying," the Denobulan doctor finally shouted, "but they *are!*"

Crusher stared openmouthed at the normally reserved physician, who was now glaring with unfettered hostility at the EMH, his jaw clenched, and breathing heavily through his nose. Elsewhere in the room, all of the medical staff had stopped whatever they were doing and turned toward the sound of the outburst.

"Gentlemen," Crusher said, her voice hard as she stepped forward to regain control of the situation, "moving them back to the colony probably won't be any more detrimental to their condition than leaving them here." She turned to Tropp. "Doctor, please coordinate the movement of the patients back to a medical facility of the Dokaalan's choosing. I'm going to have Captain Picard secure permission for me to remain with them and monitor their condition. If there's any change, I'll inform you immediately."

"And what should I be doing?" the EMH asked.

"Deactivating," Crusher snapped. "Computer, end EMH program."

The holographic doctor had no chance to say anything in rebuttal before he flickered and faded from existence, leaving Crusher and Tropp alone with their newest patient. Looking down at the prone form of the Dokaalan healer, Crusher shook her head. "I'm sorry, Nentafa," she whispered. "I feel like I've failed you."

Glancing around the isolation area, she grimaced at the sight of the patients in their weakened condition, with too many indicators on their medical monitors blinking warning red. Was she helping them—or forsaking them—by sending them back to their own hospital?

"Doctor," Tropp said, "it might be prudent for me to continue our research here. In the event we do find a new course of treatment to try, there would be nothing to stop us from administering it at the colony's hospital."

Crusher was unable to resist regarding the Denobulan with a look of mock suspicion. "A minute ago you said we were out of options and that there was no chance of finding anything new."

Shrugging, Tropp replied. "I was simply trying to get the EMH to shut up. Have I mentioned yet how much I despise those things?"

Despite all the frustration and tension and feelings of helplessness that had consumed her during the past several hours, Beverly Crusher allowed herself a welcome laugh.

Maybe we're not finished here just yet.

Chapter Twenty-five

THOUGH HIS SMILE might say otherwise, Lieutenant Diix was not a happy person.

"And this is the matter-antimatter reaction assembly, or what we call the warp core," the Andorian engineer said, walking backward with his arms up and pointing with both hands toward the massive pulsing cylinder that was the dominant feature of the *Enterprise*'s engineering section. "It is the very heart of the ship. In addition to being our primary source of propulsion for faster-than-light travel, it also provides power for many of our other onboard systems."

While it was not a verbatim recap of information found in the ship's technical specifications, Diix knew it was more than enough for his audience. That it might take months if not years for these people to even begin grasping the concepts behind modern warp-drive technology did not seem to dampen their enthusiasm. The group of Dokaalan guests had listened with rapt attention from the moment they had stepped aboard the ship, all fifteen of them hanging on his every word.

Or was it twenty? Diix had not bothered to count. It was bad enough that he had been sentenced to the role of tour guide. Hall monitoring would simply rub salt in the wound.

And if that were not enough, he and the rest of the engineering staff had to deal with modified special life-support requirements in deference to the Dokaalan contingent. While some of the other engineers enjoyed bounding about the room in the reduced gravity, it was definitely not one of Diix's preferred pastimes. Why had he been picked for this task? There were other engineers on staff who were better suited to playing host for the delegation, and Commander La Forge knew that.

Perhaps he should be grateful for the assignment and consider that it, like everything else they had discovered since the *Enterprise*'s arrival in the Dokaalan system, was actually an unexpected and welcome deviation from what many believed would be a tedious mission.

All that changed, of course, after the discovery of the Dokaalan mining outpost and the hundreds of people stranded there. The boring, pointless mission was gone now, replaced by a unique opportunity to learn about a group of incredibly resilient people. His admiration for the Dokaalan had only grown upon learning that they, working with a level of technical knowledge more than two centuries behind that of the Federation, had charged headlong into an endeavor as daunting as terraforming a planet. As an engineer, Diix could not wait for the chance to examine the technology they had literally invented out of necessity in order to realize such a grandiose dream.

He was disappointed that Commander La Forge had

not selected him for the away team to Ijuuka on an inspection tour of the Dokaalan's atmospheric processors. There would be other opportunities, of course, but that did not help him right now, not as he was attempting to explain the inner workings of the *Enterprise*'s warp drive.

I should be thankful, he decided as he finished glossing over the finer points of the propulsion system and his audience continued to regard him with silent wonderment. *They could have spent the last hour asking all manner of inane questions.*

He retracted the thought a moment later.

"What is antimatter?" asked one Dokaalan.

"How fast does your ship travel?" inquired another.

"What do your antennae do?"

It was a supreme act of willpower for Diix to retain his fixed smile. Taking a moment to insure that no anger would reveal itself through his voice, he said, "Ladies and gentlemen, this concludes our tour. I'm afraid my duties won't let me stay with you any longer, but the engineering staff will be happy to answer all of your questions. Thank you for your time."

Finished with his presentation, Diix turned and headed without preamble to the chief engineer's office. Even as he crossed the room toward the small alcove and the sanctuary it offered, he smiled as he watched the enthusiastic Dokaalan converge on those members of the engineering staff not fast enough to get out of sight before being cornered by one of their visitors.

His own respite would be short, however. With Commander La Forge off the ship, Diix was in charge of engineering until his return. That meant making sure the duty roster was up to date and that any assignments tasked for the current duty rotation were completed before the shift change.

The door to the office opened, but Diix stopped at the threshold as he realized that the room was not empty.

"Lieutenant Tyler?" he said to the young human woman seated behind the desk and working intently at the computer terminal. "What are you doing here?"

Tyler had flinched visibly at the sudden opening of the door. It was obvious that she was as surprised by Diix's arrival as the Andorian was to see her in the first place. For a fleeting second the human's expression almost seemed to be one of guilt, but for what reason?

"I'm preparing the deuterium consumption report," Tyler said, her eyes shifting to the computer console, which Diix noted had been turned from its customary position so that its face could not be seen from the door.

Surprised by the answer, Diix shook his head. "Commander La Forge told *me* to do that."

"I see," the other engineer replied. There was a slight pause where she said nothing else, instead tapping a command string into the computer terminal before rising from her seat. "I guess we have some kind of misunderstanding, then."

His eyes narrowing in suspicion, Diix stepped farther into the office, the door closing behind him. "I should say so. The assignments are clearly indicated on the duty roster. I was given the task of preparing the deuterium report, and you were supposed to be on the detail replacing that port nacelle power coupling. If there has been a change in the assignments for today, I have not been informed." He was not surprised when Tyler moved to block him from coming around the desk. Obviously she did not want to see whatever was displayed on the computer terminal.

Surprise did come, however, when the human calmly reached out and plucked Diix's combadge from his chest.

"What the hell are you doing?" he exclaimed. He instinctively reached to grab the communicator back, noticing for the first time that the other engineer was wearing a phaser. There was no time to ask why before Tyler drew the weapon and fired.

The orange beam enveloped the Andorian and his body disappeared.

Using a phaser on such a powerful setting would normally have registered with the ship's internal security sensors. Kalsha remembered this fact only the moment after deciding the Andorian would have to be killed in order to preserve the security of the mission. Thankfully, it had taken little effort to encode an override to the security grid capable of blinding the sensors to his weapon's use. He wondered if he would have time before leaving the ship to learn why these people insisted on storing weapons anywhere but a designated armory. Such information might prove useful during future operations.

It is a question for another time. Continue with your mission.

One positive aspect of killing the Andorian was that Kalsha would now be able to assume the form of the dead engineer. That at least was a less risky proposition than continuing on with his impersonation of the human. Moving so that he was not visible through the window, Kalsha reached for his left wrist and tapped it. The human woman's pinkish skin and the dark material of her uniform vanished, replaced by the metallic exoskeleton of his mimicking shroud.

The body-enveloping garment was a most-favored tool of those in his particular profession, having proven quite useful during many of his past assignments. Even in its natural state, the shroud provided effective camouflage for nighttime operations, but its true value lay in its array of built-in sensors and holographic emitters. When activated and used properly, they provided the shroud with the means to replicate nearly any humanoid form.

It had allowed him to assume the form of a Dokaalan visitor, blending in with the rest of the contingent as they were led through the *Enterprise* and allowed to inspect some of the ship's most sensitive areas, waiting for his chance to get to the chief engineer's office and the relative privacy he needed for the next phase of his mission. Clearly, the ship's crew did not believe these people might be engaged in any kind of suspicious activity. Such trust and complacency would yet prove to be their undoing.

Embedded in the garment's left arm was the shroud's control pad. Kalsha tapped a key and compact digital text began to scroll on the pad's miniaturized display screen. When he found what he wanted, he entered another command and the shroud's emitters came to life once more.

An effective technique imparted long ago by his instructors was always to keep the shroud's passive sensors activated in order to scan anyone he encountered while on assignment. After all, one never knew when it might be necessary to disable a subject and quickly assume that person's identity. Now, for example.

In response to his commands, the Starfleet uniform re-materialized. This time, however, his skin was blue, his hair white instead of black, and antennae jutted from the top of his head.

You make a fair Andorian, Kalsha decided as he reviewed his new appearance in the reflective surface of a deactivated monitor set into the office's rear wall. He had re-created the engineer down to the last external detail, with only one adjustment to make. Manipulating the control pad once more, he looked down at himself and watched as the image of the communicator badge on his chest disappeared. He nodded in satisfaction as he reached for the actual combadge he had taken from the Andorian and affixed it to his own tunic. So far as the *Enterprise*'s computer and its network of internal sensors were concerned, the presence of the communicator was the same as tracking Lieutenant Diix.

A glance through the window separating the office from the rest of the engineering section confirmed that no one else had taken notice of anything happening in here. Though he had come perilously close to compromising the entire operation, the sigh he released was born more of disappointment than relief.

Unlike many of his peers, Kalsha had no passion for killing. There had been several occasions where he had killed without hesitation, his body and mind reacting in accordance with his training. In each of those instances he had done so because he was forced to conclude that assasination was the only option available to him.

This was one of those occasions.

It had been a risk assuming the form of the human woman, but it would have been even more hazardous had Kalsha chosen to mimic someone who would be recognized as not being part of the crew. Even with a complement as large as the one on this ship, the possibility of someone taking issue with a perceived stranger was too great too ignore.

He had not been comfortable with that choice, either, arguing with his superiors that someone might notice the irregularity of a person being in the main engineering section when they should have been elsewhere. The empty space occupied only seconds before by the Andorian had given credence to his suspicions.

How many more would have to die in order to preserve the secrecy of the operation? That the arrival of the Federation starship had introduced a complication into the carefully crafted plan was an understatement of enormous proportions. Given the Federation's predilection for interfering at the precise inopportune moment no matter the issue, he wondered if their training academies offered a curriculum to foster such talent.

As Kalsha had told his superiors at the pre-mission briefing, concealing their efforts from the Dokaalan was a simple task, yet doing so in the presence of the Starfleet captain and his crew was something else entirely. If left to their own devices, they would eventually surmise that something more than the Dokaalan's heroic yet futile efforts was in play here. Already they were sending specialists to inspect the massive planetary reformation operation currently under way on the fifth planet, and what if they should find something?

A moot point now, of course, Kalsha conceded regretfully. There was nothing for him to do now except carry on with his own assignment. Returning his phaser to its holster at his waist, he entered a new command string to the computer terminal, removing the coded override to the security grid. An additional few keystrokes succeeded in wiping away any trace that he had infiltrated the computer's labyrinthine operating system.

Despite its sophistication, Federation software technology possessed a variety of flaws that were ripe for exploitation by someone possessing the necessary skill. He thought such weaknesses would have been identified and remedied by now, especially given the number of times an enemy had taken advantage of a Starfleet computer system for one reason or another. In fact, Kalsha recalled with a smile, this crew had fallen victim to such attacks more than once.

Hard lessons always take the longest time to learn, he reminded himself.

With his new identity in place, Kalsha could now sit at the chief engineer's desk and work, secure in the knowledge that so far as the rest of the department was concerned, Diix was simply carrying out his assigned duties. He would need that time and freedom, for even though he had succeeded in infiltrating the ship's vast computer network to this point, that was child's play compared to the task that now lay before him.

The information he truly needed, that pertaining to the only member of the crew who was a true threat to their plans from an intellectual as well as a physical sense, was sure to be among the most closely protected data in the system. Penetrating the multiple levels of computer security without his efforts being detected would require every bit of his technical prowess.

Still, Kalsha would find it. There was no choice, not if their plans here were to have any chance at success.

Chapter Twenty-six

"HAVE I MENTIONED how much I hate wearing these things?" Geordi La Forge asked, his voice echoing in the helmet of his environment suit.

To his right, Lieutenant Taurik replied, "Not today, though I do recall several instances during my first assignment to the *Enterprise* where you expressed similar displeasure. Shall I recount some of the more colorful descriptions you employed on those occasions?"

La Forge chuckled in spite of his discomfort, the laughter a welcome sound within the confines of his helmet. He had never enjoyed wearing the suit, or the "standard extra-vehicular work garment," as it was known in Starfleet-speak. It was true that the SEWGs had been modified and improved over the years, and the current model was far superior to the version he had worn once or twice during his first year after graduating from Starfleet Academy.

Come to think of it, he remembered, *the ones we used at the Academy were even worse.*

The engineer in him reminded himself that the current model of SEWG was the most advanced such garment created by Federation science, ideally suited for working in the harsh vacuum of space as well as the unforgiving environments of countless worlds on which Starfleet personnel might find themselves. If properly used, a SEWG was capable of supporting its wearer for several hours while drifting in open space. According to its technical specifications as well as the *Starfleet Survival Guide,* the suit was even capable of surviving planetfall in the most extreme of emergency scenarios.

None of which made La Forge feel any better whenever he found himself forced to don one of the suits in the course of carrying out an assignment. He had no plans to test that last claim, anyway, and secretly wondered if the person responsible for writing those specs possessed either a perverse sense of humor or perhaps just a death wish.

"I think I'm okay this time," he said. Looking over at Faeyahr, the Dokaalan engineer who was currently acting as their guide, he added, "Besides, any bad feelings I might have go away whenever I look at what you have to wear."

Unlike the clean and sleek environmental suits he and Taurik were wearing, Faeyahr was dressed in a getup cobbled together before their sojourn to the planet's surface. The suit itself was a bulky affair consisting of a heavily padded undersuit over which the Dokaalan wore a dull gray insulated coverall. His helmet was large and bulbous, a metal shell that housed a wide glass faceplate. La Forge could plainly see the squat tube running from the neck of the helmet to the Dokaalan's mouth, no doubt providing a source of water or whatever these people consumed to ward off dehydration.

"Such is the life of a laborer," the Dokaalan replied, the thin line of his mouth forming a smile. Despite the fact that he appeared to be a specimen of superior conditioning, if the muscled physique La Forge had seen earlier was any indication, he still bent slightly under the weight of the respirator tank he carried on his back. Unlike the Starfleet officers with their suits' atmospheric regeneration systems, the Dokaalan workers were forced to carry oxygen and other gases necessary for their survival with them into these cruel environs, including the arid, dusty, and quite poisonous atmosphere of Ijuuka. It was not unlike the methods used by humans on Earth during the dawn of their space age.

On top of everything else, the Dokaalan people were contending with gravity that, while still lower than Earth-normal, was still more than four times that which they had lived with among the asteroids for generations. Those personnel who had been assigned to work on Ijuuka had become accustomed to the conditions here, but La Forge could tell that Faeyahr was earning the steps he took.

Yeah, the engineer conceded, *I don't have it so bad after all.*

"We are almost there," Faeyahr said as the trio approached the processing plant and its main control center.

Rising several hundred meters out of the valley created between towering mountain peaks, the structure was a conglomeration of immense, rectangular buildings connected by a spider's web of conduits, funnels, and metallic grating. It reminded La Forge of the giant ore-processing facilities on Delta Vega, Janus VI, or any one of dozens of uninhabited worlds in the more remote regions of Federation space. The plant was large enough that it had been visible even from high orbit, and the energy readings it gave off as he navigated their shuttle-craft down through the atmosphere were on a level he had not seen except in larger power generators employed on some densely populated worlds, such as those used to power the massive planetary computer system on Bynaus.

Though he probably should have stayed on the *Enterprise* to oversee the reconfiguration of various systems affected by the asteroid field's background radiation, La Forge had been unable to resist the notion of inspecting the atmospheric processing plants for himself. With a smile of satisfaction, he reminded himself that his team of engineers had already done exceptional work to modify some of the ship's compromised systems. Tractor beams were now functional, though their range and power were limited. Transporters had been certified for nonliving matter, and tests were still under way to make them safe for humanoids. Phasers were still offline, but so far that had not presented a problem.

No, La Forge decided, *my people are handling things just fine without me looking over their shoulder,* which of course left him to marvel in what he was observing now.

"I said it before and I'll say it again," he offered as they passed through the plant's inner perimeter fence, "what you've done here is amazing, Faeyahr." Looking around at the mammoth processing complex, he nodded in sincere admiration. "I can honestly say I've never seen anything like it."

Regarding the *Enterprise* chief engineer, Faeyahr replied, "Considering what I have seen of your tools and ship, I find that surprising."

La Forge shrugged. "You shouldn't dismiss your own capabilities so easily. In fact, if we get the chance, I wouldn't mind a crack at flying one of those skiffs of yours."

The Dokaalan technical specialist had ferried over to the starship from one of his people's own vessels using a small craft he had called a "skiff," which turned out to be very similar in form and function to the standard workpods employed at Starfleet orbital dockyard facilities. According to sensors scans La Forge had taken while the ship was in flight, the tiny two-person ship was not only fast but also maneuverable, and would therefore seem ideal for navigating the asteroid field. For use at various exterior mining locations, the skiffs also featured remote-controlled maneuvering arms and even small laser drill emitters, making the craft quite versatile indeed.

As for the processing plants they were now touring, La Forge and Taurik had learned during their earlier visit to the first such facility that the power requirements for the network of fifty-six processing stations around Ijuuka were answered through the virtually inexhaustible geothermal energy siphoned directly from the molten depths of the planet itself. The scheme spoke volumes about Dokaalan ingenuity and skill, demonstrating that at least in this regard, they were actually more advanced than many societies with comparable levels of technology, progressing to the use of such efficient and environmentally friendly energy resources faster than a good number of their contemporaries.

"It has taken a great deal of time and effort to reach this point," Faeyahr said as they neared the airlock that would allow them access to the plant's control center, "but we still have a long way to go."

That much was true, La Forge knew. Even after decades spent cleansing the atmosphere, the network of processors was still a generation away, at minimum, from achieving its goal.

The engineer was familiar with the terraforming accomplishments of Kurt Mandl, Pascal Saadya, and the late Gideon Seyetik, of course, not to mention, he thought with a shiver, his personal experience with the notorious Project Genesis. While those efforts were examples of far more advanced techniques than what was occurring here, the Dokaalan's was still an efficient operation, one of the finest examples of planetary reformation La Forge had yet seen. Even landmark terraforming efforts, such as that on Acheron or Dr. Mandl's long-abandoned project on Velara III, had not operated in so fluid a manner despite benefiting from the most advanced facilities and techniques devised by Federation science.

His thoughts were interrupted as the trio proceeded deeper into the processing station. They passed several Dokaalan along the way, with many of the workers stopping their activities to get their first real look at their visitors.

"Welcome to our new home!" one greeter offered, smiling as he stepped forward. The muffling effect created by both his own suit helmet and La Forge's did nothing to diminish the man's fervor. The expression warming the Dokaalan's blue features showed not a hint of unease or distrust, and the engineer could not resist returning his infectious smile.

A similar welcome had been extended to them during

their inspection of the other station earlier in the day. He saw that, as in the first plant, a good number of children were employed here, performing as apprentices alongside their adult mentors and demonstrating their own levels of enthusiasm. They hurled questions at a rapid-fire pace, and the Starfleet engineers were hard-pressed to even acknowledge them all, let alone provide answers.

Just as he had during that prior event, La Forge now noted a whole host of reactions to their arrival, ranging from animated greetings such as the one they had just received to others who simply stood back and watched with varying expressions of wonder and, in a few cases, suspicion.

It's going to take them a while to get used to us, he reminded himself, unable to blame any of the Dokaalan who might be a bit on edge given the circumstances. He held little doubt that their current multipronged predicament was not helping to ease the stress.

The *Enterprise* engineers followed as Faeyahr led them to an elevator that would take them up to the plant's main level and the control center. The elevator itself was little more than a metal cage with a lever used to control the car's movement through the vertical shaft extending from ground level up to the structure's highest point.

As had been indicated in the design schematics for the processing stations provided by Science Minister Creij, this facility was very similar in construction to the one they had visited earlier in the day. Just as starships and their interiors tended to evolve from the same basic template in order to reduce the acclimation time spent by Starfleet personnel when transferring from one duty assignment to another, the processing centers were designed in much the same manner. There were variations in the external configuration of the buildings to account for the differences in terrain, of course, but the interior details of the structures they had seen so far were practically identical to those at the first plant.

"You might be pleased to know," Faeyahr said as the elevator car ascended under the Dokaalan's control, "that this station currently holds the record for most consecutive work shifts without an accident. There has not been a single mishap here for nearly three hundred cycles."

In fact, La Forge was quite impressed. Given the immense power and maintenance requirements for each of the processing complexes, he simply assumed that work-related injuries or even deaths would be a normal occurrence. He was quite happy to be proven wrong. "That says a lot for your safety measures and leaders."

Nodding, the Dokaalan replied, "Most of the plants have excellent safety records, but a few have been plagued by misfortune, particularly in recent times. Our lead engineers believe that these malfunctions are symptoms of the atmospheric generators reaching the end of their operational lifetimes. Breakdowns are occurring more frequently, which is inevitable the longer we continue forward with the project, and all we can do is plan for those eventualities and minimize the risk to the workers. So far, our leaders are pleased that we can maintain a high standard of safety despite technical problems."

Taurik turned to La Forge. "Commander, it is possible that examination of the information we have gathered during these inspections may yield alternative procedures that can extend their equipment's life span while at the same time allowing for the increase of intervals between periodic maintenance."

Seeing the confused expression on Faeyahr's face, the chief engineer smiled. "That's his way of saying we might be able to help you."

Once the elevator had reached its destination at the plant's main level, the trio entered the airlock leading into the regulated environment of the facility's command center. La Forge would have loved to discard his EVA suit for a while, but they would only be here long enough to get an overview of the plant's operation and current progress before returning to the shuttlecraft.

Removing his helmet, he noted that the air had a definite metallic tinge to it, but La Forge still breathed a sigh of relief as he drew in his first lungful. At the moment, he welcomed any air that did not come from his own atmospheric regenerator.

Small favors, and all that.

"Greetings!" offered an elderly Dokaalan as he rose from his station at the front of the room. Bowing formally in the *Enterprise* officers' direction, he added, "We were told to expect visitors today. My name is Alerott, and I am the director of this facility."

After introductions were made, Alerott spent several minutes giving the Starfleet engineers his informal tour of the control room, pointing out the current status of the plant's atmospheric processing efforts. Just like its counterpart at the first plant, the control room here was a functional collection of computer consoles and banks of gauges, dials, and a variety of status indicators. La Forge was surprised to find that unlike the other facility's command center, where several of the consoles had been configured for automated monitoring, here most of them were being manned by workers.

Taurik noticed it, too. "Alerott, if I may ask a question: Is something unusual happening?"

The elderly director's expression turned to one of worry. "Not at all. Everything is operating well within normal parameters. Why do you ask?"

"From what we understand," the Vulcan replied, "these facilities are capable of functioning almost exclusively under automated controls overseen by their central computer system. With that in mind, there would seem to be an excessive number of personnel on duty here."

Alerott abruptly laughed in response to the query. "We like to do things a bit differently here, Lieutenant. I have worked at this facility since its activation, and even after all this time I have never been completely comfortable allowing a machine to do my work." Still smiling, he shook his head. "My daughter tells me that I should open my mind to new ideas, but I have always been rather slow in that regard. Besides, it keeps me active and at my age that cannot be a bad thing. Would you not agree?"

Sensing that Taurik might want to debate the illogic of not employing available automated measures, La Forge quickly replied, "I can't argue with that, sir." He grinned as he noticed the lieutenant's quizzical expression.

"Well," Alerott said, holding his arms out to indicate the control room, "what do you think of our remodeling effort?"

" 'Incredible' isn't too strong a word," La Forge answered. "We have people back home who are responsible for projects like this, and not only will they be interested in seeing what you've done here, I guarantee they'll be tripping over themselves to get out here and see it for themselves."

Nodding, Alerott replied, "I have heard of your captain's offer to assist us. While others might feel the need to decline such generosity, I have no such false pride. There is no shame in being shown a better way to do something, after all." A beeping tone from one of the consoles behind him caught the Dokaalan's attention, and he glanced at it before turning back to his visitors. "If you will excuse me a moment," he said with an almost paternal smile, "I must now go watch over my subordinate."

As he returned to his work, La Forge and Taurik found themselves allowed to wander the control room, spending the next ninety minutes or so overseeing the operation. It was obvious from the way the technicians carried out their responsibilities and communicated with one another that they were well versed in their roles. Even when a hydraulic failure was reported in one of the power generator's cooling plants, a repair crew was dispatched with nary a fluctuation in what was obviously a well-rehearsed routine. La Forge found himself impressed yet again with their hosts.

It was Taurik, however, who spoiled his good mood.

"Commander," he said as the engineers made their way back toward the airlock, "I was able to scan the computer system tasked with overseeing the main atmospheric processors, but I am confused by some of my readings."

"How so?" La Forge asked.

"As we have been told, the software protocols used by the computers at all of the plants are of a uniform nature, designed to keep the impact of the reformation process balanced across the entire planet. However, if my tricorder readings are correct, it would seem that the protocols in use at this facility are deviating from that norm."

His brow furrowing in concern, the chief engineer said, "Could it be a computer error?"

"I find that unlikely," Taurik replied. "None of the system's error-tracking programs appears to be registering anything out of the ordinary. From my preliminary readings, I suspect this deviation is deliberate. The changes being introduced by the new formulae are subtle, so minute as to avoid detection by any of the system's fault-discovery software." He paused, his right eyebrow rising as he considered his own words. "It is also possible that the oversight protocols themselves have been modified to allow these deviations to function undisturbed. I would need more time to test my hypothesis, however."

Turning the Vulcan's theory over in his mind, La Forge found himself not liking what he was coming up with on his own. "How long do you think this has been going on?"

"I cannot say for certain without a more thorough investigation of my findings," Taurik said, "but from my initial review I believe these changes are not meant to produce immediate results. Instead, they appear designed to introduce a cumulative effect over time. The changes to the software may have been in place for years."

From what La Forge had gleaned from Creij's design schematics, the vast array of complex mathematical calculations used to constantly monitor the processing stations' operation were designed to adapt to the ever-changing nature of the environment the Dokaalan were creating. Separate computer software was required to oversee the reformation protocols, constantly on the watch for errors that might introduce dangerous elements into the new atmosphere. The need for accuracy was far too great to think that a deviation such as Taurik was describing could be accidental or even the fault of computer error.

"If you're right," he said, "then that means we're talking about the work of an experienced software engineer. How many people among the Dokaalan population have that kind of skill, along with the opportunity to make their changes and keep an eye on things to see that no one else figures out what's going on?" It was a physical effort to keep from looking over his shoulder at any of the Dokaalan workers. Who among them, if any, might be a suspect?

Despite the misgivings held by many, La Forge was convinced that the very future of Dokaalan civilization would almost certainly reach a point where a project as bold as terraforming a planet would become critical to their survival. This was especially true if they were unwilling to relocate to another world. Still, he knew that many Dokaalan were against the idea, preferring instead to stay among the asteroids where they had at least come to terms with their situation and had devised ways to handle most of the difficulties.

But were any of them capable of sabotage to further their desires?

Chapter Twenty-seven

ABLE TO USE the relative solitude offered by the chief engineer's office, Kalsha had plumbed the *Enterprise*'s massive computer core, scouring its extensive databases for the information he sought. With each step, he deleted all traces of his search before the computer's security protocols even knew he was intruding, just as a fugitive on the run might brush his own tracks from a dusty path so as to stay hidden from his pursuers.

His work was meticulous and precise, but slower than he would have preferred. Still, he knew that to work in haste here and now was to invite discovery. The slightest misstep could bring an end to his mission—to everything they had been working toward. One tug on any loose thread he left behind could unravel the entire fabric of what he was attempting to accomplish.

Therefore, he sat at the workstation, slowly weaving his way through the computer's vast databases and using the opportunity to copy into his newly acquired Starfleet tricorder any and all information he thought would be useful against his unwitting hosts.

No reason to let all of this work go to waste.

After nearly two hours of careful searching, Kalsha finally had been able to forge access to the high-clearance portions of the computer's data banks. It had required every bit of his technical expertise to penetrate the security surrounding that area of the ship's main computer storage without alerting anyone else to his covert activities.

Despite the effort and the risk accompanying it, he had succeeded in finding the information he had been sent to obtain: the complete technical schematics for the *Enterprise*'s android crew member, Lieutenant Commander Data.

While much information had been gathered about the android in the past, one of the key facts that had proven elusive was how to deactivate it. Kalsha had briefly considered trying to destroy Data outright, but that was far too drastic an action. The *Enterprise* crew would certainly exhaust every available resource trying to locate the responsible party, which would of course risk exposing the entire mission and was therefore out of the question.

As he scanned the schematics, it took little time for him to learn about the emergency manual control located on the android's back. If he could get to that switch, he would be able to disable Data easily. Unfortunately, that was only a temporary measure and one the *Enterprise* engineers would be able to diagnose easily. Further, it would only serve to ignite suspicion among the crew about who might have triggered the switch, and that was attention he did not need at this juncture, not when there was still so much to do.

There had to be another way, something more subtle. If he could devise a method to render the android inoperative in a manner that left it intact yet unable to function, such a mystery might turn the engineers' collective attention away from other duties and devote much time to determining the scope of the problem and finding a solution. Such a plan, if successful, would allow Kalsha even more freedom in which to operate.

A perusal of Data's maintenance and diagnostic logs revealed something promising. Apparently an incident had occurred that required the *Enterprise*'s captain to deactivate the android when it began to malfunction. The chief engineer had modified a tricorder to emit a pulse of energy transmitted at a particular frequency, something called an "actuation servo," that resulted in a shutdown of Data's neural net and disabled him until such time as the ship's engineering crew was able to repair the android.

It stood to reason that such a pulse, modified properly, could fuse the circuitry of Data's positronic brain irreparably. The specifications for the actuation servo were recorded here in the diagnostic logs, providing Kalsha with everything he needed to devise a new protocol for his purposes.

His work completed, he reminded himself that in order to perpetuate his disguise, it would be necessary for him to risk doing what he had sought to avoid: interact with members of the ship's crew. It was an aspect of his assignment that he had quickly come to loathe. For one thing, he had discovered that humans, who made up a large portion of the *Enterprise*'s crew, emitted a distasteful odor, one the ship's atmospheric systems seemed unable to remove from the air.

Resigning himself to the idea, he rose from the desk, pausing a moment to examine his reflection in the deactivated wall-mounted monitor and insure that his outward appearance of Lieutenant Diix was still in place.

He certainly had not meant to insinuate himself among the crew using such a conspicuous persona. In fact, his goal would have been better served had he remained in the role of a lesser officer, one with computer access but fewer responsibilities to others. Instead, his new position of leadership was an unanticipated result of being interrupted by the luckless Andorian.

Still, assuming the identity of Diix brought with it a new opportunity, something he slowly realized as he strode past other Starfleet engineers busying themselves with their various tasks. As Kalsha made his rounds, his "fellow officers" went out of their way to inform him about their progress toward their designated objectives; assignments the Andorian must have doled out before his demise. They also freely entered their personal computer-access codes in his presence, something they certainly would not have done had they realized that the open tricorder in his hand was attuned to capture those code sequences so he might make use of them later.

All about him, computer stations and monitors provided a wealth of information about the status of nearly every major shipboard system. The engines, environmental control, even the weapons and defensive systems were all observed here. On one monitor Kalsha even noted the current status of the ship's deflector shield energy modulation. An enemy would surely find that bit of intelligence invaluable during an attack, yet here it was for anyone to see. Did these people know nothing about operational security?

Of course, the officers had no reason to suspect that anything untoward might be going on here. There was nothing about him that appeared overtly out of place, let alone a threat to the ship. The mimicking shroud's advanced arrays made certain of that, yet Kalsha still harbored heightened senses of alert and vulnerability as he interacted with the crew. Occasionally he stopped to listen to another crew member's report, nodding silently with presumed interest or understanding before informing the unsuspecting engineer to carry on with their duties. He hoped his charade was enough. Acting out of character from his adopted persona could well draw attention, so he erred on the side of discretion, allowing the shroud's sensors to passively scan his surroundings and gather information.

Kalsha approached one of the consoles encircling the room's dominant feature, the warp core that was the heart of the starship's propulsion system. Towering overhead and extending twelve decks through the middle of the ship's secondary hull, it pulsated with life as it controlled the reaction of matter and antimatter to generate the massive energy required to propel the vessel at faster-than-light speeds. Unleashed, that energy carried the potential to obliterate the ship and its occupants in the blink of an eye.

And by their own design, here it stands . . . so vulnerable.

"Lieutenant?"

Turning quickly, he found himself facing a female alien dressed in a Starfleet uniform. She was blue-skinned and devoid of hair, and it took Kalsha a moment to remember that this was a Benzite. That in turn helped him to draw the officer's name from the list of engineers he had earlier committed to memory.

"Yes, Ensign Veldon?"

"I caught you," the officer said, smiling.

His eyes narrowing, Kalsha slowly drew a breath, preparing for what might come next. "I am not sure I understand."

"I caught you staring at the reactant flow," the Benzite said. "I get mesmerized by it myself, sometimes."

She was attempting to connect with him on some conversational level, Kalsha realized. He was not at all interested, but tried to feign it. At least she did not smell as bad as her human counterparts.

"We all get drawn to our jobs by something, I suppose," he said, smiling politely and stepping away from the warp core. "If you will excuse me, I need to get back to those status reports."

Veldon nodded knowingly. "Oh yes. Commander La Forge gets cranky when those reports are late."

Moving away from the ensign, Kalsha decided he had done enough interacting as he headed back to the relative safety of the chief engineer's office. Once there, he could begin testing a few of his newly acquired passcodes to see if they might yield access to other areas of the ship's computer.

He forgot all about that, however, when his quarry stepped onto the main engineering deck.

It was his first sighting of the gold-skinned android since boarding the vessel, but Kalsha's people had learned a great deal about Data's capabilities in the past. While he did not know many details about the mechanism itself, he knew enough not to let his wits down in its presence. He kept his stride, thinking it best to avoid the android altogether.

It, however, had other ideas.

"Excuse me, Lieutenant Diix," Data said. "I have been ordered by Captain Picard to research possible refinements of the Dokaalan terraforming procedures. I would like to gather some data in engineering, if I may."

"Certainly, sir," Kalsha replied. "I am sure you know your way around."

The android nodded. "Of course. Thank you," it said as it stepped around him toward a computer console. "I am attempting to gather information that we might compare with the findings of Commander La Forge upon his return to the *Enterprise*. We may be able to suggest options for accelerating the terraforming process in such a manner that we would still be able to respect their wishes of not interfering to any significant degree."

"That is interesting," Kalsha said, actually meaning it. The task of transforming the planet's atmosphere into an environment capable of sustaining life was a long one, even prior to his people's arrival. Unwilling to risk discovery by the Dokaalan, they had found it necessary to adapt to their own primitive terraforming techniques. If the Federation could offer less time-consuming alternatives, then so much the better.

He nodded politely. "I will leave you to your work, Commander," he said before turning and nonchalantly moving to another workstation.

This was a perfect opportunity to strike, he decided as he observed the android engrossed in its work. Deactivating it here and now would elicit immediate confusion among the other engineers, and they would certainly waste no time turning to the sudden problem in their midst. Further, there would be little time to suspect any one person, especially him, of being responsible for causing Data's abrupt malfunction.

Pretending to study the status displays on the computer terminal before him, Kalsha pulled his tricorder from the holster at his waist and activated it. He called up the actuation protocol he had created, verifying that it was ready to execute at his command. The pulse would be effective only within a small radius, no more than five meters, he suspected, but the workstation he currently occupied was within that distance.

Kalsha took one last look at the android, marveling once again at the speed at which it was able to input and extract information from the computer. Reports of its physical capabilities, he noted, had not been exaggerated. It would be a shame to lose such a valuable specimen of artificial intelligence, but it was a small price to pay in order to insure the success of their larger mission. Besides, with the technical specifications he had copied from the *Enterprise*'s computer, it was entirely possible that, one day, a duplicate of Data could be made.

Slowly, he slid his thumb across the tricorder's face and over its recessed keypad, at the same time taking one last look around to verify that no one in the engineering section was paying attention to him.

"Lieutenant Diix," Data suddenly said, looking in Kalsha's direction at the exact instant he pressed the transmit key. "I wonder if I might—"

It stopped in midsentence, its mouth remaining open as if to pronounce the next word. Joints locked in midmotion as the android was turning from its workstation, momentum carrying it off balance until it tipped over and fell like a rock to the carpeted deck.

"Commander Data!"

Kalsha heard the cry from behind him even as he moved from his own workstation, already assuming the role of concerned colleague. All around him, engineers were scrambling across the room toward their fallen comrade. Trying to appear as alarmed as everyone else, he knelt beside Data and held his tricorder over the android in an effort to appear useful. He took the opportunity to look at Data's face, looking into its yellow eyes and seeing no glimmer of activity.

"What happened?" asked a light-haired crewman whom he could not identify.

"I do not know," he replied. "He was just standing here and then he collapsed."

Suddenly Data blinked. Once, twice, then a dozen times before his eyes began to sweep from left to right.

What? How was this possible?

"I . . . I . . . I-I-I-I," it stammered, remaining motionless while emitting the sound but still causing one of the kneeling engineers to jump back.

Another crewman, an ensign he knew only as Leisner, said, "We should run a diagnostic." He looked to Kalsha, "What do you think, Diix?"

Kalsha, still trying to figure out what he had done wrong in trying to disable the android, scrambled for something to say that would not raise suspicion among the other engineers. His efforts were hampered as the human engineer, Leisner, knelt closer, the odor emitted by his body launching an all-out assault on Kalsha's nostrils.

"I have suffered . . . a catas . . . trophic failure of my . . . neural net," Data said, its voice sounding broken and digitized. "I must shut . . . down to run in . . . ternal diagnos . . . tics. Do not attempt . . . repair. Inform Com mand . . . er La Forge."

Kalsha struggled not to fidget in front of the other engineers. What if he had only inflicted minor, easily reparable damage? All his efforts might well have been wasted. Relieved that the engineers had in effect been instructed to leave Data alone for the time being, he nodded. "It is probably best to do as he suggests. His own diagnostic abilities can do more for him than we can until Commander La Forge returns."

Beside him, Ensign Leisner said, "It might help if we move him to his diagnostic alcove."

Nodding in agreement, Kalsha organized the engineers to raise Data from the deck, a task easier said than done owing to the android's weight, which was of course far greater than that of a living humanoid of comparable size.

As the other officers maneuvered Data into the alcove specially constructed for use by the *Enterprise* engineers when performing diagnostics and maintenance on the android, Kalsha could only puzzle over why the actuation servo he had programmed had failed to work properly. He activated his tricorder again and reviewed the unit's scan log from the point when he had triggered the pulse, frowning as the recorded data showed a deviation in the frequency and intensity he had selected.

How had that happened?

Something, another energy source, had interfered with the actuation protocol at the time of execution. What could be responsible for that, especially at such a close range? Then it struck him, and he nearly cursed aloud at the realization.

The mimicking shroud, with its own contained power source, had to be the culprit. In his haste, he had failed to modify the servo's frequency to compensate for the interference generated by the garment. Reports submitted by other operatives in the past had detailed malfunctions in weapons and equipment later attributed to the shroud's energy field. How could he have forgotten something like that?

He tried to shake off his frustration at his foolish error. In fact, he had been lucky indeed that the pulse had not caused an adverse affect on the shroud itself, something else he had failed to consider when devising his plan.

Fool! I need to exercise greater care, or I risk compromising everything.

With Data now ensconced in his diagnostic alcove, he watched as Ensign Leisner activated a control that locked a pair of metal bands in place across the android's chest.

Pointing to the Benzite ensign, the engineer said, "Veldon, set up a terminal to monitor the progress while Data runs his diagnostics. We'll use that to see if we can figure out what happened."

Kalsha regarded the android's immobile form with its frozen, impassive face and its yellow eyes staring blankly back. Had the actuation servo been enough to permanently incapacitate Data's neural net, or had he caused only slight damage that could be remedied in short order? If Data could be repaired, either through his own efforts or those of the other engineers, it was entirely possible that the android would be able to identify

Kalsha, or Lieutenant Diix, rather, as the one responsible for the injury inflicted upon him.

"We need to report this to Commander Riker," Veldon said, looking uncertainly at Kalsha.

Kalsha nodded. "Of course." Doing so would expose him to contact with senior members of the ship's crew, but there was no avoiding that now. Having assumed the identity of the senior engineer on duty in the absence of Commander La Forge and Lieutenant Taurik, it was his responsibility to speak on behalf of the engineering section. All he could hope for was that the conversation that was sure to come would be as brief as possible.

Assuming what he hoped was a convincing air of worry, he tapped the combadge he had confiscated from the real Lieutenant Diix prior to killing him. "Engineering to bridge. Commander Riker, we have a serious problem down here."

Chapter Twenty-eight

PERHAPS IT WAS just his imagination, but La Forge was sure that there was more of an edge to the attention he and his companions were receiving from the Dokaalan.

Not everyone, he thought, trying to soothe his rising anxiety. Quite a few of the workers they passed in the corridors of the processing plant's main level continued to exhibit the same type of curiosity and warmth toward the visitors as La Forge had seen all day.

Still, he had not mistaken the look of keen interest on the face of Alerott and his assistant as he and Taurik had left the command center, had he? Were his eyes playing tricks on him? Had Taurik's report touched off a streak of paranoia?

Perhaps, but it also was possible that something out of sorts just might be going on here. If an act of sabotage was under way, then lives could be in danger. He and Taurik had a responsibility at least to investigate the possibility.

When they were once more sealed inside their environment suits and making their way back down to the ground via the utility elevator, La Forge turned to Faeyahr. "I'd like to take a look around the main processing area, if that's all right with you. What do you say?" He forced himself not to glance at Taurik as he made the request, fearful that the engineers' Dokaalan guide might notice the action and get suspicious.

Suspicious of what? La Forge asked himself. He had no reason not to trust Faeyahr, after all. So far as he could tell, the Dokaalan had been entirely forthcoming about all aspects of the processing plants and his people in general. However, the very reason he could have been assigned as their escort might be to insure that the Starfleet engineers did not stumble across anything incriminating if indeed a scheme of some sort was under way. If that was the case, then who could they trust?

No one, La Forge decided. *At least, not yet.*

Until he was certain of what, if anything, was behind the strange readings Taurik had discovered, it seemed that the best course of action would be to avoid raising the suspicions of anyone, Faeyahr included.

Frowning, the Dokaalan replied, "I am not sure why that would be necessary, Commander. The machinery in use here is virtually identical to that at the plant we visited earlier today. I doubt you will learn anything new about it or any of its components."

It was a valid point, La Forge knew. Considering that all of the complexes across the planet were working toward the same goal, it seemed apparent that there would be little room for deviation from one location to the next. They had spent a great deal of the morning touring the various sections of the first plant, learning about its cycle of operation, performance record, safety and security systems, and so on. With all of that accomplished, there seemed very little need to repeat the process again at this location. Taurik's tricorder scans of the facility would provide more than enough insight to the entire process and would make for an interesting review once the engineers got back to the *Enterprise.*

Think fast, Geordi.

As it happened, Taurik bailed him out.

"We completed our tour of the facility so quickly that there was insufficient time to inspect everything with the detail we would have preferred," the Vulcan said, holding up his tricorder for emphasis. "If I were able to record scans of areas at this location that are comparable to those we reviewed this morning, I will have a complete record of a processing plant's cycle of operation."

La Forge had no idea just how lightly Taurik might be treading the line between truth and falsehood, but his explanation certainly sounded convincing. The chief engineer added, "Besides, since these guys operate their control center differently than the other plant, what with employing more people instead of relying on automation and all, they might have a few other differences in some of the other areas, too." He shrugged, trying to play up the role of intrigued fellow engineer as well as that of interested tourist. "And, the more information we have, the better our chances of being able to offer assistance in helping you speed things up."

Faeyahr considered the engineers' words for a moment before nodding. "When you put it that way, it is a sound suggestion." La Forge waited until the Dokaalan's attention was diverted before casting a relieved expression in Taurik's direction.

The elevator slowed to a stop and the trio emerged onto the plant's ground floor. Passing through another airlock, after which they could once again remove their suit helmets, they proceeded down another narrow corridor that in short order opened into the plant's massive, amphitheater-sized central area.

Just as La Forge had expected, the interior layout of this facility matched that of the first plant in most of the major details. The storage tanks and power generators used to drive the continuous cycle of transforming Ijuuka's inhospitable atmosphere occupied the bulk of the complex floor, situated in five rows of six units. Each of the individual generators was connected to a power distribution grid that in turn directed the energy created here to the suite of eight atmospheric processors occupying the facility's middle levels.

As the engineers and their guide moved farther into the facility, La Forge that saw in addition to the constant machinations contributing to the plant's normal processing operations, a good deal of maintenance was taking place. One Dokaalan was occupied with welding two pieces of metal railing together, for what, the *Enterprise* chief engineer could not tell. Others were involved with the repair of a storage tank, using a type of handheld, air-powered tool to replace the rivets holding the container's outer skin to its frame.

"The trouble with this type of work is that it is very labor-intensive," Faeyahr explained as they walked, "not only with the day-to-day tasks but also in the maintenance and repair aspects. I suppose it is yet another price to pay for our eventual success."

"That's pretty much how it is with anything worth doing," La Forge replied, smiling despite the unease he felt over what Taurik had shown him. "Of course, I'm sure you and your people learned that a long time ago."

"Agreed." The Dokaalan reached out and placed a blue hand on the engineer's shoulder. "We see many things in much the same way, my friend. The more time we spend together, the greater my belief that your arrival here is a gift from Dokaa. She has finally seen fit to deliver us from our trials and offer us salvation, but we must be willing to accept it from the hand of a stranger."

"Would she mind if you took the help from a friend?" La Forge asked. It had been easy to see past the idea of simply aiding the Dokaalan for the engineering exercise it presented and embracing the idea of doing whatever he and the rest of the *Enterprise* crew could do to offer these people a better life. After all they had been through and despite the success they had wrought through sheer audacity and their unyielding will to survive, the Dokaalan deserved a break.

And they were not the only ones who would benefit.

A seemingly unending string of crises, from the second Borg invasion to the long-lasting and still to be fully determined effects of the Genesis Wave, to say nothing of the Dominion War, had all conspired to take their toll on the Federation in recent years. Rebuilding or replacing all that had been lost, if indeed that was possible, would take years. Along the way, La Forge hoped that people would take a moment now and then to remember what had made everything they had fought for worthwhile in the first place.

And part of that rebuilding, he mused, *means making a new friend once in a while.*

The biggest question to be answered at the moment, however, was whether they had stumbled into the middle of a societal quarrel caused by the massive terraforming project. Any assistance the *Enterprise* and the Federation could provide might eventually do more harm than good if the grand plan to create a new home for the Dokaalan was already sowing strife among the people. By all accounts, the idea of abandoning the mining outposts, which despite their obvious limitations had been the only home many of these people had ever known, was obviously not sitting well with some segments of the populace.

His attention was drawn to Taurik as the lieutenant, tricorder in hand, approached them from around the side of a gargantuan support column. "Commander La Forge, there is something here I think you should see." He pointed to a collection of storage tanks, towering above them on the plant floor. "I am detecting a secondary power source operating in that vicinity. It is small and isolated, not connected to the facility's main power supply."

Despite the Vulcan's typically stoic demeanor, La Forge still recognized the hint of concern in his voice. "I don't suppose you're going to explain it as a portable power source for some of the workers' tools or something like that."

Taurik shook his head. "While it appears that the energy readings are emanating from a portable source, the readings themselves are inconsistent with anything the Dokaalan have at their disposal."

Frowning at that and not liking the possibilities the junior engineer's report was conjuring in his own imagination, La Forge said, "Let's take a look." He paused a moment, looking around the floor of the plant to see if they were being observed. No one seemed to be taking an overt interest in them, but that did not ease his apprehension. "But try to act casual about it."

He ignored Taurik's puzzled expression as the trio made their way without hurry toward the storage tanks. Doing his best to play the part of intrigued visitor, La Forge made a point to ask questions about the plant and its operations to Faeyahr for the benefit of the Dokaalan workers they passed. All the while he let his eyes play over the surface of the machinery, allowing his ocular implants to search for anything out of the ordinary that might provide a clue for Taurik's power readings.

Then he saw it.

"What is that?" he asked as his eyes found the small, oblong device hidden away within a mass of pipes jutting from the side of one tank. "Whatever it is, it looks like it's hooked into the flow system directing the different chemicals up to the atmospheric processors."

Leaning closer for his own look, Faeyahr shook his head. "I have never seen anything like that before."

"That is because it is not Dokaalan in origin," Taurik, keeping his voice low. He looked around him before adding, "Commander La Forge, my readings show that this is an improvised device, constructed from components likely salvaged from a variety of sources. Its outer casing is composed of cast rodinium. So far as we have been able to determine, that element is not indigenous to this region of space."

"Rodinium?" La Forge repeated. He knew that the substance, one of the hardest known to Federation science, was used by many races, most notably the Cardassians, in the building of their space vessels. Early Federation deep space outposts, specifically those erected on and beneath the surface of asteroids, were constructed with exterior hull sections crafted from the robust material. Ordinarily, it would make perfect sense for the Dokaalan to employ the substance in the creation of their own facilities. The only problem with that idea, if La Forge's quick calculations were correct, was that the nearest source of the mineral was dozens of years away in a Dokaalan spacecraft traveling barely above the warp-speed threshold.

So, where had it come from?

"An alien power source?" he said, remembering not to speak too loudly. "But whose? And what the hell is it doing here?"

Taurik held up his tricorder. "According to my scans, the device is designed to introduce subtle variations into the chemical composition of the storage tank's contents. The alterations are very minimal, nearly invisible except to an intensive scan. It is unlikely that any of the testing equipment available to the Dokaalan engineers would detect these deviations."

"Sort of like the software modifications you detected earlier," La Forge said. "Are they related?"

"It is possible," Taurik replied. "The device does contain a form of transceiver assembly that would allow it to receive instructions from a remote source."

Faeyahr stepped closer, his expression a mix of confusion and disbelief. "Are you saying that someone else like you has been doing something to our work here without our knowing about it?"

Shaking his head, La Forge replied, "We're not sure, Faeyahr, but it's beginning to look that way." To Taurik he said, "But if someone else were here, we should have been able to pick up some sign of them before now." The *Enterprise* had detected no sign of other spacecraft anywhere in the system, even before the ambient radiation from the asteroid field had begun to interfere with the ship's sensors.

"Could they have arrived after you," Faeyahr offered, "and kept their presence a secret?"

"Unlikely," Taurik said. "If my readings are correct, then like the software modifications I found earlier, the changes being introduced into this storage container are designed to do so over a lengthy period. If the incidents are related, then what we have found is a scheme that has been in operation for quite some time."

This situation was becoming more unpleasant with each passing second, La Forge decided. "I think the tour's over," he said. "We need to report this to Captain Picard." Unfortunately, that would take time. With the *Enterprise* still orbiting the Dokaalan central habitat among the asteroids, communications would be hopelessly scrambled by the field's background radiation. That meant flying back to the ship, which of course entailed getting back to the airlock and retrieving their suit helmets before making the walk across the open space to the landing field where their shuttlecraft waited.

Piece of cake, right?

Wrong, he decided, as they approached the service corridor leading to the airlock and found two large Dokaalan workers waiting for them.

Unlike everyone else working in the complex, these two were dressed in what La Forge took to be uniforms, single-piece green garments that contrasted sharply with their pale blue skin. They wore no insignia to offer clues as to rank or position, but the highly polished black belt and boots, to say nothing of the cylindrical object in a holster at each Dokaalan's waist, told the chief engineer that these were a variety of law-enforcement official.

"Commander La Forge?" one of them asked. "Forgive the intrusion, but the minister of security has asked us to find you. There is a situation that he feels requires your attention."

"What is the meaning of this?" Faeyahr asked, displaying irritation rather than concern toward the two new arrivals. "Is something wrong?"

Obviously annoyed at the direct question, the other Dokaalan replied, "Minister Nidan will explain everything when we arrive. He has asked us to escort you to the secondary control center." He held up an open hand to indicate back the way the trio had come.

For the first time since arriving in this system, La Forge wished for a working phaser. "We'd love to stay and chat, but my captain's expecting us back on our ship. Has this been cleared through him?"

"He is being notified as we speak," the first Dokaalan said.

The sales pitch might have worked if his companion had not chosen that particular moment to place his hand on the holster attached to his belt. He realized his mistake, too, but not before catching La Forge looking at him. The chief engineer's eyes locked with the

Dokaalan's and in that instant, both men knew the ruse was over.

"Commander!"

La Forge heard Taurik's warning the heartbeat before the Dokaalan's hand cleared his holster with whatever weapon it contained. He caught a blur of motion as the Vulcan rushed forward, his right hand reaching to squeeze the juncture between the Dokaalan's neck and shoulder. The security officer's eyes rolled back in his head and he collapsed, falling like a broken doll to the floor.

To his credit, the man's companion did not freeze in reaction to Taurik's sudden preemptive strike. Instead he moved to his right and reached for his own holster, managing to clear the weapon and bring it up. La Forge saw light reflecting off metal before there was a flash of energy and something screamed past his shoulder. Then Taurik had closed the distance between himself and the Dokaalan, rendering him unconscious alongside his friend.

"What manner of weapon is this?" Faeyahr asked as he jumped forward, grabbing the security officers' fallen armaments. "Security officers carry stun batons, but they are a contact weapon. I have never seen anything like this before."

"Probably the same people who planted that power source on the storage tank," La Forge said as he took one of the weapons from Faeyahr, frowning as he got a closer look at it. Bulkier than a standard Starfleet-issue phaser, it was composed of a squat cylindrical body connected to a stubby handgrip. It had two power settings, clearly marked in Federation Standard: "Stun" and "Kill."

"I'll be damned." He held it up for Taurik to see. "This looks like a first-generation phase pistol."

Taurik nodded as he took the other weapon from their Dokaalan companion. "You would be correct, Commander. This model has not been in use by Starfleet personnel for approximately two hundred years, though they are occasionally available from various illegitimate sources."

"Yeah, but it's an easy bet that the Dokaalan don't do a lot of business with the Orion Syndicate or their black market," La Forge replied. "And besides, these are the first ones we've seen since we've been here. I'm guessing there's not a lot of them, and their owners probably want to keep them low-profile." It was yet more evidence that someone more advanced technologically than the Dokaalan was operating clandestinely here, but who? What would be the gain?

"Do not move!" another voice abruptly shouted from somewhere behind them before the whine of another phase pistol resonated in the corridor. It struck the wall near La Forge, and the engineer instinctively moved away from it as he backpedaled for the airlock.

"Commander," Taurik said as he took one of the confiscated weapons from Faeyahr. "They are bringing reinforcements. We must leave now." La Forge looked up to see more Dokaalan in green uniforms running down the long corridor in their direction.

"We have to warn the captain," he said as he pushed Faeyahr through the airlock door, then waited for Taurik to go in before following after them and sealing the hatch shut.

"None of them are wearing suits," Faeyahr said as he reached for his helmet and put it on, "but more security moderators may be waiting for us outside."

Dayton Ward & Kevin Dilmore

"I do not see any alternative," Taurik countered as he pulled the lever to open the airlock's outer door. To the trio's joint relief, the area outside the facility appeared to be deserted, for now at least.

How long is that going to last? La Forge wondered as they ran for the landing area.

Chapter Twenty-nine

WILL RIKER ENTERED the engineering section to find the entire staff gathered, more or less, near Data's diagnostic alcove. He watched for a moment as the officer in charge, Lieutenant Diix, attempted to assert his authority by giving instructions to the various engineers in the room.

Having listened to Lieutenant Diix's vague report only moments before, he could not help the anxiety he felt as approached the group. The Andorian engineer had requested Riker's presence down here, rather than providing a complete report over the ship's intercom. As he observed the scene in engineering for himself, he realized that Diix's suggestion had been the correct one.

Riker could hear the Andorian stammering a bit as he issued instructions, and he paused several times to review whatever notes he might have entered hastily into the padd he carried. He knew the young officer was juggling the responsibilities of presiding over the very heart of the starship along with the current problem he faced, and that strain was beginning to reveal itself.

Time to help the man out, he mused.

"What happened?" he asked in what he hoped was his best mentoring voice as he stepped closer to the diagnostic alcove and the immobile form harbored inside it. He listened with growing worry as Diix, the senior engineering officer on duty while Geordi La Forge was off the ship, provided a complete recounting of the moments up to and following Data's abrupt collapse.

"We thought it best to put him here for the time being, given his instructions," Diix explained, indicating the dormant android.

"*His* instructions?" Riker asked as he studied his friend's inanimate face.

"Yes, sir," Diix said. "After he collapsed, he spoke just long enough to tell us not to attempt any repairs and to notify Commander La Forge of the situation. We only moved him to the alcove so we could monitor his internal diagnostic protocols and try to make sense of whatever they might find."

Riker nodded, noticing a hesitation in Diix's words that he chalked up to the events of the last few minutes.

"I know you're doing what you can," he said, hoping his tone sounded more reassuring to Diix than it did to himself. He tried to remember that, just as the medical staff would spring to action were a biological crew member injured on duty, there was no doubt that the *Enterprise*'s complement of engineers were acting with similar concern and haste to aid Data in a time of need.

Yet, as he studied his friend's unmoving form, his face still frozen as if in the middle of a sentence, the first officer felt a knot of worry forming in his stomach. With his incomparable physical and cognitive skills, Data had proven himself time and again to be an invaluable member of the crew. Riker's first instinct as Data's friend was to order the engineers on hand to spare no effort in getting the android up and running again.

As the starship's acting commanding officer, however, he was well aware of the pressures facing the group of people surrounding him. Pulling all of them from their assigned duties to focus on Data posed a potentially worse problem than having the android out of commission. The engineering crew needed to stay on their toes in regard to every system on the ship, particularly given the hazardous environment of the Dokaalan system. Regardless of the value his friend represented to him and the rest of the crew, Riker was reminded of the hard fact that he could consider no one irreplaceable.

Data himself would tell you that.

"Ensign Veldon," he said as he turned to the Benzite engineer manning a portable field-use monitor that had been wheeled next to the alcove and linked to its emergency access ports, "what can you tell me?"

Veldon indicated the scrolling stream of computer data on the portable console's primary monitor. "The commander's internal diagnostics are indicating that his positronic pathways have suffered a cascading failure. It appears he is attempting to isolate the ones that are no longer operational."

"So part of his brain is still working?" Riker asked.

Nodding, the ensign replied, "Apparently, but there's no way yet to tell which part. He definitely has no control over his motor skills." The Benzite paused to enter a new string of commands. "He might be able to find his way around some of the affected pathways, but even if he does, we have no idea how long that might take."

Riker tried to translate for himself what the engineer was saying. "It almost sounds like he's had a stroke."

Veldon turned to look at him and offered an appreciative smile. "That is an accurate analogy, Commander."

Riker had seen Data absorb all manner of punishment over the years that required physical repairs, but he had always harbored the notion that whatever was broken on his friend could be identified and repaired. Each time there had been a malfunction in the past, they had found a way to help the android, and the first officer wanted to believe that would be the case now.

So why did he feel this situation was different? Was it because of the way Data's debilitating condition had been portrayed, as though he had fallen ill from a disease that had no known cure? Lieutenant Diix had described the cascading wave of circuitry and relay burnouts as though it had affected Data as an individual. This breakdown, if it could not be corrected, seemed to carry the potential to alter Data, even more so than his emotion chip's removal.

Seeing Data in this condition only served to demonstrate again that no matter the sophistication of his friend's software or the ways in which experience helped to shape him as an individual, he was still, at the end of it all, a machine.

Riker himself had almost proven that fact too well more than a decade ago during the landmark legal proceeding that established that Data was a sentient being and entitled to civil rights as recognized by the Federation. Ordered by Starfleet's Judge Advocate General to serve as prosecutor at the hearing, it had fallen to Riker to prove that Data was simply a machine and nothing more, a notion he had not believed then and certainly did not accept now. Despite that, it was a fight he had very nearly won, and also was one of several dark incidents from his life that he wanted to forget. He instead chose to retain the memory, along with the lessons he had learned about his friend that day.

Turning to Diix, Riker asked, "According to your report, you were the one of the closest people to him when this happened. Do you have any idea what might have caused it?"

"We are currently examining several theories, sir," the Andorian replied. "One is that he may have somehow been affected by the radiation surrounding us and generated by the asteroid field. I have ordered a check of all deflector-shield systems to insure that some form of radiation we might have previously failed to detect is not penetrating the hull."

Riker nodded approvingly. "I take it you haven't found anything on that front."

"No, sir, but at the very least it will rule out a cause if we find nothing. Our other ideas mainly revolve around Commander Data himself, and potential faults that might lie within his internal software. However, given his operational record I find that unlikely, too." He shook his head. "I am sorry, sir, but I have only limited expertise with Commander Data's construction and internal systems. Commander La Forge is rather protective of him when it comes to maintenance and diagnostic matters, you understand."

Riker could not help smiling at the image that evoked. "Only too well, Lieutenant. Commander La Forge is very much the mother hen when it comes to Data." Indicating the android with a nod of his head, he added, "Given that he's told you to let him run his own diagnostics, I think you're right. We'll let him work the problem himself until Geordi gets back."

The smile faded, however, as he regarded his friend once more. Though he had faith in the rest of the engineering staff when it came to the *Enterprise* itself, Diix was right when he said that no one else knew Data the way Geordi La Forge did.

When is he due back again? Not for a while yet, according to the last report he had received from Lieutenant Vale. Shaking his head, Riker dismissed the melancholy feelings. Until La Forge returned, Diix was the officer in charge, and he as well as the rest of his staff needed to be reassured of that fact.

Turning to face the engineers gathered nearby, the first officer said, "I want you to know that I appreciate your efforts to this point. I know it's difficult when you're working a problem that you've never faced before, but if Starfleet didn't have confidence in your abilities they wouldn't have posted you to the *Enterprise* in the first place. Don't hesitate to report anything you find to Lieutenant Diix, no matter how inconsequential it may seem." To the Andorian he added, "Keep me informed, Lieutenant."

"We'll make it so, Commander," Veldon said.

Leisner grimaced and slapped the Benzite on the shoulder. "Oh, very cute," he said, his tone teasing.

Riker grinned, allowing himself a moment to enjoy the light demeanor exuded by the collection of fresher faces at the stations surrounding him. Mixing up the duty rosters had turned out to be a good idea, he decided, and it seemed to be popular among the ranks; it broke up the routine.

What I wouldn't give for an hour of routine right now.

"Lieutenant," Riker said to Diix after a minute, "come with me, please." He noticed the Andorian's eyes widen a bit at the request, and they walked to the chief engineer's office in silence as the first officer mulled what he wanted to say. It certainly would do no good at all for him to add to Diix's anxiety level as long as he remained in charge.

Once inside the office and with the doors closed behind them, Riker gestured for Diix to take the seat behind the desk as he took one of the empty chairs in front of it. "How do you think things are going down here, Lieutenant?"

Obviously caught off guard by the question, Diix paused a bit before answering. "Given the circumstances, I think the crew is doing its best."

"And you? How are you doing?"

Riker saw the veneer of reserve crack just slightly as the Andorian appeared to weigh his thoughts. "To be very honest," he replied, "I have found all of this to be very unexpected."

"Don't let it shake you," Riker said, smiling. "I know this position is the first time you've been in command when things aren't going well."

Diix nodded. "That it is."

"If I might offer some advice?"

"Certainly," the younger officer said.

"You've got good people who know their jobs," Riker continued, trying not to sound condescending, "which takes a lot of the pressure off of you from the start. Just go about your business and let them go about theirs. They *want* to work for you, so let them."

Riker was well aware that his leadership methods were not as rigid or forceful as those demonstrated by more seasoned officers in the fleet. He had learned over the years that the reins of command rested more comfortably in his hands when they were loosened a bit, especially where his *Enterprise* shipmates were concerned.

With so many of the senior staff off the ship or, in the case of Data, wholly unavailable, it fell to junior officers like Diix to take charge of the less experienced personnel. It was trial by fire, so to speak, a time-tested approach used to determine who possessed those qualities both tangible and indefinable that conspired to make a true leader. Riker felt Diix possessed those qualities, and hoped that the encouragement he offered the younger officer might help him to relax and allow him to focus on his duties rather than on his own expectations of what a leader should be.

"Thank you, sir," Diix said. "I will bear that in mind."

As he watched Commander Riker depart the engineering section, presumably to resume his duties on the bridge, Kalsha waited until the human was safely out of earshot before allowing himself a sigh of relief. He had been able to field the first officer's questions easily enough, though he had to admit that part of the reason for that was the general, nonaccusatory nature of the human's queries.

Still, it had been a challenge. Riker smelled no better than any of the other humans, after all, a condition made worse by the confined space of the chief engineer's office.

Kalsha had been able to imbue enough truth when deception was required that it made telling the lies easier. It was a trick he had learned long ago during his earliest days as a covert operative, and the human Riker had not been any the wiser. He had asked his questions and given his motivational speeches without any idea that he had been staring into the face of the enemy.

While he had prepared himself for a more intensive questioning session as Riker demanded answers for what had happened to the android and who or what might be responsible, Kalsha was not surprised that the first officer did not begin voicing allegations about anyone who might be a culprit for the damage done to Data. After all, the actuation servo used to deactivate the android had gone undetected by anyone in the engineering section. There was nothing to suggest that anything untoward had occurred here.

At least, not yet.

With the android safely housed in his alcove, there was no way Kalsha could approach him or make another attempt to deactivate him permanently without the risk of drawing attention.

He was still angry with himself over his having miscalculated the requirements of the android's shutdown protocol. The possibility existed that Data would reactivate and perhaps even devise a solution to repair itself or offer information to the engineers directing them toward a course of action. What if its internal sensors had detected or even recorded the pulse Kalsha had sent? It would provide the crew with the first clue that something sinister might be happening in their midst.

Kalsha could not dwell on that. The only thing for him to do was carry on in his persona of Lieutenant Diix and continue with his mission, only now he would have to move faster in the event the engineers did manage to make some progress in their investigation. He would have to be more careful from this point on, of course. If another suspicious act were to occur before he could complete his primary task and escape the ship, the crew would certainly believe they were under some form of attack and would enact appropriate countermeasures. Even on a ship this size and with his mimicking abilities, Kalsha had no illusions that he could evade their security forces for any prolonged period.

Relax, he tried to assure himself. *By the time that happens, it will be too late.*

He reached for the padd on his desk, the one he had been using to further his disguise as just another *Enterprise* engineer, when a new thought suddenly gave him pause.

The private talk with Commander Riker had been interesting, to say the least, and Kalsha could not help the fleeting feeling of admiration he felt for the human, despite the odor that seemed to be an unavoidable trait of his species. It was obvious from his demeanor that Riker was a benevolent leader who cared a great deal for those under his command. In all his own experience as a soldier and later a spy, Kalsha had never enjoyed the guidance of someone so devoted to his duties as well as to those who served under him.

It was a stark contrast from the methods of intimidation and brutality routinely practiced by superiors he had known during his career. Kalsha could not help but wonder if the performance and morale of his own military might have benefited from the effects of more leaders like the human Riker. Such qualities might well have made the difference during the last war.

Enough, he scolded himself, forcing the wayward thoughts from his mind and reminding himself to return his focus to the task at hand. Still, as he retrieved his padd and made his way from the office, intent on carrying out his mission, Kalsha allowed himself one last brief moment of resignation.

It would almost be a shame, he decided, when Riker died along with the rest of the ship's crew.

Chapter Thirty

WHEN HE SAW no sign of activity near the shuttlecraft, La Forge knew that something was up.

"It doesn't make any sense that they wouldn't have somebody waiting for us," he said as he ran, his breath becoming labored with the effort of jogging in the environment suit. "Where are they?"

Running alongside him and to his right, Taurik replied, "Perhaps the incident inside the complex unfolded too rapidly for whoever is trying to detain us. They may not have expected resistance."

La Forge shook his head. "Maybe, but I'm betting that they're also trying to keep this low-key." Indicating Faeyahr, he added, "Whoever's playing around behind the scenes here, they're doing it without the knowledge of at least some of the Dokaalan. They may be trying to keep their presence a secret. If that's the case, then they'll be looking to catch us quickly and quietly. That might give us a bit of an advantage, at least until we get off the planet."

Behind him, Faeyahr asked, "Why would someone want to interfere with what we are doing here? What do we have that anyone could want?" La Forge noted that the Dokaalan's breathing was even heavier than his own. Despite being acclimated to the heavier gravity on the planet's surface, Faeyahr was probably not accustomed to this type of exertion.

"That's what we're hoping to find out," the chief engineer said, "but to do that we're going to need help. That's why we need to get back to the *Enterprise.*"

He heard the telltale beep of Taurik's tricorder and turned to see the Vulcan slowing to a walk in order to study the device. Then the junior engineer pointed toward another storage building to their right.

"Three life-forms have just emerged from the far side of that structure," he reported. "They are armed, two with older-model Klingon disruptors and one with what appears to be a Bajoran phaser."

"Interesting mix," La Forge said. Whoever they were dealing with, he theorized, they used whatever materials and weapons they could get their hands on. Was all of this the work of some type of rogue group? Were they dealing with a band of pirates or profiteers manipulating the Dokaalan's situation for their own benefit?

He knew they had only seconds before the new arrivals saw the trio running for the shuttlecraft. Studying the nearby structure with his ocular implants, he determined that it was nearly one hundred meters away. How fast could their pursuers cover that distance? Were they accurate marksmen with their eclectic collection of weaponry?

There was only one way to find out.

"Keep moving," he said, taking off toward the shuttle-craft with a renewed energy. As he ran, he tapped his suit's communicator. "La Forge to shuttlecraft *Ballard.* Initiate prelaunch sequence."

"Acknowledged," replied the feminine voice of the shuttle's onboard computer.

The first shot came just as he reached for the panel set into the small vessel's hull to open its rear hatch. Orange energy struck the ground near his feet and he turned to see three figures heading toward them, eighty meters away but closing the distance rapidly even while dressed in bulky environment suits similar to Faeyahr's.

"Inside!" he yelled. "Taurik, get us ready for take off."

As Taurik and Faeyahr scrambled aboard the shuttle-craft, La Forge sighted down the length of his phase pistol at one of their pursuers and fired. The beam lanced forward from the weapon and struck the figure in the chest but he continued forward, the weapon having had no noticeable effect.

Uh-oh.

Backing into the *Ballard* and slapping the door control, La Forge fired the weapon again and achieved the same result. The Dokaalan kept running as if hit by nothing at all.

"Hang on, Commander," he heard Taurik say from the shuttle's cockpit. "I am initiating liftoff."

La Forge fell onto one of the passenger couches as the tiny vessel's engines flared to life and he felt the shuttle move beneath his feet. He could tell by the craft's movements that Taurik was wasting no time with niceties, pushing the *Ballard* to maximum thrust the moment they left the ground. The engineer was pushed into his chair as the ship banked sharply and accelerated, the view through the forward canopy that of clouds rushing past as the shuttle headed straight up and away from the planet's surface.

"Go to full impulse power as soon as we're clear of the atmosphere," he said a moment later as the craft leveled off and he could rise from his chair. Removing his SEWG helmet, he made his way forward to the cockpit and dropped into the copilot's seat. "Our friends down there are sure to have buddies of their own somewhere. Any signs of pursuit?"

"Affirmative," Taurik replied immediately, pointing to the console set between the two pilot seats and indicating the series of displays there, which showed data generated by the shuttle's array of external sensors. "Five small vessels are on separate intercept courses near the outer boundary of the asteroid field."

"Skiffs, most likely," Faeyahr said, rising from his own chair to lean over La Forge's shoulder.

Taurik nodded. "You are correct. Sensor readings show that the vessels are similar to the craft you piloted to the *Enterprise* earlier today."

"Any weapons?" La Forge asked. He knew that the Dokaalan ships were very similar to Starfleet workpods, but it did not mean that their mysterious pursuers had not modified the vessels in some way for their own needs.

"None that our sensors have detected," Taurik replied. "They are equipped with the same array of maneuvering arms and laser drill emitters, but that is all."

Frowning, La Forge shook his head. "Well, not really. Those things are fast, and their pilots are probably better at maneuvering through those asteroids than we are. We're not home free just yet."

"And they may have additional ships waiting for us within the asteroid field," Taurik added. "Sensors are unable to penetrate the radiation to any significant degree."

Wonderful, La Forge thought, remembering the care he and Taurik had been forced to exercise when traveling to Ijuuka from the *Enterprise* earlier in the day. They would have to slow their speed once they entered the field itself, nullifying their lone advantage against their pursuers. The *Ballard* possessed no weapons of its own, and they would be flying with compromised instrumentation as well.

"Somebody doesn't want us to get back to the ship, all right," he said. Things were unfolding much too rapidly for this to be the work of mere pirates or rogues, La Forge decided. Whoever they were, they were using technology more advanced than that available to the Dokaalan, and they were working very hard to capture the Starfleet engineers. Obviously, he and Taurik had uncovered something that someone wanted to keep quiet. Though it seemed that the majority of the Dokaalan were oblivious of the skullduggery taking place in their midst, La Forge wondered how many might actually be involved in this affair. Who could be trusted?

"Taurik," he said as he studied the sensor images that showed the current position, course, and speed of their pursuers, "can you plot an evasive course?"

"The approach vectors of the pursuing ships are such that it is likely we will encounter at least one of the ships if we continue to travel in the general direction of the *Enterprise*," the Vulcan replied. "I can plot a course that will take us away from the ship, but we would risk encountering other vessels that we have not yet detected."

"In other words, better the devil you know." Checking his own console, La Forge sighed in resignation. "I'd rather keep heading for the ship. If we can get close enough, their sensors might be able to detect us if we run into trouble." Looking over his shoulder, he said to Faeyahr, "You need to get back in your seat. This is liable to get a bit bumpy before it's over."

At La Forge's prompting, Taurik guided the *Ballard* into the asteroid field, retarding the shuttlecraft's speed as the first of the enormous masses of rock slipped past the edges of the viewport. Given their proximity to some of the asteroids, La Forge could not even order the use of the ship's deflector shields as a defense against collision, lest the shields interfere with the shuttle's maneuvering ability.

He forced himself to relax his clenched jaw.

"Sensor effectiveness is down sixty-eight percent," Taurik reported. "I have lost track of three vessels. One of the remaining two is maneuvering in behind us while the other is approaching from the port side forward. Both ships are closing."

"Trying to pinch us," La Forge said. He considered increasing their speed but almost as quickly dismissed the idea. They were already traveling as fast as he dared and while he considered himself a more than capable shuttlecraft pilot, he knew that neither he nor Taurik could navigate the asteroid field with the same audacity as their pursuers.

Movement in the corner of his eye made him turn to see a Dokaalan skiff coming around one of the larger asteroids, accelerating as it cleared the massive rock. Even from this distance the chief engineer could see through the two-person craft's canopy and into its cockpit, where only one of its pilot seats appeared to be occupied.

Then he felt the shuttlecraft bank to starboard as Taurik attempted to evade the approaching vessel. Outside, the skiff flashed in the viewport, so close that La Forge could see the join lines between hull plates before it passed by, disappearing somewhere behind them.

An alarm suddenly blared in the shuttle's small cabin, followed by the voice of the computer. *"Warning. Incoming vessel on collision course. All hands brace for impact."*

"Behind us," Taurik called out just before the entire shuttle shuddered around them. La Forge felt them shoved off course even as the Vulcan fought to retain control of the craft.

"Is he crazy?" La Forge asked, to no one in particular.

Next to him, Taurik nodded. "Such aggressive behavior would seem to indicate that they are willing to go to great lengths to secure our capture."

"But ramming us?" Faeyahr said, the higher pitch in his voice a strong indicator of the Dokaalan's anxiety. "What do they gain from that?"

"It keeps us from reporting what we've found," La Forge replied. "That might be good enough for them if they can't catch us." He checked the damage-control monitor on the console near his left hand. "Minimal buckling to the aft hull. I don't read any damage to the skiff, though."

Maybe shields wouldn't be such a bad idea after all, he mused. His hand moved toward the controls that would activate the *Ballard's* deflector shields. The motion was stayed as Taurik guided the shuttlecraft close enough to an asteroid perhaps half the size of the *Enter-*

prise that the chief engineer thought he might actually be able to reach out and touch the rock's craggy surface. It was a maneuver that would have been impossible had the shields been activated.

"Nice flying, Taurik," he commented, though the Vulcan said nothing, his attention focused instead on his controls.

Faeyahr said, "The skiffs are heavily plated for protection in external mining sites. They can withstand serious collisions, even at these speeds."

The shuttle trembled again, but the impact was not as severe this time. *"Warning,"* the computer said, *"outer hull breach in aft section."*

"They are firing at us with their laser drill," Taurik said. He tapped new commands to his console and the *Ballard* banked again, this time to port as the Vulcan guided the ship around a larger asteroid. "It was only a glancing blow, but a well-aimed shot might be able to penetrate the hull."

"Well, let's make sure we don't give them that shot," La Forge replied. He looked over his shoulder to Faeyahr. "Anything else about those ships you can tell us?"

The Dokaalan nodded. "They are fast and maneuverable, but their engines are not that powerful. We tend to avoid approaching the larger asteroids at faster speeds because their gravitational pull can be dangerous at close range. Your ship's engines are stronger, so you may not have to worry about such things."

"It's not like we can ignore it, but it might be something we can use if things get tight." Returning his attention to his console, he checked the sensor display, shifting the information being transmitted by the ship's scanners until he found what he was looking for. "Taurik, maneuver us in close to that big asteroid at bearing ninety-seven mark four."

"Aye, sir," the Vulcan replied, his fingers entering the necessary commands. Outside the shuttle's viewport, La Forge saw the asteroid he had selected, an immense hunk of rock perhaps half the size of a small moon.

The computer's proximity alert sounded once more just before another bump rattled the inside of the shuttle-craft. La Forge was nearly thrown from his seat as Taurik struggled to keep the vessel on course. Another alarm blared in the cabin and a status indicator on the damage control monitor flared crimson.

"I'm getting tired of being a punching bag," the chief engineer muttered.

"We are venting drive plasma from the starboard nacelle," Taurik said. "I have to shut it down."

La Forge nodded. Leaving the drive plasma to vent uncontrolled risked its ignition by the shuttle's engine, which would almost certainly result in an explosion large enough to destroy the ship altogether.

He shook his head in frustration. "A single phaser bank would be more than enough to keep them off our back."

"Perhaps it is an enhancement we can investigate upon our return to the *Enterprise,*" Taurik offered. Were it not for their present circumstances, La Forge might have laughed at the Vulcan's deadpan reply.

Suddenly, inspiration struck.

"Ease our speed back," he said. "Let them catch up." Though he did not look up from his station, he could feel stares from both Taurik and Faeyahr.

"Closer?" Faeyahr repeated. "Commander La Forge, what are you doing?"

"I've got an idea," La Forge said, his fingers moving over his console.

The results of his actions were immediately noticeable to Taurik. "Commander, you have instructed the computer to open our port engine coolant interlock. I submit that this is not the best time to purge our plasma exhaust."

"Let them get closer," La Forge said, his attention focused on his console's status readings. "This is going to get a little dicey." Looking to Taurik, he asked, "You ever hear of the Kolvoord Starburst maneuver?"

"I have," Taurik replied. "It is an intricate aerobatic maneuver involving five ships traveling in tight formation, then crisscrossing each other's path at close range and igniting their drive plasma. The resulting visual effect is said to be quite stimulating. Is it your intention to vent and ignite our drive plasma in a similar manner?"

La Forge nodded. "Thank our friends for shooting up the starboard engine and giving me the idea." Of course, he did not need to say that it was a dangerous maneuver, almost as likely to flash back and destroy the shuttle itself as it was to ignite the plasma trail he was about to create.

Of course, Taurik held no such misgivings.

"Commander," Taurik said, "Starfleet Academy banned cadets from attempting the maneuver more than a century ago due to the extreme risks involved."

"I know all about the risks," La Forge replied. The maneuver had been attempted illegally by five Academy cadets a decade ago, one of them Wesley Crusher, and had resulted in the death of one of the participants.

So let's hope I have better luck, he thought grimly.

Taurik pointed to the sensor display. "Ship approaching aft, range two kilometers and closing."

"Hang on," La Forge said, watching the monitor and waiting until the gap separating the *Ballard* from the incoming skiff was less than a kilometer before his finger stabbed a control on his console.

The interior bulkheads vibrated as the drive plasma vented and made contact with the superhot engine exhaust. In his mind's eye he saw the ignited plasma trail flared out behind the shuttlecraft, likely washing over the forward surface of their pursuer's ship.

Then the ship rocked violently to starboard and alarms blared inside the cabin as consoles throughout the shuttle's interior blinked crazily or went dark altogether. Taurik was thrown to the deck but La Forge managed to stay in his chair, and found himself scrambling to keep the ship from careening out of control.

"What's happening?" Faeyahr cried out.

"We've lost the port engine," the chief engineer replied, pinned into his chair as he fought to reach his console. "Inertial dampeners are out."

Regaining his seat, Taurik reported, "Attitude control is offline, Commander. I am having difficulty maintaining our course."

"Restart the starboard engine," La Forge ordered. "It's all we've got left." Glancing briefly at the sensor display, he added, "That blast must have damaged the other ship, too. It looks like they're drifting."

"They may be the more fortunate," Taurik said. "Helm control is becoming more difficult, and the starboard engine has lost too much plasma. It will not restart."

This is definitely not good, La Forge thought as he studied the status monitors. Systems all over the ship had been affected by the plasma explosion, and the trouble was mounting with each passing second.

"Commander!" he heard Faeyahr yell out from behind him and the chief engineer looked up to see the immense asteroid looming in the viewport.

"Taurik!" he shouted. "We need thruster control now!"

"I am trying, sir," the Vulcan replied. "The controls are sluggish."

Even from this distance, La Forge he could make out the rock's craggy features, towering peaks contrasting sharply with deep canyons cloaked in shadow. A ship the size of their shuttlecraft could fall into one of the asteroid's numerous chasms and never be found.

And they were heading straight for it.

Chapter Thirty-one

"HE'S STILL RUNNING his own internal diagnostics, sir," Commander Riker's voice said through Picard's combadge. *"So far, he hasn't said anything else since it happened."*

Standing in the Zahanzei Council's meeting chambers on the Dokaalan central habitat, Picard frowned as he listened to his first officer's report. "And a cause still hasn't been found?"

"No, sir. The engineering staff is working on it, but they don't know if the problem is with Data himself or if it's the result of an external source. They'll know more when Data's diagnostics are complete."

In the years since Picard had known him, Data had proven to be a startlingly robust individual, a pinnacle of cybernetic engineering as envisioned by his creator, Dr. Noonien Soong. Though he had suffered injury on several occasions, those instances were almost always caused by the influence of an outside element working against him.

Therefore, to hear about his sudden incapacitation was troubling to say the least.

"While I have full confidence in the engineering staff," Picard said, "no one knows Data's systems like Geordi. Has there been any word from him?"

"Not yet, sir," Riker replied, *"but communication between here and Ijuuka is compromised due to the radiation field, and he's not supposed to be back for a few hours."*

The captain sighed in resignation. "Keep me informed, Number One. Picard out." With the connection severed, he was once again reminded that there were occasions where he could only stand by and wait for others to do their jobs, and that this was one of them.

Such is the double-edged sword of command.

For a brief moment Picard felt a twinge of apprehension. He considered himself a self-reliant individual unafraid to make even the most difficult decisions required of his position, but as a leader he had long ago learned the virtue of accepting and acting on the counsel of the officers under his command. It was therefore disconcerting when one or more of his most trusted advisors was unavailable to him, an admission he had not made even to Deanna Troi during their private conversations.

Logic quickly reasserted itself, however. La Forge was off the ship carrying out Picard's orders and would be back in short order. Once apprised about Data, the chief engineer would expend all energy and resources to determine a cause and a solution for his friend's condition.

So, why did Picard still feel uneasy?

"Captain?" Troi prompted as she stepped closer, having stood to the side as Picard received Riker's report.

Shaking his head, he said, "I don't like the timing of

this, Counselor. It's decidedly convenient given the circumstances." He glanced over his shoulder to where Hjatyn and other members of the council stood in a circle talking amongst themselves. "For the sake of appearances, however, I think it best that we not discuss this in front of the others." If something odd was going on, he did not want to alert anyone to the idea that he might be suspicious.

Troi replied, "I understand, sir."

"Have you detected anything else from any of the council members worth noting?"

"Nothing more than I already reported, sir," the counselor said. "The security minister, Nidan, maintains a suspicious attitude, but I attribute that to the nature of his responsibilities. Hjatyn has been most forthcoming regardless of the questions I've asked, but I still sense caution when he answers even though he does a remarkable job of concealing it. Other members of the council continue to demonstrate a growing sense of comfort and trust at our presence." Frowning, she added, "And there are those whose enthusiasm seems to have dampened somewhat since our arrival."

"How so?" Picard asked.

Pausing a moment before replying, Troi shrugged. "It's almost as though one or two of the council members have had a change of heart, or perhaps they've begun to doubt their original feelings about us. Minister Creij, for example. At our first meeting, she was among the most vocal of our supporters, but now I sense hesitation when she talks to me."

"Is it possible," Picard said, "that she feels our presence here might somehow be threatening to her work?"

They had quickly learned that the Dokaalan were a proud people, steadfastly determined to see the transformation of Ijuuka into their new home through their own efforts. Though Minister Creij had welcomed any suggestions by the *Enterprise* crew that might accelerate the terraforming process, had she done so simply for the sake of politeness? Did she privately harbor feelings of resentment and fear at being upstaged by people with advanced technology?

Troi replied, "I don't know, sir, but my instincts tell me that's not the reason."

The captain nodded. "Well then, we should continue as we have and see where it takes us." It was a weak and undesirable plan, but given the circumstances it was the only course of action open to him.

For now, anyway.

Their attention was drawn to a door opening at the far end of the council chambers, allowing Dr. Crusher to enter. Picard knew that the physician had transferred her remaining Dokaalan patients, left over from the mining outpost rescue operation, to the central habitat from the *Enterprise* several hours earlier. According to her last report, she had been monitoring their condition since then, and he could see by the expression on her face that she too still seemed to be troubled.

"Doctor?" he prompted as she approached them.

Crusher attempted to affect a smile, but it was forced and she seemed to realize it as she exhaled in apparent frustration. "I've just spent the last three hours in their medical center with my patients. Three hours ago most of their major internal organs were on the verge of collapse, and there was nothing I could do to stop it. Now their condition is improving with every minute, and I didn't do a damn thing to cause it."

"You're still learning about Dokaalan medicine, Beverly," Troi offered. "Surely their doctors know how best to treat their own people, even though you've done wonderfully in such a short time."

Shaking her head, Crusher replied, "I could accept that if it were the case, but their doctors didn't do anything either. Besides, it wasn't just the five miners we rescued. One of their doctors was on the *Enterprise* with me, and he began to present the same symptoms as the others." Waving her hand to indicate their surroundings, she added, "Something here is affecting their physiology, something that causes a negative reaction when its influence is removed, and I think I've got an idea what."

"The radiation," Picard said.

"Exactly," the doctor replied. "It was like what happens to addicts suffering withdrawal symptoms when whatever substance causing the addiction is removed."

Picard nodded. "On the ship and with the shields up, the radiation would be blocked, at least enough to deprive the Dokaalan of whatever benefits they receive from the radiation." It was an interesting notion, he conceded. "Could it be a by-product of their having lived out here all these years? Their physiology would have had to acclimate to the environment, but in only a few hundred years?"

"It's not out of the question, Captain," Troi said. "Remember the colonists on Tau Cygna V?"

It took Picard a moment of sifting through his memory to recall the *Enterprise*'s mission to that planet, where a Federation colony ship, the *S.S. Artemis,* had ended up. The mission had arisen after the Sheliak, a reclusive race with whom the Federation had a strained relationship for more than a century, exercised their rights as owners of Tau Cygna V and demanded the colonists leave or face extermination. Picard had managed to resolve the dispute between the Sheliak and the colonists, but only after a great deal of assistance from Data.

"Their descendants eventually adapted to the hyperonic radiation on that planet," Troi continued. "It's entirely possible that something similar has happened here."

Crusher replied, "I agree. I'll need time to set up some new tests to be sure, but it would explain their reaction both here and on the ship."

"Proceed as you think best, Doctor," Picard said. Shaking his head, he added, "Well, this will certainly make my next report to Admiral Nechayev more interesting." He had dispatched a status report the previous evening, transmitting it along with his log entries back to Starfleet Command via subspace. With the background radiation still presenting an obstacle to communications, Data had programmed an unmanned probe to navigate out of the asteroid field and to the perimeter of the Dokaalan system in order to transmit the information.

No doubt that report already was stirring up controversy in the hallways of power back on Earth, and Picard was reasonably sure that Alynna Nechayev was enjoying every minute of it. It was an image that almost made the captain smile.

But not for long.

An earsplitting klaxon suddenly blared, echoing in through the council chambers and nearly making Picard jump out of his skin. "What is that?" he asked.

"It is an emergency alert signal," Hjatyn said as he broke from the circle of other council members, shuffling as quickly as his aged body would carry him toward the control room Picard and his people had visited earlier. The captain followed after with Troi and Crusher behind him.

The command center was a rush of activity, with Dokaalan technicians scrambling from console to console and warning lights flashing for attention on a number of workstations around the room. Though the alarm was not sounding in here, Picard's ears were still assaulted by bursts of static washing over someone yelling out in a panicked voice.

"What is it?" Hjatyn asked as he entered the room.

Turning from where he watched over the shoulder of a technician manning one computer console, Nidan replied, "Mining Station Twelve is reporting an explosion. We are still trying to gather information, First Minister."

At that moment, Picard's combadge chirped for attention and Riker's voice called out, *"Riker to Captain Picard."*

"Picard here. Go ahead, Number One."

"Sir, we're picking up a massive detonation on one of the nearby mining outposts," Riker said as he sat in the captain's chair on the bridge of the *Enterprise.* "Sensor scans are still fuzzy, but it was large enough to detect even through the interference."

"Are you able to ascertain the extent of the damage?" Picard asked.

Rising from the center seat, Riker replied, "No sir, we'd have to get closer for that. Request permission to render assistance."

"Absolutely," the captain said. *"Set a course for the outpost immediately. We'll catch up in the shuttle-craft."*

Riker nodded to Kell Perim at the conn. "Prepare to get under way, Lieutenant." He saw the look of uncertainty in Perim's eyes, but the Trill officer said nothing as she turned back to her station and began entering the necessary instructions to her console.

"Number One," Picard's voice said over the intercom, *"Minister Hjatyn has told me that there are more than eight hundred people on the outpost, and reports are coming in that several areas have experienced explosive decompression. Their life-support systems appear to have sustained damage as well. The Dokaalan are dispatching rescue ships, but they won't be able to get there as quickly as the* Enterprise. *Time is of the essence, Will."*

"We're on it, Captain. Stand by," Riker said as he stepped toward the conn and ops stations and laid a hand on Perim's shoulder. "Kell, you sure you can handle this? If you think you need help, just say the word."

There was no mistaking the nervousness on the lieutenant's face even as she nodded in response. "I think so, Commander. I'm no Data, but I'll have the computer helping me."

While she was of course no match for Data's superior reflexes and experience, Perim was an exceptional pilot in her own right. Riker had faith in her ability to navigate the *Enterprise* through the asteroid field, knowing she would call for assistance if she felt it was warranted.

Smiling, Riker patted her shoulder. "You'll do fine," he said before turning away from the forward bridge stations. "We're getting under way now, Captain."

"Good," Picard replied. *"We'll be right behind you."*

"We'll leave a light on for you, sir," the first officer said, smiling to himself as he settled once more into the command chair. "Helm, move us out," he said.

Perim nodded. "Aye, sir."

On the main viewer, the colossal asteroid that was home to the Dokaalan's central habitat drifted beyond the left edge of the screen as the *Enterprise* turned on its axis to align itself with its new heading. Seconds later, the shift was over and the ship began to move forward.

"Lieutenant Vale," he said, "contact sickbay and notify Dr. Tropp to prepare triage measures, just like last time. Cargo holds, shuttlebays, whatever he needs. Let him know that Dr. Crusher will be in contact shortly with more instructions, but for now he's in charge."

"Aye, sir," Vale replied.

All around Riker, members of the crew set to their various tasks. Left with nothing do to except sit quietly and wait for the situation to evolve, he once again noted the ratio of alpha-shift crew members to those brought on duty as replacements for officers otherwise unavailable for one reason or another.

While he knew that every member of the crew was qualified to carry out his or her responsibilities, Riker could not deny the unease he felt at not having his most trusted colleagues by his side. He glanced at the chair to his left, the one normally occupied by Deanna Troi and which now of course was conspicuously empty.

Watching Perim's fingers move over her console, Riker tried to conjure some of the confidence he hoped to have given her for himself. Despite her own skills, it was hard not to think of the sometimes harrowing passage Data had provided during the *Enterprise*'s first journey through the asteroid field. Though the android had shown no signs of strain or unease during that earlier crossing, Riker had to believe that it had been a trying experience even for his friend's extraordinary talents.

"Number One," Picard said, interrupting his thoughts. *"We've received new information from the outpost. They believe the explosion wasn't an accident."*

A sudden chill ran down Riker's spine at the report. Someone had deliberately caused such catastrophic damage, possibly resulting in the deaths of hundreds of people? There had been discussions about those among the Dokaalan opposed to the terraforming process and how some had taken to sabotage, but on this scale? If such people were indeed operating in the shadows among the Dokaalan, what else were they capable of doing? Did they pose a threat to the *Enterprise* and if so, would they attempt to take action against the ship as he and the crew tried to render assistance to the outpost victims?

There's nothing you can do about that now, he admonished himself. *Shut up and play the cards you're dealt.*

"Understood, sir," he said simply. What else was there to say? It did not matter to the people on the outpost that there might be others seeking to harm him and the crew. It was not relevant to those same people currently in distress that Data was not here, or that several of the people he trusted most were off ship. The people on that asteroid could not wait for circumstances to be ideal before a rescue was attempted. They were in trouble, they were dying, and they needed help.

Right now.

About the Authors

DAYTON WARD has been a fan of *Star Trek* since conception (his, not the show's). After serving for eleven years in the U.S. Marine Corps, he discovered the private sector and the piles of cash to be made there as a software engineer. He got his start in professional writing by having stories selected for each of Pocket Books' first three *Star Trek: Strange New Worlds* writing contests. In addition to his various writing projects with Kevin Dilmore, Dayton is the author of the *Star Trek* novel *In the Name of Honor* and the science fiction novel *The Last World War.* Though he currently lives in Kansas City with his wife, Michi, Dayton is a Florida native and still maintains a torrid long-distance romance with his beloved Tampa Bay Buccaneers. Readers interested in contacting Dayton or learning more about his writing are encouraged to venture to his Internet cobweb collection at ***http://www.daytonward.com.***

After 15 years as a newspaper reporter and editor, **KEVIN DILMORE** turned his full attention to his free-lance writing career in 2003. Since 1997, he has been a contributing writer to *Star Trek Communicator,* writing news stories and personality profiles for the bimonthly publication of the Official *Star Trek* Fan Club. Look for

About the Authors

Kevin's interviews with some of *Star Trek*'s most popular authors in volumes of the *Star Trek* Signature Editions. On the fictional side of things, his story "The Road to Edos" was published last year in the *Star Trek: New Frontier* anthology *No Limits*. With Dayton Ward, he has also written a story for the anthology *Star Trek: Tales of the Dominion War* and seven installments of the continuing e-book series *Star Trek: S.C.E.*—with more to come. A graduate of the University of Kansas, Kevin lives in Prairie Village, Kansas, with his wife, Michelle, and their three daughters.

The saga continues in May 2004 with

STAR TREK®
A TIME TO HARVEST

by
Dayton Ward & Kevin Dilmore

Turn the page for an electrifying
preview of *A Time to Harvest.* . . .

Will Riker's stomach lurched as the *Enterprise* moved around yet another large asteroid, rolling to port and allowing the massive hunk of rock to slip past.

"Sorry about that, sir," Lieutenant Kell Perim called over her shoulder from where she sat at the ops console. Her fingers moved with the grace of a concert pianist's as she entered commands to her console, which were in turn translated into instructions for the ship to maneuver through the Dokaalan asteroid field. "This last stretch is going to be a little rough."

Riker almost laughed out loud at the lieutenant's comment. The Trill officer had worked at the same pace since leaving the Dokaalan central habitat for the now-crippled Mining Station Twelve. Riker wondered when she might tire—and whether that might happen before they reached their destination. For the third time in an hour, he felt compelled, pulled almost as if by tractor beam, to take the helm and fly the ship himself, but knew better than to act on that impulse. His place was the one he currently occupied—the center seat, in command of this mission, and trusting the people around him to do their jobs.

"Now you tell me." He tried to let a bit of his natural joviality lace his words, just enough to reassure Perim of his confidence in her skillful navigation through the asteroid field. Like everyone else on the ship and particularly those with a prime vantage point on the bridge, he knew that any travel through the seemingly endless expanse of tumbling asteroids drifting between them and hundreds of injured—most likely dying—Dokaalan was fraught with hazards at even the slowest speeds.

That danger was magnified as the *Enterprise* pushed forward as fast as Perim dared, responding with all due haste to a call for help sent from one of the Dokaalan mining outposts. Captain Picard had been with First Minister Hjatyn and other members of the Dokaalan leadership caste when the call came, and had dispatched the ship to respond to the outpost's plea as quickly as possible while he, Dr. Crusher, and Counselor Troi caught up to them in their shuttlecraft.

Now the lives of more than eight hundred people were hanging on the ability of Commander Riker to move the *Enterprise* through this asteroid field, and complicating the matter even more was the information that Picard had shared with him: that the explosion at the mining outpost might have been an act of sabotage. Was someone, some group of Dokaalan, trying to instill terror in the rest of the community? Were they extremists pursuing some as yet unknown agenda and hoping to extract a measure of conciliation from the Dokaalan leadership? If so, how far were they willing to go for their cause? Was the *Enterprise* in danger?

That this was the second such rescue mission they had mounted since arriving in the system was also a point not lost on Riker. The first instance had possessed its share of obstacles, but the *Enterprise* crew had successfully rescued all but a small number of Dokaalan miners from their damaged outpost. A sour taste still filled the first officer's mouth at the thought of those they had failed to save, a feeling that had not lessened no matter how much he had tried to dwell on the hundreds of victims that had been rescued.

We'll just have to do better this time, won't we?

Further complicating things for Riker was a short-handed command staff to aid him through the rough spots. As well as not being on board to oversee the chaotic triage operation that was sure to come once the ship reached the outpost, Geordi La Forge was still off the ship, examining the Dokaalan's terraforming operation on Ijuuka, and Data had, for reasons unknown, fallen victim to some sort of as yet unexplained breakdown. Engineering had been attempting to diagnose the cause of the android's incapacitation, but that effort was now sidelined as they worked to prepare the ship for the upcoming strain on its systems and resources.

Additionally, and though he would not admit it to anyone else, Will Riker also missed the comforting presence of Deanna Troi. Not only did she provide him with his own emotional anchor, but her empathic abilities were an unmatched gauge for the mental well-being of the crew. At a time like this, such insight would be invaluable.

Well, he reminded himself, *you don't have it, so you're just going to have to get by without it.*

"I'm picking up fluctuations in the inertial dampers," Perim said, not taking her eyes from her console. "I think the background radiation must be affecting them somehow."

Not for the first time, Riker quietly cursed the asteroid field and its troublesome varieties of ambient radiation, which had plagued the *Enterprise* since it arrived here. Several of the ship's systems—transporters, tractor beams, sensors, and now the inertial dampers, to name but a few—had been disrupted by the constant assault of the potentially deadly radiation permeating the region.

Commander La Forge and the engineering staff had been able to tune the vessel's deflector shields to screen out the harmful rays, but the continuous need to keep the shields activated was beginning to take its toll on systems all over the ship. The shields also required repeated retuning in order to deal with varying levels of radiation as the *Enterprise* moved through the asteroid field.

Just another day in the Dokaalan system, Riker mused, sighing heavily.

Don't miss

STAR TREK
A TIME TO HARVEST

Available May 2004 wherever paperback books are sold!

Printed in the United States
By Bookmasters